Signet

The Dead

Wives Society

"Scotia MacKinnon is tough, clever, interesting,
and believable."—Carolyn Hart

Sharon Duncan

Author of *A Deep Blue Farewell*

SIGNET

$5.99 U.S.
$8.99 CAN.

ISBN 0-451-20949-4

9 780451 209498

50599

S ▷ EAN

Praise for the Scotia MacKinnon mysteries

The Dead Wives Society

"Who will be the next member of the Dead Wives Society? Scotia MacKinnon, police-officer-turned-private-eye, who lives aboard a boat in Friday Harbor, a day's sail from Seattle, sets out to answer just that question, although she doesn't know it at first. What seems to be a routine missing person's case soon leads MacKinnon on a trail of deciet, murder and espionage.

"Sharon Duncan has done it again, in this third installment of her Scotia MacKinnon series. Her writing grabs you with its subtle irony, insider humor, and is chock full of eccentric characters so skillfully penned, you'd swear they're real!" —Sheriff Michael A. Hawley, author of *Double Bluff* and *Silent Proof*

A Deep Blue Farewell

"Satisfyingly complex with unexpected twists . . . I highly recommend *A Deep Blue Farewell* as well as its predecessor to readers." —The Mystery Reader

Death on a Casual Friday

"Move over Millhone. There's a new girl in town. [Scotia MacKinnon] is the most believable new private eye in half a dozen years. . . . The action unfolds with wit, grace, and tension, and the climax . . . is gripping." —Joe Gores, author of The DKA File novels

"Fans of female P.I.s are going to cheer the arrival of Scotia MacKinnon. Appealing and intelligent, she's a welcome addition to the ranks." —*Romantic Times*

"[Duncan] has hit a level that it takes some authors many books to achieve." —*Mystery News*

"You'll love this snappy mystery debut!" —Dorothy Cannell, author of the Ellie Haskell mystery series

"Sharon Duncan makes her debut with an intricate and interesting novel." —BookBrowser

THE DEAD WIVES SOCIETY

A SCOTIA MACKINNON MYSTERY

SHARON DUNCAN

A SIGNET BOOK

SIGNET
Published by New American Library, a division of
Penguin Group (USA) Inc., 375 Hudson Street,
New York, New York 10014, U.S.A.
Penguin Books Ltd, 80 Strand,
London WC2R 0RL, England
Penguin Books Australia Ltd, 250 Camberwell Road,
Camberwell, Victoria 3124, Australia
Penguin Books Canada Ltd, 10 Alcorn Avenue,
Toronto, Ontario, Canada M4V 3B2
Penguin Books (N.Z.) Ltd, Cnr Rosedale and Airborne Roads,
Albany, Auckland 1310, New Zealand

Penguin Books Ltd, Registered Offices:
80 Strand, London WC2R 0RL, England

First published by Signet, an imprint of New American Library,
a division of Penguin Group (USA) Inc.

First Printing, August 2003
10 9 8 7 6 5 4 3 2 1

 REGISTERED TRADEMARK—MARCA REGISTRADA

Printed in the United States of America

PUBLISHER'S NOTE
This is a work of fiction. Names, characters, places, and incidents either are
the product of the author's imagination or are used fictitiously, and any resemblance to actual persons, living or dead, business establishments, events, or
locales is entirely coincidental.

BOOKS ARE AVAILABLE AT QUANTITY DISCOUNTS WHEN USED TO PROMOTE
PRODUCTS OR SERVICES. FOR INFORMATION PLEASE WRITE TO PREMIUM MAR-
KETING DIVISION, PENGUIN GROUP (USA) INC., 375 HUDSON STREET, NEW YORK,
NEW YORK 10014.

For the Schmooze,
for Sam,
and for Jean Claude.
Que descansen en la paz.

There is a danger for him who taketh the tiger cub, and danger also for who so snatches a delusion from a woman.

—Old Persian proverb

PROLOGUE

Nowhere is it written that a private investigator has to like her clients. Not even a private investigator who hangs her shingle in the harborside village of a remote Pacific Northwest island. I did not like Chantal Rousseau from the first moment I laid eyes on her. Or perhaps from the moment I first heard her name.

It was a hot Saturday morning in July. Very hot for the San Juan Islands, where the average summer temperature is seventy-two degrees. I had my head wedged into *DragonSpray*'s engine compartment and was attempting to insert the pry bar between the engine block and the alternator so I could tighten the fan belt when the phone rang. I expected a call from only one person: Nicholas Anastazi, my significant other, a Seattle maritime attorney who was planning a birthday dinner party for himself at his house on Crows' Nest Drive and was flying up from Seattle that morning with one of his business partners.

I gingerly extricated my head, wiped my hands on a rag, and managed to grab the portable phone seconds before my voice messaging service would have snatched the call. It was Nick. He and Andy Cooper had arrived on schedule. Andy's wife Crystal had driven up several days ago.

"The dinner for four is going to be for six," he said. "Crystal Cooper coerced me into including a new

Friday Harbor doctor. Her name is Chantal Rousseau and she's bringing her mother, who, according to Crystal, is a Berber tribeswoman."

"Interesting. Anything I can bring?"

"It's all under control. But, Scotty, could you come early? I thought maybe we could spend some quiet time together before anybody else gets here."

"I'll be there by two."

Nick's house has a spectacular view of the Strait of Juan de Fuca and the city of Victoria, British Columbia. He loves to entertain there. Years of bickering over a property settlement with his former wife would have made the house beyond his budget, but after representing a Microsoft executive whose litigious nature exceeded his cash flow, Nick ended up with the house in lieu of a well-earned fee. It had been two weeks since I'd seen him; I wished it were just the two of us celebrating his birthday. I sighed, returned to the engine, finished the adjustments to the bolts that would tighten the tension on the fan belt, and checked the level of the transmission fluid.

DragonSpray is a 38-foot sloop-rigged sailboat, my live-aboard home at slip G-73 at the Port of Friday Harbor. I bought her from a retired cruising couple after I moved to San Juan Island from San Francisco and hung out my shingle for "S. J. MacKinnon Investigations." *DragonSpray* was in Bristol condition when I bought her. About the only expenses I'd incurred— except for the ongoing challenge of maintaining the brightwork—were for every-other-year haul-outs and bottom painting.

The transmission fluid registered right where it should be on the dipstick and I checked the drip from the stuffing box, which appeared to be normal. One of the automatic bilge pumps and the radar had both been malfunctioning the last time Nick and I had been out cruising, and I'd noticed that the winches needed lubrication. The winches could wait for another day, the radar was beyond my expertise, and the bilge pump would have to be replaced on my next trip to Seattle. I closed the engine compartment and put the toolbox away. With a towel, a clean pair of sweats, shampoo supplies, and wild raspberry body lotion in a canvas bag, I headed up to the Port building for a shower.

The sky was cloudless, the temperature around eighty-five degrees, and there was a light breeze out of the east. For the better part of the year, Friday Harbor is a sleepy port village of a few thousand souls located halfway between mainland Washington and Vancouver Island. It rains ten months out of twelve here and most travelers prefer to head for sunnier climes. But come July and August, summer sailors and powerboaters arrive, the big white ferries disgorge masses of humanity onto Front Street, and both the main street and the docks at the port begin to resemble New York City at lunch hour. Just before I got to the ramp leading up to the main dock, I stepped around two suntanned eight-year-olds attempting to lower a crab trap into the harbor. Outside the fish vendor's shack, I dodged a thin blonde with an overloaded and out-of-control dock cart.

Half an hour later I was back on *DragonSpray,* showered, shampooed, and fragrant. I put on a blue shirt and a pair of white shorts and regarded the long hanging locker that housed my schizophrenic wardrobe. On the left side of the locker were the denim skirts and cotton shirts, wool sweaters, bib overalls and blue jeans that comprised my working and boating wardrobe. By their side, on padded hangers, hung the velvet tops, silk skirts and black, mid-thigh cocktail dress I bought a few months ago for visits to Seattle.

The two faces of Scotia MacKinnon.

I grabbed the hanger with the black dress, zipped it into my travel bag, threw a change of underwear and toiletries into another small bag and locked up

DragonSpray, eager to see my beloved and learn more about the Berber tribeswomen.

My ten-year-old gray Volvo is not what you would call a performance car. It has more than 200,000 miles on the odometer, is usually covered with San Juan Island glacial fines, a.k.a. dust, and Nick has suggested numerous times that I replace it. I pressed the accelerator, turned the ignition key, and wanted to scream.

The battery was dead.

And for no good reason. Neither the lights nor the radio had been left on and I'd installed a new battery not more than six months ago. *Merde!* Now I'd be late arriving at Nick's, even if I could get the attention of Tom's Taxi within the next hour. Which on a Saturday in July was unlikely. I couldn't find my cell phone, which meant I'd probably left it on the boat. *Merde encore!* I scrambled out of the car and slammed the door in frustration. I was about to lock it when a faded red Morris Minor stopped beside me. The carrot-colored hair and grinning face of the driver belonged to Zelda Jones. Zelda is my office mate and on-call research assistant, a computer genius and graphics artist cum events arranger. Like the proverbial Cheshire cat, she often materializes at unexpected times.

"You look less than happy, boss."

"I'm due at Nick's in fifteen minutes and this effing car has a dead battery."

"Hop in; I'll drive you."

I frowned. "If I don't get it charged now, I won't have a way back to town on Monday. Nick will be flying back early with Andy." Besides, an investigator with no vehicle is a poor investigator.

"Leave me the keys. I'll have Sheldon take care of it and we'll bring it out to Nick's on Sunday."

I breathed a sigh of relief, transferred my overnight and dress bags to the backseat of the Morris, and folded myself into the passenger seat. "You've saved my life."

"Or at least given you more time for hot sex." Zelda smiled wickedly, did a tire-squealing U-turn, and raced out of the parking lot and down the hill.

I buckled the seat belt, wondered about her mind-reading skills, and inquired what had brought her into town. "I thought you had a big date with Shel tonight."

"I do. He's taking me to the Spinnaker for dinner."

"So why the long face?"

"I just *know* he's going to ask me to marry him."

"Good grief, woman! I thought marriage was the number one priority in your life."

She sighed and turned right onto Second Street without signaling. "I know, I know. He's tall and handsome and makes beaucoup bucks and half the women on San Juan Island, single or married, would kill for a date with him."

Sheldon Wainwright was a ship's pilot, stationed in Port Angeles on the Olympic Peninsula. When he wasn't guiding container ships into the Straight of Juan de Fuca, he hung out at his aunt's house in Cape San Juan, ever hopeful that his adoration of Zelda might be requited.

"But?" I prompted.

"But he's so . . . predictable. So . . . ordinary. No surprises, no—" She floundered, uncharacteristically at a loss for words. We came to a brief stop at Blair Avenue and continued up the hill. "He's like a *husband*. Always there." She shrugged. "Besides, Jean Pierre's on his way back to Friday Harbor."

Jean Pierre was the hired skipper of a classic wooden yacht that had been anchored at Roche Harbor for several weeks in the spring. Zelda and Jean Pierre had had a brief romance before the yacht left for Alaska.

"Anyway, the reason I came into town was to do some work on the O'Banion wedding."

"The writer?"

She nodded. "Bronwyn O'Banion. She's driving me crazy."

"How so?" B. K. O'Banion was a local celebrity, a historical-romance writer. Though judging from the one novel I read, there was more soft porn than history in her work. Browyn lived on neighboring Lopez Island.

"She's changed her mind about the color of the table linens and now they've moved the wedding date up to two weeks from today."

"Who's she marrying?"

"Some wealthy dude from Portland. Name's Wes Caswell. I'll meet him this week when they write their vows. He's taking her to the South Pacific for their honeymoon. Tahiti, I think. But he's not the problem. It's her. She wants everything to be perfect, like a happy-ever-after scene from one of her novels."

"Where's she getting married?"

"At the château she built on Lopez after she sold movie rights on the last novel. The wedding and reception are going to be in the walled garden." She sighed, downshifted, and made a left hand turn onto Douglas Road. "And when I finish with the bride, I'm meeting Abby."

"What's Friday Harbor's ex-con up to?" Abigail Leedle is a seventy-something retired biology teacher and a wildlife photographer. She and Zelda were the founding members of the Coronas, a group of environmentally-minded feminists. Last spring Abby took exception to a sportswear magazine that tried to do a photo shoot at one of the island's historical parks and spent a brief sojourn in the San Juan County jail.

"She's got a boyfriend."

"Abby? !"

"He's writing a book here and Abby's renting him

the studio over her garage. He's one of the geologists that predicted the Mount Saint Helens eruption and now he's tracking the Cascadia subduction."

"What's a Cascadia subduction?"

We turned right at the state park and headed up West Side Road. The little Morris slowed and Zelda downshifted. "I'm clueless. Ask Nick."

"Tectonic plates are the large crustal plates that move around on the rims of continents," Nick explained. "The San Juans have their own plate. Someone told me the San Juan Plate is sliding slowly under the North American Plate. It's called subducting. Actually, I've heard the rumor that the San Juan Plate is stuck and not sliding anymore."

"So we're going to have a rather large tremor one day," I guessed, watching Nick trim two large leeks, chop them, and add them to the olive oil in the soup pot. Small piles of minced garlic and chopped fresh ginger waited on the cutting board. "What's on the menu tonight? Can I do anything?"

"The hors d'oeuvres tray is chilling. You're going to assemble the salad while I do the soup. My butcher prepared the lamb so it's ready for the oven. Crystal Cooper's bringing a pilaf to honor her Moroccan friend. And I picked up the lemon granita at Tino's Deli."

"Tino's old family recipe, I imagine."

"Naturally. Handed down from his great-great-grandmother."

"Where are the salad ingredients?"

"Bottom right-hand drawer of the fridge. Here's the recipe." He handed me a clipping from an old edition of *Food and Wine*. "And the salad bowl."

I glanced at the clipping, found the greens, and moved to the wet bar. "Tell me about the Moroccan guests."

"Chantal Rousseau is an internist and Crystal's best

friend. Her mother's name is Raheela. As I understand it, Dr. Rousseau has accepted a job at the medical clinic in Friday Harbor and is in the process of
moving up here with her mother."

"How did Crystal meet a French Moroccan doctor?
I thought her latest cause was adopting Bosnian
orphans."

"Crystal got incensed over the plight of the Afghan
women, so she joined a human rights group in Seattle.
Muslim Women United, or something like that. Chantal founded it."

"Chantal is from Morocco?"

"She was born in Paris. Her father was French, a
diplomat, I believe. Her mother's family are tribal
Berbers. The parents met at brides' fair, whatever that
is." He added the garlic and ginger and a pinch of salt,
then peered at the recipe through his reading glasses.

I spread the wet leaves of romaine between paper
towels and blotted up the moisture. "Do Berbers
speak Berber?"

"Most Berbers speak a language called Tamazight."

"How erudite you've become, Mr. Anastazi."

He peered at me over the top of the glasses and
grinned. "Crystal prepped me after she found out my
knowledge of geography ended at the Himalayas and
the Mediterranean Sea." He added a can of chicken
broth and several cups of water, covered the pot, and
began to set up the bar. "I've got a new client who
also appreciates martinis. He just came back from
London and said there are only two places over there
where you can get a good martini. One is the American Bar off the lobby of the Savoy Hotel, where they
charge fifteen dollars for the expertise. And the other
is the Stafford Hotel in St. James's Place where the
price is twelve dollars." He raised the sleeve of his
shirt to check his watch. "Our guests are not arriving
until six thirty. I stacked the dishes and utensils on
the table. You know where the wine glasses are. If

you'll set the table, beautiful lady, we'll have time for a nap. That is, if you'd like a nap." He tilted my head back and gave me a long, suggestive kiss. "And in case I haven't told you recently, you have fabulous legs."

The Coopers, accompanied by two women; one late thirties, one approaching sixty, arrived at six forty. The older woman, swathed from her ankles to the top of her head in a filmy blue garment, lived up to my image of a Berber tribeswoman. But any preconceived notion I'd had of a Muslim feminist bore no resemblance to the feral, green-eyed female with long, long chestnut hair and exotic makeup who accompanied her. I took one look at Chantal Rousseau's ankle-length, silky white gown that bared one dusky shoulder and her hat—a toque, actually, with appliquéd flowers in shades of jungle green—and doubted that Friday Harbor was ready for such a creature. When I saw the expression on Nick's face as the foursome came through the door, I knew *I* wasn't.

Andy made the introductions. Chantal's handshake was firm. Her pale green eyes with their outer circle of dark green searched my face and then she turned to Nick with a dazzling smile. Her mother Raheela's handshake was limp and ladylike. Like her daughter, she had green eyes, but the dark hair under the filmy silk scarf showed many threads of gray. I stole another look at Friday Harbor's newest answer to Dr. Kildare, picked up the tray of fresh vegetables and yogurt dip, and began circulating with a forced smile on my face. While I trust Nick implicitly, Chantal Rousseau was quite a package of provocative femininity. Suddenly my sexy little black cocktail dress seemed awfully retro and I knew it was going to be a long evening.

A large woman, Crystal Cooper arranges her blond hair in a tight chignon. She bears a striking physical resemblance to her husband, Andy, a graduate of Stanford Law. Their politics are also similar: activist,

liberal, and articulate. Crystal and Nick's former wife
were once—perhaps *still* are—best friends. Crystal's
favorite dinner conversation revolves around remem-
brances of times past, often followed by meaningful
glances toward me, the evil husband stealer. Which
I wasn't.

When I first met Nick, I was working for a security
firm in San Francisco. He was a six-foot-four, forty-
something, George Clooney look-alike handling admi-
ralty law cases for a California Street megasize law
firm. I lost my heart the first time I saw Nick, but he
was married. Several years later, one of the senior law
partners died, one of the junior partners was disbarred
for something unbecoming an attorney, and Nick's
wife started a torrid affair with their financial advisor
and asked for a divorce. Nick along with two other
associates, Andy Cooper and Tony Nakaro, made a
break for Seattle and set up their own firm there.

The Coopers moved over to the long windows overlooking the water. At the bar, Nick poured Sapphire
gin from its distinctive blue container into a silver
shaker. "Shaken not stirred," he proclaimed face-
tiously, adding the vermouth.

"Just like James Bond," Chantal murmured. Her
voice was soft, her accent more French than Middle
Eastern.

Nick gave her an appreciative glance. "Are you an
Ian Fleming fan?"

Chantal looked at her mother. "We both are."

"I have all the Bond films on video," Nick said,
pouring the shaken-not-stirred libations into the waiting glasses. "Perhaps we should have a movie party."

Over my dead body.

"We would be *enchantées,* Nicholas."

She pronounced it "Neekolás," and I thought I was
going to be sick.

Nick handed the delicate crystal glasses around. Ra-

heela declined the martini and Nick offered her a glass
of Pellegrino water instead.

"A toast," Crystal Cooper proposed. "To Friday
Harbor's new physician and to the liberation of all
women in veils. May they enjoy health, wealth, and
love."

As we raised our glasses, I saw Raheela frown and
something like a shadow pass over Chantal's smooth,
dusky face.

Over the lemon granita and coffee, while Nick gave
Raheela and Chantal a tour of his video collection,
Crystal suggested that perhaps I could help the two
women "adjust" to island life. "Just help them fit in,
Scotia. Chantal's recently gotten divorced. Her husband was a Brit. She was mad about him and the
divorce was devastating for her."

Most divorces are devastating in one fashion or another. However, any sympathy I might have had for
Dr. Rousseau's marital trauma had flown right out the
window when she started fawning over Nick. Trauma
from divorce was one thing; using Nicholas Anastazi—
my Nick—for her recovery was another. I also suspected that the new doctor would not be open to the
suggestion that if she wanted to fit into island life, she
would have to wear underwear and discard her stiletto-
heeled strappy sandals and iridescent gold eye shadow.
Ergo, I didn't pay much attention to her parting promise to call me. Or perhaps my memory lapse was
caused by the interlude in Nick's moonlight-bathed
bedroom that followed the guests' departure.

Thinking back on it now, I should have paid more
attention.

PART 1

1

The Washington State ferry boat Kaleetan *rounded the tip of Shaw Island and thrust its bow into the swift currents of San Juan Channel. On the upper observation deck of the green and white vessel, a dark-haired man of medium height pretended to stare into the foamy white bow wave. His restless, golden brown eyes were obscured by the tinted aviator glasses perched on his slightly Semitic nose. A 380 Walther PPK 9 was hidden under his well-tailored navy blue blazer. The other ferry passengers, July tourists in shorts and sandals, milled around him, leaning over the high metal railing in the warm afternoon breeze, jostling for a glimpse of the infamous black-and-white orca whales.*

The man in the blue blazer was Michael Farraday, code named Falcon. Like many other ferry passengers, he had driven up Interstate 5 from Seattle to Anacortes in his rental car, arriving at the Anacortes ferry terminal in time to make the 2:50 sailing for Friday Harbor on San Juan Island. However, unlike the other passengers, Farraday was neither a local islander returning home nor a summer vacationer. He courteously detached himself from an attractive female who'd offered to show him around Friday Harbor after they arrived and strolled along the starboard deck. Hands in his trouser pockets, he pondered the assignment he'd accepted. An assignment that had led him from his comfortable flat

*in London's St. James's Place to an archipelago of re-
mote, sparsely inhabited islands off the coast of Washington State.*

The assignment, in the arcane parlance of the intelligence community, was a "wet operation": search out
and eliminate a highly placed British agent, code named
Polo, who had disappeared while on assignment in Istanbul. Before vanishing, Polo had sold British intelligence to the Iraqis and caused the death of five people,
including two other British MI-6 agents and an American woman who was a U.S. embassy employee. Farraday had received the assignment directly from the
Director General of MI-6, the arm of British military
intelligence dealing with espionage overseas. No other
person had been present at the early morning meeting
at Thames House. Faraday knew that the DG must
have already received tacit approval from the prime
minister for the task to be delegated. He also knew he
had been chosen because he was one of the best marks-
men in MI-6.

"Friday Harbor. Now arriving Friday Harbor," a
voice announced over a loudspeaker.

The ferry made a slow turn to the left past Reid Rock
and Farraday glimpsed his destination: a picturesque
village rambling up the rocky hillside above a harbor
filled with sailboat masts. A red-and-white seaplane tax-
ied slowly away from the breakwater, accelerated across
the water with a roar of its engine, and was airborne.

Farraday opened the heavy door that led to the inside
observation lounge and mingled with the throng headed
for the narrow stairway to the car deck. His rented
turquoise Subaru was the first car in the center lane
behind the walk-on passengers and bicyclists. The ferry's engines reversed and the front of the vessel met the
off-loading ramp with a small thud. Farraday unlocked
the Subaru and ducked into the driver's seat. The ferry
crew secured the huge docking lines around the bol-
lards, signaled to the first cars, and Farraday drove off

the ferry behind the cyclists. Scanning the crowd of faces waiting for the arriving passengers, he slowly drove past the ice cream parlor, around the ancient madrona tree, and left on Spring Street, his thoughts on the wily prey he had tracked more than halfway around the world.

On the Monday following the birthday dinner Dr. Chantal Rousseau did call and make an appointment for one o'clock. She arrived promptly and seated herself in the white wicker chair beside my desk. It was the hottest day on record for the San Juans. The California couple—my landlords—who bought and renovated the Olde Gazette Building where my office is located had not considered air-conditioning to be a necessity and the temperature had been climbing for the last two hours. I tried to raise the casement window behind my desk a few more inches in hopes of enticing a breeze from the harbor and only succeeded in breaking a thumbnail. Although my regard for the good doctor had not improved since meeting her on Saturday, and her lemon yellow linen suit with a mid-thigh skirt, alligator pumps, and charcoal eyeliner were eminently more appropriate for downtown Los Angeles than my funky office on Guard Street in Friday Harbor, I was not one to turn down the possibility of a fee.

"Can you help me find my ex-husband?" she asked. "He stole my investments. Nick says you are an investigator. Will you help me find Forbes?" Her grasp of English pronunciation and grammar had improved significantly since Saturday night.

I reached for the background information form I fill

out on new clients and removed a small tape recorder from the bottom left-hand desk drawer. "May I record our conversation?" If I accepted the case, I would have her sign my contract for investigative services, which gives me written permission to record our conversations. If she didn't, I'd delete the recording.

"Of course."

"First of all, why do you want to find your ex-husband?"

"He took all of my money, even my son's college fund." She frowned. "I know everybody thinks doctors are rich, but I had to borrow money to get through medical school. And then I helped my first husband get his Ph.D. It took me a long time to get any money saved." She sighed. "It is not just my money he took. He stole my mother's wedding dowry and her antique tapestries and I had to sell my condominium in Seattle."

"Let's start with your ex-husband's name, last known address, and social security number."

"His name is Forbes Cameron. After he filed for divorce this past May, he was staying at the Rose and Thistle Club in Seattle. It's a residence club. Forty-three Carlyle Place. And before that at our condominium." She supplied a street number and social security number.

"Date and place of birth?"

"March 28, 1960. He was born in Scotland. Edinburgh, I think."

"You have a copy of his birth certificate?"

She shook her head.

"Parents' names?"

"His father died a long time ago. His name was Peter."

"Peter Cameron?"

"I think so."

"His mother?"

"Elizabeth."

"Is she still living?"

"She died about fifteen years ago."

"Mother's maiden name?"

Another shake of the head.

"Any siblings?"

"Two sisters. Millie and Marianne."

"Married names?"

"Millie's name is Thatcher. She lives in London and raises dogs. Marianne is married to someone named Ashburn. Brian . . . or maybe Bruce. They have a sheep ranch in Australia. I don't have their addresses."

"Does Forbes Cameron have a business?"

"Strome Investments in Seattle. But it's closed now."

"You have a copy of your marriage license?"

She opened the thin maroon briefcase on her lap and extracted a sheaf of papers. "I made copies for you. It's all here: the license, the prenuptial, the power of attorney, and the divorce papers."

I scanned the documents quickly. As is customary in prenups, there were lists of assets with which each of the parties was entering the marriage. Chantal's list was modest and included three mutual funds, one parcel of real estate in Seattle, some furniture and personal possessions, and a trust account in her son's name. The list for Forbes Cameron comprised an extensive list of investments, two antique cars—a Bentley and a Rolls—a two-year-old Jaguar XJ8, and real estate in Washington, California, and Florida. The terms of the prenup stated that each of the parties would keep the property they entered the marriage with and share equally in the appreciation of any joint investments or acquisitions after the marriage. All standard stuff. What struck me as not so standard was the mutual durable power of attorney clause attached to the prenup that gave each of the parties permission to buy, sell, invest, or liquidate any of the assets of the other.

"Why did you sign this power of attorney?" I asked.

She shrugged. "Forbes was a financial advisor. He was going to help me with my investments. He said we needed to get my money in some better funds and stocks with a higher yield so my son would have enough for college. And it would be easier if he didn't have to bother me with signing papers all the time."

"Did you have a lawyer review the agreement before you signed it?"

"No."

"Why not?"

"It would be wrong. As if I did not trust him. My father always took care of financial matters for my mother. And I thought Forbes would do the same for me."

I took a deep breath. This woman was a doctor, probably in her late thirties or early forties. She must have spent at least eight years in one or more institutions of higher learning and then a number of years as a resident and an intern and in practice somewhere. And yet with one stroke of a pen she had given another person complete control over her entire financial life. Which is what often happens when life is negotiated in a bedroom.

I turned my attention to the divorce papers. "Where is the final decree?"

"It was . . . was never filed. A week after I received a copy of the petition, I got a note from Forbes saying he had to go to Scotland. A death in the family. He said he'd stay in touch."

"So you're not divorced?"

She stared at me. "I guess that's right."

I stared back at her. *She guessed.*

"After a month, I tried to call his attorney." She gestured to the documents I was holding. "At the phone number for the law firm on the divorce papers. Lockerbie and Skye. But the phone number didn't exist. I couldn't get a listing for the firm." She began chewing on her right pinkie nail. "And when I checked my investments, they were gone."

"Gone, as in sold?"

"Yes. I called my father's attorney and he checked on it. All the mutual fund companies had received an order in writing and a copy of the power of attorney and Forbes had liquidated the investments. Even my son's college fund."

"What about Forbes's assets? It was a mutual power of attorney. You could have liquidated his assets, couldn't you?"

"They were phony. All of them, even the real estate. If he has any assets, they aren't the ones he put in the prenup."

The scam was dazzling only to the uninitiated. "And the condominium? Did he sell that, too?"

"That's all I had left. When we got married, I sold the little house I was living in with my son and made a down payment on the condo. The payments were more than I could afford, but Forbes said he was having funds transferred from an offshore account and he would take over the mortgage. I sold it last week so I could buy the condo here in Friday Harbor." She smiled. "The Seattle property was in both our names, so I used the power of attorney."

The only smart thing she'd done since she met him. "Whose idea was the divorce?"

"His. He said our marriage was . . . a mistake. He was really sorry. He said he was still grieving over Gwendolyn, his first wife."

"What happened to Gwendolyn?"

"She was stabbed to death when she found a burglar in her flat."

"When did this happen?"

"Right after they were married, I think. In London."

"Was her murderer ever found?"

"He said the police never found anyone."

"Did he have close friends in the area?"

She shook her head. "He said he'd rather spend his time with me."

"What kind of work did he do before he came to the U.S. ?"

"He was in the diplomatic service. A commercial attaché in the Middle East and then in South America."

"Was he an attaché when you met him?"

"No. He left the diplomatic service after they made him do something unethical. He said all governments are decadent, so he opened his own firm in Seattle to do financial consulting. Helping people with investment portfolios. He's very intelligent and has degrees in economics and finance."

"How did you meet this man?"

"At one of Crystal's dinner parties. She introduced me."

"Do you know where she met him?"

"At a charity ball. He was with some English people. He spoke French and Arabic and she thought he would be perfect for me."

"Where are Forbes's degrees from?"

"The one in economics is from Cambridge and he . . . I think he got another degree from Princeton."

"Is he an American citizen?"

"No, but he has a green card."

"Any club memberships or professional associations?"

"A financial advisors' association. He used to go to dinner meetings. I don't remember the name of it."

"Were you ever in his office?"

She nodded. "It was a very nice office, in a building on Sixth Street. Near the Crowne Plaza Hotel."

"You ever see any of his clients?"

"No." She hesitated. "Forbes had clients from all over the West Coast. He did portfolio management for a fee. He mostly communicated with them by phone and e-mail."

"Your Forbes Cameron sounds like a very well educated professional. Professional con man, that is."

She blinked her jungle-cat eyes. "You mean . . . he
may have done this before?"

"It all sounds too smooth for a novice, Dr. Rousseau. He's probably covered his tracks well. Forbes
Cameron may be an alias. On the off chance that I
find him, what would that accomplish?"

"My father's attorney says since he misrepresented
his assets in the prenuptial agreement, and the mutual
power of attorney was a part of the agreement, we
could make him pay restitution for what he stole from
me. That's why I hired the other investigator."

"What other investigator?"

"I hired a P.I. in Seattle."

"If you already have a P.I., why do you need me?"

"He was killed."

"Killed? How?"

"He was leaving his office in Pioneer Square. There
was an article about it in the newspaper. It says his
wallet and briefcase were stolen." She handed me a
clipping.

Pioneer Square is a twenty-block area of historical
brick buildings near the Seattle waterfront consisting
of galleries, bookstores, eateries, and sports bars.
After dark, it's not one of the safer areas in the city.
I read the brief news clipping. Sanford Whiteley, a
Seattle private investigator, had been shot on June
28—only a couple of weeks ago. An occupant of the
same office building had been leaving a few seconds
behind Whiteley, saw Whiteley fall to the sidewalk,
and called 911. No one else noticed anything and there
were no suspects.

"Did this Whiteley uncover anything on Cameron?"

"He called me the day he was murdered. He said
he had a report for me. We were going to meet the
following Monday."

"Did he work for a security firm or alone?"

"I only talked to him by phone, but I think he worked alone. Sometimes a woman answered the phone. I'm sure his murder did not have anything to do with me," she said, watching my face. "Pioneer Square is not a safe place at night. And I need your help. It's not just the money. It's a question of family honor."

"Why family honor?"

"Forbes told my mother she should have insurance on her old tribal tapestries and jewelry. It was her family's wedding dowry to my father and it's been in her family for a long time. Forbes said he would get them appraised for her."

"And?" I asked, already knowing the answer.

"He said he got the appraisal and was talking to an insurance broker."

"And of course the jewelry and tapestries disappeared along with Forbes."

"Yes. Will you help me find him? If it's a question of your fees, I got a good price for the condo. I can pay you. Will you get my mother's dowry back?"

"My fees are the going rate, but if we get into recovery of stolen property, it could get expensive. If he's gone back to the U.K., you might want to hire an investigator over there."

"I didn't tell Forbes everything. I keep cash in a safe-deposit box. I can pay you."

I opened the right-hand drawer of the desk and pulled out a copy of my "Contract for Investigative Services," which includes my fee schedule and requires a retainer up front. "Read it. If it sounds okay and you can handle the fee, sign it on the bottom."

She scanned it quickly, ignored the fine print, and signed it. I imagined she had signed the prenup the same way.

"Have you found any unusual activity on your credit card since he left?"

She shook her head. "No. My attorney said to cancel my MasterCard. I did and got a new Visa card."

"Would you happen to know of any credit cards your husband used? Or have a copy of the card numbers?"

She frowned and pulled a small checkbook in a maroon cover from her briefcase. "I don't think Forbes ever used a credit card. I remember he always carried cash. He said it made life simpler."

And made him more difficult to trace.

"Did you have a joint account for household bills?"

"Yes, but I've closed it."

I glanced at Cameron's list of assets. "Did he drive the Jaguar?"

She nodded.

"I'd like the license plate number, if you have it. And in case he's still in Seattle, names of any places he used to hang out. Like a favorite bar or restaurant."

"I'll look, but I don't think I know the license plate. He didn't usually go to bars."

"Any favorite restaurants you two went to?"

"The White Orchid. And the Hunt Room at the Sorrento."

The White Orchid is an upscale Seattle waterfront restaurant and the Sorrento Hotel is Seattle's oldest and most romantic lodging establishment, a long-ago residence of the Vanderbilts, the Ballards and the Guggenheims. Nick and I have broken bread at the Hunt Room, the hotel's elegant dining room, on several memorable occasions.

Dr. Rousseau wrote out a check for the retainer, pulled an eight-by-ten photograph from her portfolio and laid it on my desk. "It's Forbes. It was taken the day we got married, last October 10th. And this is an e-mail I found on my laptop. It was deleted, but I found it in the computer's trash file."

I examined the attractive, intelligent face of the well-dressed forty-something man in the photo. "Handsome devil, isn't he?"

She narrowed her eyes. "A devil, yes." She glanced at her watch and stood up. "I have to leave. I should be at the clinic now."

"What's the e-mail?"

"It's to a friend of his who lives in London," she said. "His name is Chris." She gathered up her belongings. "And before you ask, no, I did not make two million dollars last year. Forbes is a . . . fucking liar." Her voice was very soft and full of venom.

"Dr. Rousseau, I want you to know that there are no guarantees I can find your husband. And very little probability of recovering your mother's property."

She smiled. "Just do the best you can."

That was usually my line. I let her leave without responding.

3

The door closed behind Dr. Rousseau. I turned off the tape recorder, fanned myself with a manila file folder, and stared out the window at the empty high school parking lot next to the tennis courts. Two teenage girls in ragged denim cutoffs were batting a fuzzy green ball around with so much energy in the heat that it exhausted me to watch them.

My new client was the victim of an accomplished con man. And there is possibly no act of deception as devastating to the psyche as becoming the victim of a sweetheart swindler. A friend of mine from my days in law enforcement in the San Diego Police Department, who worked on fraud cases, once told me that all the sweetheart con artists she knew possessed the attributes of psychopaths. But even when the swindlers were caught, it was very difficult to prove intent, to prove that the money they had stolen wasn't a gift from the girlfriend or fiancée.

I considered the photo of Forbes Cameron that my new client had left. He had a regal head with professionally styled light brown hair. Dark brows above guileless, inviting dark blue eyes. A straight, Anglo-Saxon nose. A blue rep tie, silky and tasteful. Well-manicured fingernails with a new gold band on the third finger, left hand. He appeared to be a happy, successful gentleman reclining against an ivory colored

sofa, one gray pin-striped leg crossed over the other.
A figure to inspire respect and trust. I slid the photo
into the file and turned to the e-mail. It was addressed
to christgood@bsglaw.uk.com sent on the 14th of September last year.

Dear Christopher,
    You are correct that it is definitely my turn
to write. I was already feeling guilty before
your letter arrived yesterday. It appears life is
treating you well. Lunch with the prince and
a new Bentley! I imagine the local gendarmes
were growing weary of chasing your old car
and it is always a good idea to change one's
M.O. frequently. Great news, your winnings
at Mundolito. And you know I am four shades
of green hearing about your evening at
Jimmy'Z. I would imagine the place was
mobbed with gorgeous nubile creatures as
always.
    Speaking of women, I haven't told you about
Dr. Chantal Rousseau, whom I met several
months ago. She's an internist with a well-
known medical group here in Seattle. After
keeping company for several weeks, she asked
me to move in with her. She has a teenage
son who's a savage. He didn't fancy me so he
moved out and is living with his father.
There is still a God. Chantal's practice is doing
rather well. I believe she made two million
dollars last year, so I was able to be helpful
with tax suggestions and investments. The
really good news is that she's agreed to become
my wife! I'm working on the standard pre-
nup, as they call them over here. La doctora
seems impressed with my financial acumen,
so I don't think she'll balk at it. This little
house is a bit of a hovel and I've talked her

*into buying a condominium on the waterfront.
The only worm in the ointment is that her
mother will be living with us and she's quite
the snoop. A Berber tribeswoman or some
such thing.*

*D.D., the moneybags from California, has
become difficult, as you warned. La berbère
caught me talking to her, but her English is
atrocious so she probably didn't understand
a thing.*

*By the by, I saw Sergei in Vancouver. My
love to your Mum. Looking forward to
seeing Annie and John. Best, F.*

So. My new client had picked a winner of a husband. The setup for the con was explicit and brazen.
It appeared that Cameron's friend Christopher lived
well. Perhaps in a manner Cameron would have liked
to mimic. I wasn't going to find him hanging out with
trailer trash in a cheap motel. He would have moved
on to some other scene of affluence, power, and gull-
ible women. Who was Sergei? Or Annie and John?
Annoyed that Dr. Rousseau had simply dropped the
e-mail on me without explanation, I phoned the clinic
and left a message for her to call me.

I riffled through my Rolodex, searching for the card
for Lieutenant Bernie Morgan, a Seattle P.D. homicide detective I'd met back in the spring while working
another case. I got his voice mail, and asked him what
he knew about the shooting of a P.I. named Sanford
Whiteley. I then checked the background interview
form against the tape recording and locked up my
files. I had an appointment at three o'clock with a
local attorney who wanted to prep me for my testimony in a child custody trial scheduled for next week.
Briefcase in hand, I was almost to the door, when the
phone rang. It was my friend Angela Petersen, who
was attempting to move from sheriff's dispatcher to

deputy sheriff, a step up that required passing three tests: one written, one physical, and one oral. She had aced the first two, and I remembered she had been scheduled for the oral exam on Saturday.

"I did it, Scotia. I got the job. You may now address me as Deputy Petersen."

"I never had any doubt that you would, Deputy Petersen." The oral exam was to be administered by Sheriff Nigel Bishop, who was on partial medical leave following a minor heart attack last spring. Nigel was not a great fan of my forthright, liberal-minded friend and a high score on the oral exam would have been surprising. I've known Angela for almost two decades, through her years as medical examiner at the San Diego P.D. and then her career advance to teaching forensic medicine at UCLA.

"Is Matt taking you out for a celebration dinner tonight?" I asked.

"No. He isn't." She sighed. "He's furious that I insisted on applying for the job and then accepted it over his protestations. When I was on the phone to my sister, he slammed out of the house and I haven't seen him since."

"I'm sorry."

A commercial fisherman, Matt Petersen spent six or so months a year in southeast Alaska. When he was in Friday Harbor, he wanted Angela at home, cooking meals, doing the laundry, and tending the vegetable garden at their old house on Griffin Bay. He had gotten into a snit when she took an administrative job with the sheriff's office a year ago, but I thought that had been smoothed over.

"Since he hurt his back a month ago Matt can't fish any more this year," Angela explained. "Now everything makes him twitchy. He'll get over it. Thank God he agreed to fill in as skipper on one of the whale watch boats a friend of his bought last year."

"You have time for a celebratory drink late this afternoon?" I asked.

"I've got a county disaster-planning meeting but it should be over by four thirty."

"George's at five?"

"See you there."

I opened my office door to the rousing strains of a German opera—something by Strauss, I guessed—and the fragrance of buttered popcorn.

Zelda was holding forth on the phone. Open magazines covered her desktop and surrounded her chair. Wedding magazines, wine magazines, culinary magazines. She was dressed in a pair of flowered cotton pajamas and pink shower clogs. Zelda goes in for theme dressing, but I couldn't think what today's might be unless she was going to a sleepover that evening. From the corner of the office, Dakota, a lean Black Labrador, reclined on his red futon and regarded her with half-closed eyes. I made my way to the table on the far wall and filled a blue bowl with buttery white kernels. Saroya, the naturopathic physician who shared the OGB lower floor with Zelda, came in, gave me a nod, and disappeared behind her door.

"It's a Vera Wang design," Zelda said firmly into the phone. "Strapless, full-skirted silk organza with cuff detail and a gigantic organza rose on the bodice." There was a pause. "The veil? Hold on." She consulted her notes. "The veil is rectangular-shaped sheer tulle, chapel length. Also by Vera Wang." Another pause. "The matron of honor is wearing petal-pink satin. And Bronwyn will have roses for her bouquet, with green hydrangea and green South African babbles." A pause. "Yes, she's going to send photos of the chateau. Thank you." She hung up the phone and twirled around.

She shook her head, eyes rolling. "That was *Village Life* magazine. Every month they do a section on celebrity weddings and they're sending someone to cover the O'Banion-Caswell nuptials and I'm going to

get a credit!" She twisted her long hair—auburn with
metallic gold streaks this week—on top of her head
and anchored it with a pencil. I sat in the chair beside
her desk and laid my interview notes on Forbes Cameron in front of her.

"What's this?" she asked.

"Info for a background check I need for my new
client. And see if you can find out who the recipient
of this e-mail is." I handed her a copy of the deleted
e-mail message from Forbes Cameron to Christopher.

"Oh, the new doctor. I saw her come in when I was
on the phone. With that body, half the guys in hard
hats in this town will find themselves with internal
medical problems. The clinic is going to be mobbed."
She scanned the interview notes. "Forbes Cameron.
Nice name."

"You have time to do it today?" Since Zelda had
added events arranging to New Millennium Communi-
cations, my research sometimes had to compete with
birthday celebrations and yachting events.

"I'll make time. You want one on your client as
well?"

"Please." I operate under the assumption that most
clients will lie to me about one thing or another.
Sometimes the lies are minor; sometimes they're significant. So I've started doing routine backgrounds
on them.

She glanced at the clock. "I have an hour before
Bronwyn comes by to bring me the vows. I found a
calligrapher to do them in a book of handmade paper
so they can keep them forever."

"Sounds very romantic. Speaking of which, how did
the dinner with Shel go on Saturday night?"

"We went to the Spinnaker and he insisted on ordering champagne," she said gloomily. "I hate alcohol
and I particularly hate champagne. It gives me a
headache."

"And then he proposed?"

"No, but it's been five years since we met. He thinks we should live together. I do *not* think we should live together. So we had a fight. After the dessert." She smiled brightly. "I should have the backgrounds on Forbes Cameron and Chantal Rousseau by five o'clock and I'll see what I can do with the e-mail. Then I'm off to a Corona meeting at the Dry Dock. Abby's got a zinger of an agenda tonight."

"More 'Tourist Go Home' stuff?"

"She found out the petition to the National Marine Fisheries to designate the orcas an endangered species wasn't approved, so she's declared July as Save the Orcas Month. She's on a tear. Says she's going to picket the whale watch boats and let the tourists know we've lost 20 percent of the orcas already."

Abby's tactics promised to keep the island hopping. Such is life on the other side of paradise.

I arrived at George's Tavern a little before five, but there as no sign of Angela. The old tavern was quiet for a July afternoon: no game of billiards in the back room and no one feeding the jukebox. Feeling somber from my prep sessions for the child custody trial, I'd stopped by the office and picked up a scribbled note from Zelda attached to a background report on Chantal Rousseau compiled by DataTech, the on-line public records retrieval system I used. I found an empty bar stool and reread Zelda's note.

The SSN you gave me for Forbes Cameron is bogus. Belongs to a woman in Florida who died ten years ago. Only thing on Forbes Cameron was a Washington State driver's license # and a King County marriage license dated October 10 last year. The e-mail address is registered to Browne, Smythe & Goodfellow, 83 Winston Mall, London. Christopher Goodfellow? Z.

"What'll it be, Scotia? The usual?" I blinked up at Lindsey, the pretty redheaded bartender who used to be engaged to Henry, my dockside neighbor. I nodded. She added ice to a glass, filled it half full with vermouth, topped it off with club soda, and added a twist of lime.

"How's Calico?" she asked. "I miss her."

"Calico is fine." I wondered if Lindsey had second thoughts about breaking off her engagement to Henry. "I was away all weekend, so Henry said he'd make sure she got fed and sheltered. I presume tonight it will be my turn. Which reminds me, I'm out of cat food."

A dark-haired man in a blue blazer and tan pants approached the bar and Lindsey greeted him with a welcoming smile. I sipped the vermouth and soda and my cell phone rang. It was Angela.

"Scotia, I'm not going to make it to George's. I'm on my way to Santa Maria to check out a prowler report. How about a rain check for tomorrow?"

"Let's talk in the morning. I don't have my calendar with me. Good luck with the prowler."

I'd only been on Santa Maria Island once. It's sparsely populated, more wooded and more mountainous than San Juan and Orcas Islands. I remembered an old stone convent nestled in a small, bucolic valley. Not a place you'd expect to find a prowler. An old Willie Nelson tune drifted down from the speakers over the bar and I felt someone looking at me. I turned toward the man in the blazer who was sitting at the end of the bar. I didn't know him, but he had lovely eyes of a tawny brown color. I returned his smile and reread Zelda's note. If Forbes Cameron's SSN was bogus, I wondered what else was bogus about him. I turned to the DataTech report on Chantal Rousseau.

She was born forty-one years ago in Rabat, Morocco to Guy Rousseau, a citizen of France, and Raheela Tabbal, a citizen of Morocco. She was a naturalized U.S. citizen. Religion, Muslim; political affiliation, Democrat. Educated at l'Université de Paris-Sorbonne, with a *License de philosophie* and a *Maîtrise de sciences et techniques*. Followed by an M.D. from Stanford University in 1987. My green-eyed client was a very educated *femme*. No trace of a record with the police, FBI or Interpol. She didn't owe any federal taxes and had a checking account at a Seattle bank with a balance of $2,456.88. Club memberships and associations included the AMA, the Association of Holistic Practitioners, and the International Fund for Muslim Women (IFMW), of which she was the president.

It was an impressive vita. Coupled with the green eyes, chestnut hair, and trim, curvy body, Dr. Chantal Rousseau was an exceptionally attractive target for an upwardly mobile con man. There was nothing in the report that contradicted anything she'd told me. I reread her memberships and associations and paused at the reference to the IFMW. For no more than one or two seconds, I recalled the number of charities for various Islamic causes that had turned out to be fronts for terrorist funding.

4

G dock is a long, long walk from the Port administration building, even in summer, but the distance provides some respite from the rowdy cruisers on the transient docks. When I got out to G-73 after my canceled date with Angela, Henry was standing on *Pumpkin Seed*'s aft deck. Calico, the previously homeless feline for whom we both provided food and shelter, balanced on the stern rail beside him. She waved her tail and rubbed against Henry's rotund midsection. "Hi, Henry. How goes it?"

"Hullo, Scotia." He scratched several days' growth of dark beard going gray, ran one hand through his ungroomed hair of the same color, and shrugged. "Lots of chores to do that I don't feel like doing."

I glanced at his 25-foot, plastic cabin cruiser. "At least you don't have any brightwork to worry about."

"Thank God for small favors. I'm a disaster with varnish." Henry is a mortgage broker for a major company on the mainland. He manages their Friday Harbor office and he's lived aboard *Pumpkin Seed* since his divorce. For much of the time that I've known him, Henry has been depressed. The only hiatus in his depression was last spring when he was engaged to Lindsey. After a series of unfortunate accidents around *Pumpkin Seed,* Lindsey bowed out of the engagement and Henry's depression returned. I haven't been very supportive of Henry's antics in the past, including being overly critical of his engagement only six months after his divorce. Just now, however, there was something about his down-in-the-mouth countenance that touched me.

"Must be kind of lonely since Lindsey left."

"Yeah." He scrunched up his face and for a minute I thought he was going to cry. "The singles scene in Friday Harbor really sucks."

"So I've heard. You know, Henry, I saw a notice in the *Gazette* this week that there are several new classes starting at the dance studio."

"I'm lousy at ballroom dancing."

"They're doing country and western and some folk dancing. There's always more women than men in dance classes."

"You know what I always wanted to learn, Scotia?"

"What's that, Henry?"

"The tango." He hummed a few bars of a tune I didn't recognize and did a sideways sashay that sent Calico leaping for the safety of the dock.

I smiled. "There are some great instructors at the studio. I'll bet you could find someone to teach you the tango."

"Yeah, maybe."

DragonSpray was uncomfortably warm. I opened the portholes in the main salon and ladled into Calico's small white bowl a portion of chopped chicken and wheat germ, a new brand with no preservatives, no additives, and no artificial color. Three messages waited on my voice mail: from my mother, Jewel Moon; from my daughter, Melissa, who was working on a Colorado guest ranch for the summer; and from Nick. I returned Nick's call and he answered on the first ring.

"Scotty, I called because I miss you. And because yesterday went by way too fast."

I took a deep breath, flooded by the images of wak-

ing in his arms yesterday morning with the sun stream-
ing through the bedroom window, of our long brunch
on the deck above blue water with the snow-covered
Olympic Mountains as a backdrop. "I know," I said
softly. "I had a hard time readjusting this morning."

"I'm stuck here in the city this weekend," he said.
"Nicole wants me to have dinner with her and her
boyfriend on Saturday and I'll be working on a brief
all day Sunday. But next week I've got a lighter load.
Could you come down for dinner on Tuesday, a week
from tomorrow? I don't have anything on the calendar
for the following day."

"Tuesday would be fine," I said, knowing that the
reason I wasn't asked to join him for the dinner on
Saturday was that Nicole was ever hopeful that
Mummy and Daddy would one day get back together.
My rare encounters with her had been decidedly cool.
"I have a new client," I said, "but hopefully I'll have
the case wrapped up by then."

He chuckled. "Let me guess. Your new client
speaks French."

"How did you know?"

"She called me at the office to get your last name
and phone number. Are you going to be able to help
her find her ex-husband?"

"I'll do my best."

"You want to drive or fly down next week?"

"Flying would be easier, since it's just for one
night."

"Let me get you a reservation and I'll call you
back."

I hung up, thinking about an empty weekend without Nick, and dialed my mother's number down in
Mendocino on the northern California coast, where
she lived with her longtime partner, Giovanni.

"Scotia, what would you think about my coming up
to Friday Harbor for a visit?" she asked. "Giovanni
is going trekking for a week in the Dolomites with his

cousin. Would that work for you, dear? I could drive
up on Friday afternoon and stay until the following
Friday."

"Coming to Friday Harbor would be fine," I said
slowly, considering that I'd just agreed to see Nick in
Seattle the following Tuesday, a rendezvous I was not
willing to give up, selfish or no. "This weekend is free,
but I'm going to be in Seattle at Nick's on Tuesday
and part of Wednesday next week."

"Oh, that's not a problem. I can entertain myself.
Maybe I could take a whale watch tour or rent one
of those mopeds to explore the island. And do you
think I could meet that friend of yours, the fox photographer who's got a book coming out? What's her
name? Agatha?"

"Her name's Abigail. I'll introduce you. What time
shall I expect you on Friday?"

"Probably late Friday night. I'll call you. How's Melissa? Did she really go off to that ranch in Colorado?"

"She's working as a waitress at the Sweet Grass
Guest Ranch in Steamboat Springs. Says she loves it."

"We would have liked her to work here this summer, but perhaps that's better for her. Do you think
she's gotten over that Brazilian terrorist?"

"He was a soccer player."

"Whatever, dear. I'll see you late Friday."

Last spring Melissa, a junior at St. Mary's College
in California, had been jilted by her Brazilian boyfriend and had run off to Grandma's to lick her
wounds, where she'd set a record for the world's short-
est career in waitressing.

I dialed the ranch number, left a message with the
hotel desk clerk, heated up some leftover spinach and
cheese ravioli in the microwave, and turned on the
TV.

I surfed the Weather Channel, learned that the Pacific Northwest would be experiencing record high

temperatures for at least three more days, clicked the Power Off button on the remote, and tried to imagine how I would entertain my mother for a week without both of us going stir-crazy on my thirty-eight-foot floating home.

Loosely speaking, *DragonSpray* is a replica of a re-built one-hundred-year-old wooden sloop—possibly a New England oyster dragger—that was given to a nearly penniless fifty-one-year-old seaman named Joshua Slocum in 1892. As every yachtie and cruiser who has read *Sailing Alone Around the World* knows, Slocum spent two years rebuilding his vessel, spent a year commercial fishing with *Spray* along the Atlantic coast, then on 24 April 1895 sailed out of Boston Harbor on a voyage that would take three years and make him the first man to single-hand around the world.

My *DragonSpray* is not exactly a "replica" of the original *Spray,* because she is constructed of fiberglass rather than wood and is not built *exactly* from the drawings contained in *Sailing Alone.* Nor, in the language of marine architecture, is she a "near copy," which would also indicate timber construction, using *Spray*'s original lines, but "with modifications." Rather, *DragonSpray* is a *Spray* "type" or *Spray* "class": She was designed and built to retain the best of *Spray*'s features, including the legendary stability and balance of the original vessel.

According to the provenance provided to me by the previous owners, a couple who spent many years cruising around the southwest Pacific before retiring to Orcas Island, *DragonSpray* is solid glass fiber using C-Flex as the base material with something called a chopped strand mat and woven roving. She was constructed with a little more than four tons of cast iron for ballast. On a less technical note, all the deck hardware, including portholes, winches, cleats, and so on are bronze, and there are no plastic fittings. All her sails—mainsail, headsail, storm jib, and cruising spin-

naker—are Dacron, made in New Zealand. And best
of all, she has a roller-furling headsail, which means
that when the wind comes up, the sail can be furled
or reefed—reduced in size—from the cockpit. A big
plus for single-handing, which I do when I can't shang-
hai a crew.

In order to make space for Jewel Moon I would
have to find another location for all the stuff I had
"stored" on board. The laundry that hadn't been
folded. A year-old stack of *Sail* magazines. Various
and sundry boat gear that had strayed from its rightful
place. I should also give the head and shower a thor-
ough swabbing and clean out the reefer, which was
developing some very exotic growths. Jewel Moon
likes to sleep late, so I could provision the galley with
OJ and croissants and leave her a thermos of coffee
each morning.

I had no intention of sending her off on a moped
tour—alone or otherwise—for the very important reason that the local islanders hate, despise, and abhor
the buzzing two-wheeled vehicles. There have been far
too many "accidents," some fatal, involving collisions
between the pesky machines and island vehicles—
large, ponderous trucks that can't seem to avoid hitting the mopeds that wander into their path. And
meeting Abigail the Whale Savior would take care of
my mother's desire for whale watching.

The phone rang.

"Hi, Mom, it's me."

"Hi, you. How's life on Sweet Grass Ranch?"

"It's cool. The guests are nice."

"Lucky you. What hours are you working?"

"This week I serve early breakfast and lunch. Next
week, I'll do breakfast and dinner. It's a really awesome place, Mom. Would you ever consider living in
Colorado?"

Give up the ocean? And misty green mountains?

And Nick? "Well, you know, we could talk about it. Have you met any interesting people?"

"Kind of. The ranch has special entertainment on Saturday nights. The last one was a cowboy poet. Mom, he was fabulous. I bought one of his books. His name is Justin. He's a cousin of the ranch owners and is going to teach a writing class in the evening for the guests. Anyway, how are you? Any new dead bodies floating around, ho ho?"

"Not exactly. Just insurance and law stuff. Not terribly exciting." Which wasn't entirely true. Even on San Juan Island, I'd had a couple of cases that had involved homicides, but I shared my work with Melissa strictly on a need-to-know basis.

"Yeah, Mom, I know. You left that stuff behind when we left San Diego. But don't you ever miss it? Being a police detective, I mean, and all that crime stuff? And weren't you on the harbor patrol or something? I kind of remember you used to work on one of the boats."

Melissa had been five when I'd graduated from San Francisco State with a degree in psychology and her father departed for the azure waters of the Seychelles Islands. I had subsequently enrolled in the Police Academy, working a variety of weekend jobs to support us, and then became a patrol officer with the San Diego Police Department. The years we'd spent in San Diego had been turbulent ones. I'd worked my way up to detective in Domestic Abuse, and after five years of trying to help beaten, battered, and abused females in dead-end relationships, including a near fatal encounter with a disgruntled, estranged spouse, I'd requested a change of assignment to the Harbor Patrol. There had also been my marriage to fellow detective Pete Santana—whom Melissa had started out despising and ended up adoring—followed by his death in a border town shoot-out with a drug dealer.

"Mother? Are you still there?"

"I'm here."

"Don't you ever miss helping those women and catching criminals?"

"The answer to that is both yes and no," I said slowly. "Or the better answer is that I burned out. I like my life here. I like to know that I'll be home every night and I don't have to look over my shoulder if I decide to go out for a late night walk. And that nobody will have to bring you news that your mother got in somebody's way. I didn't want to make you an orphan."

Mentally, I added: *And, yes, Melissa, sometimes I feel guilty that I left. Even sadder, though, is that sometimes I can't feel anything.* To survive those San Diego years I put my feelings on hold, got desensitized. It's never quite gone away.

There was a silence on her end. Then a soft, "Thanks, Mom." Another pause. "Have you . . . do you ever hear from my father? You know, since the time he sent a birthday card when I was ten?"

"No, I haven't, Melissa." And that's all I could say. I had already made every excuse in the book for the tall, tawny-eyed, terribly sexy young man I'd met the day I was standing in line to register for my first semester of college. And because he was standing in line for Psych 101 and I was supposed to be in line for Library Science 101, I switched lines. And ended up chasing wife abusers and drug runners in high-speed boats instead of cataloging volumes of poetry.

Robert Frost was right. The road we choose makes all the difference.

"It's okay, Mom. Maybe sometime he'll get his act together and want to see me. How's Grandma? Is she upset that I didn't come back to Mendocino for the summer?"

"Grandma's fine. She's coming up to the island on Friday to visit for a week."

"To visit you? Is that okay? I mean, you guys don't

get along very well. Like you have some issues, I think."

I smiled. She was right. We did have "issues." Issues having to do with the fact that my mother, born Barbara Baskin, only daughter of a respectable couple from Newton, Massachusetts, had changed her name to Jewel Moon and gone off to Cape Breton Island in Nova Scotia, Canada to study Gaelic dance. She'd fallen in love with a Cape Breton fisherman, produced me, and then abandoned me when I was five because "the horizons were too narrow" in St. Ann's Bay.

"It's okay, we'll get along." My cell phone sounded. I pressed "Answer" and asked the caller to hold. "I've got another call, Melissa. Talk to you later?"

"Sure, Mom. Love you."

"Love you, too." I hung up and turned back to the cell phone. It was Lt. Morgan of the Seattle P.D.

"I checked the homicide you asked about, Scotia. Whiteley was shot at 7:08 P.M. on June 28 outside his office building at First and Yesler. Someone leaving the building at the same time saw him fall, ducked back inside, and called 911. No other witnesses. When the patrolman got there, Whiteley was dead. One 25-caliber bullet to the heart. His briefcase was missing, but not his wallet. His wife in hysterics couldn't think of anyone who would want to kill him. Any particular reason you wanted the information?"

"Whiteley was investigating the ex-husband of one of my clients. Supposedly he had information he wanted to share with her. Could you give me the wife's telephone number?"

"Sure. It's a listed number."

I wrote the number on an envelope and thanked him.

"Gimme a call when you make it to the big city," he suggested.

I promised I would, put away my cell phone, and dialed the number on the landline. It rang four times.

"Susan Whiteley." She didn't sound hysterical, but she did sound harassed and impatient.

"Mrs. Whiteley, my name is Scotia MacKinnon. I'm doing some investigative work for Dr. Chantal Rousseau. I've just learned about your husband's death and I apologize for bothering you. I understand your husband was also working for Dr. Rousseau before his death."

"I don't know. He didn't talk about his clients. What do you want?"

"Dr. Rousseau said he had some information he wanted to share with her. I thought he might have left a report in his files."

There was silence on the other end. "Sandy's briefcase was stolen when he was killed. And when we were burglarized, his files were ransacked."

A red light went on in my head: The killer had shot Whiteley, stolen his briefcase, hadn't found what he wanted, had gotten his home address from ID in the wallet, had broken into his residence. "When were you burglarized?"

"Three days after the shooting. They only took the new TV, but the apartment is still a total mess. And I'm sure the cops are going to do the same thing about the burglary they did over Sandy's murder. Zilch."

Morgan hadn't mentioned the burglary.

"I assume your husband had a computer. Was that stolen or damaged during the burglary?"

"Yes, we have a laptop. They didn't get it, because I've been staying with a friend in Tacoma since Sandy was shot. I had it with me. Good thing, too. It was brand-new."

"Would it be possible for you to check the files on the laptop? See if there's anything labeled Rousseau or Cameron?"

"Sure. Hold on."

Several minutes went by. "There's a file for Rousseau."

"Could you e-mail it to me?"

"Yeah, but it will be late tonight. I'm on my way out."

"Tonight will be fine, thank you."

"Hold on, There's something else. An e-mail came in after Sandy . . . after Sandy was killed. It's from . . ." She paused. ". . . from People Recovery International. A report on some dude named Campbell. Frederick Campbell. That have anything to do with your client? You want that too?"

Frederick Campbell. Forbes Cameron. Could just be. "Yes, please forward that to me as well." I supplied my e-mail address. "Mrs. Whiteley, it's possible your husband's death and the burglary are related. The burglar may be back."

"I know. I'm moving out tomorrow. I'm going back to Montana to live with my sister."

"Please be careful when you go out tonight."

"Yeah." The line went dead.

I made a cup of Sleepytime tea, performed my bedtime ablutions, caught a glimpse of myself in the mirror, and decided my hair was overdue for a trim. I crawled into my bunk where I lay awake for a long time thinking about a wife who was killed by a burglar and a P.I. who was killed and then burglarized. Just before I drifted off to sleep, I wondered if there was more to Forbes Cameron than just a handsome con man.

5

I slept fitfully and woke a little after six on Tuesday. Calico lay snuggled against my right leg on top of the white comforter, one paw over her eyes. The distant buzz of a small outboard motor disturbed the early morning silence. *DragonSpray* rocked gently, fenders creaking against the dock. A cool, salty early morning breeze drifted through the open porthole. I inhaled the smell of algae and creosote and rotted wood, the harbor odors of fish and kelp. Without disturbing Calico, I slid from under the comforter and into a pair of gray sweats. Canvas bag in hand, I headed up to the Port building. The sky was cloudless. A light breeze was blowing out of the east.

I had the women's shower room to myself. Eyes closed, water cascading over my head, I poured on the shampoo and thought about what I wanted to accomplish that day. Assuming Whiteley's widow had made it back from wherever she was going last night, I'd find her husband's file and the People Recovery Report when I got to the office. I needed to talk to Dr. Rousseau about the e-mail to her husband's friend, Christopher, and see if she knew "D.D.," identified in the e-mail as "moneybags." And who was Sergei?

It was seven fifteen when I got back to *Dragon-Spray*. I fastened the damp towel to the lifelines with a clothespin. Scrunched against one of the bulkheads,

I shook out my wet locks to air dry and contemplated my three other open cases: the contentious child custody case I'd been prepped for yesterday, which was set for trial on Thursday morning; my ongoing search for an elusive sailor named Harrison Petrovsky, whose last communiqué came from Singapore; and a background check for a woman in Seattle on a man she'd met though an upscale singles organization. At seven thirty, a plaintive *meow* drew me back down to the cabin. I spooned a large serving of Healthy Cat onto a saucer, poured a glass of orange juice for myself, and headed for my locker in the master stateroom. The travel bag I'd taken to Nick's on Saturday was hanging on the back of the cabin door. I unzipped it and removed the little black cocktail dress I'd thought was the height of chic until Chantal Rousseau had pranced in with her off-the-shoulder creation. I hung my dress back on the right-hand side, and from the left-hand side I chose my favorite pair of soft, faded blue jeans and an oversize white linen camp shirt.

I made it four blocks uphill to the bakery by eight fifteen. Carrying two warm pecan sticky buns and a Seattle morning paper tucked in my rucksack, I arrived at the Olde Gazette Building just as the Morris Minor pulled to the curb. Zelda had the convertible top down and she crawled out of the ancient vehicle juggling a stack of magazines and file folders. She was wearing a hot pink lace tank top with a scalloped neckline and a long, black peasant skirt. Given the dampness of her long hair, she couldn't have been out of the shower more than ten minutes.

"Homework?" I inquired, unlocking the front door of the building and giving her a hand with the teetering stack of yellow and green file folders.

"*Over*work is more like it." She pushed the sunglasses with lipstick-red frames up on her nose. "After you left yesterday, I took on another event. A retirement dinner dance on a megayacht for some bigwig

from Boeing. Fortunately, it's not until September or
I'd have to clone myself twice." She staggered over
to her desk, let her burden slide down on the desktop
and sniffed. "I smell fresh pastry. You wouldn't have
stopped at the bakery, would you?"

"Matter of fact, I did." I dropped the files on her
desk.

"Maybe got some of those pecan sticky buns?"

"Yup." I headed for the stairs, eager to see if Susan
Whiteley's e-mail had arrived.

"Any chance you got more than one?"

"Yup."

"Want to trade it for a cup of New Millennium all
organic Honduran java?"

"Deal," I agreed from the top of the stairs, fumbling
for my keys. "Have to check something first."

My answering machine's red light was blinking. I
ignored it and downloaded new e-mails, which contained the forwarded People Recovery Report and the
Rousseau file Whiteley had never had a chance to
share with his client.

The file commenced with notes from Whiteley's first
telephone conversation with Dr. Rousseau, followed
by three "Activity Reports" and an "Invoice for Investigative Services." Page one detailed the same
background information Chantal had given me—last
known addresses, DOB, SSN, names of friends, known
hangouts, etc., etc. There was one category I hadn't
covered—"eccentricities and idiosyncrasies"—which
for Forbes included "likes monogrammed personal
items: handkerchiefs, shirts, cuff links; enjoys Ba-
roque music."

Pages two and three summarized three surveillances
Whiteley had completed on the subject, Forbes Cameron. After six hours across the street from the Rose
and Thistle Club, 43 Carlyle Place, Seattle, Washington, on Wednesday, June 25 at 5:39 P.M., Whiteley had
picked Forbes Cameron up as he was leaving the club

and followed the subject, who was driving a silver gray Jaguar XJ8 with license tags 843LEP, to Mama Wanda's, 813 Maple Avenue. Subject left the XJ8 in valet parking and dined with an attractive, well-dressed blonde of thirty-something wearing a gold wedding ring. Whiteley had attempted to put a bug on the Jaguar, but the valet lot was fenced and the security guard vigilant, so he went to the bar and observed the couple until 10:36, when they left the restaurant. The woman departed in a taxi and the subject signaled the valet for his car. Whereupon Whiteley opted to follow the woman, whose destination was the Evergreen Arms Apartments on Compton Place. After paying the taxi driver, the woman disappeared inside the secured building. As soon as the woman was inside, Whiteley approached the doorman with a scarf and said the woman who had just come in had left it in the taxi. The doorman took the scarf and without revealing her name, said that he would return it to its owner.

"That must be a doozy of a report." Zelda put a red ceramic cup of steaming coffee on my desk and headed for my rucksack. She grinned and pulled the white bakery sack from the front pocket. "Good thing I'm honest. You were so engrossed I could have taken off with the whole bag. What're you reading?"

"The dead P.I.'s report on Forbes Cameron."

"What dead P.I.?"

I explained the demise of Sandy Whiteley. She stared at me. "And I suppose his death had nothing to do with Dr. Rousseau?"

"Don't know yet. At any rate, Whiteley was pretty creative. Listen to this:

> On Thursday, June 26, subject did not leave the Rose and Thistle until 6:45 P.M. I followed subject on foot to the Sorrento Hotel, 900 Madison Street, where subject met the same blond woman he had dined with the night before and

also a tall, thin sandy-haired man of forty-something with a curly beard and moustache. The man wore a gold wedding ring. The three were shown to a table in the Hunt Room. For a sizeable tip [see item #3 on attached invoice], I persuaded the maître d' to seat me at the closest table—I told him they were English movie stars—which was two tables away. I was able to hear only fragments of their conversation. They appeared to know each other well and laughed a lot. At one point the woman shared several photographs with subject. All three spoke British English. I heard subject call the woman "Annie." Following dessert and after-dinner glasses of what looked like port, the sandy-haired man paid the bill with a credit card and they departed. I then repaired to the bar—"

Zelda burst out laughing. " 'Repaired?' What's this dude think he's writing? The Great American Novel?"

"He's actually quite literate. Wouldn't be the first P.I. who decided to make a buck on his cases. Anyway, he goes on.

I then repaired to the bar and spent the next two hours schmoozing the barmaid—a comely English lass from Devon, if you can believe it. I told her I was a reporter with Rolling Stone and said it would be worth a hundred dollars to my editor [see item #4 on invoice] if she could confirm the identity of the sandy-haired man. Whereupon she checked the credit card receipts and reported that the bill had been paid by J. Taylor-Bickford III. I confided that he was Mick Jagger's London banker and took my leave."

"So who're all these people?"

"Hold on. There's more." I scanned page three: The

following day, June 27, Whiteley found a telephone listing for J. and A. Taylor-Bickford, with no address, and
called the number. A woman with an English accent
answered. Whiteley identified himself as the maître d'
from the Hunt Room, said a monogrammed gentleman's
handkerchief with the initials F.W.C. had been found at
their table and asked where he should return the item.
The woman laughed, said something to someone with
her about 'Freddy's hankies' and instructed Whiteley to
send it to the Rose and Thistle Club on Carlyle Place,
if he could get it there before two o'clock, because "Mr.
Campbell" was leaving for Los Angeles. And if he
couldn't, it wouldn't be the end of the world.

There the report ended.

I checked the Rousseau file, compared the surveil-
lance report with the e-mail to Christopher, and bingo!
Forbes Cameron had been dining with Annie and
John Taylor-Bickford on June 26 in Seattle. But had
Whiteley delivered the fictitious handkerchief? Had he
met "Freddy"? I glanced back over the report.

"And?" Zelda prompted. I shared Whiteley's June
27 surveillance, as far as it went. Below, Zelda's phone
began to ring. "Probably the secretary from Boeing."
She swallowed the last bite of sticky bun, grabbed her
coffee cup, and clattered down the stairs.

I nibbled on my own sticky bun and absently sipped
the coffee. The red light on the answering machine
demanded attention. The message was from my friend,
Jared Saperstein, the *Friday Gazette* publisher. Would
I like to meet him for lunch at the Drydock at one?
He had something he wanted to show me. I called
back, accepted the invitation, and turned to the last
page of the Whiteley file, the confidential report on
Frederick W. Campbell, compiled by People Recovery
International, which had arrived after Whiteley's
death.

Sharon Duncan

People Recovery International (PRI)
Confidential dossier #AU765-SW
Frederick W. Campbell

SSN: none
Last known address: Sadri Ahsik Soikak 19, Bey-oglu, Istanbul, Turkey
Telephone number: unknown
Date/Place of birth: March 28, 1958; Edinburgh, Scotland
Parents: Peter Campbell (deceased 1979) and Eliza-beth Fleming (deceased 1984)
Father's occupation: veterinarian
Mother's occupation: novelist
Siblings: Marianne, Millicent (birthdates not available)
Education:
1966–69 Bishop's Stornbridge, Hertfordshire
1969–75: Eton. Excelled in sports and languages (French and Russian)
1975–79: Cambridge University, Trinity College. Read economics; first in Russian language; 1979: passed Foreign Service Office examination
1981: Master's Degree in National Security Strat-egy, National War College, Washington, D. C.
1982: Monterey Language School, Monterey, Cali-fornia; studied Arabic
Career: 1983–2000 British Military Intelligence (MI-6): Postings: Sophia ('84–'86), Moscow ('87–'89), Riyadh ('89–'92), Bogota ('93–'95), Rabat ('95–'97), Istanbul ('97–?)
Marital history: 1983 Married Gwendolyn Godfrey (deceased 1985), daughter of Sir Francis and Lady Henrietta Godfrey of London
Politics: Unknown; parents were Conservatives

Club memberships and associations: White's, London
Banking/investment history: unknown
Police record: none
FBI record: none
Interpol record: not available
FIT taxes due: N/A
Childhood hobbies: horseback riding, swimming
Credit rating: unavailable

Frederick Campbell was a beautiful piece of work. A Scots lad with two sisters, a literary mother, and a father who was a veterinarian. I didn't know anything about Bishop's Stornbridge, but Eton and Cambridge impressed me. A public school education followed by eighteen years in British Military Intelligence. A master's degree from the National War College. A widower at twenty-seven. The rest of it, with a few discrepancies, more or less matched the Forbes Cameron fragments I'd gotten from Dr. Rousseau.

Apparently Whiteley had extrapolated the "Freddy" and "Campbell" from his telephone conversation with Annie Taylor-Bickford and ordered the background report. I scanned the PRI report again. What happened after Istanbul? Is that when Frederick became Forbes Cameron? Zelda's note said the only relevant info she'd found on Forbes Cameron was his marriage license to my client and a Washington State driver's license. And according to Dr. Rousseau, his name had been on the deed to the Seattle condo Dr. Rousseau had disposed of with the help of the power of attorney. But there were no credit cards, no federal tax notations, no bank or investment accounts for Forbes Cameron.

Sanford Whiteley, a fairly creative investigator, had tried to track down Freddy by calling the Taylor-

Bickfords, and had probably spoken to Anne. Anne had blown Forbes's cover.

The next day Sanford Whiteley was dead.

I felt a chill despite the heat and called Dr. Rousseau at the medical clinic, leaving my name and phone number. Then I tried her home phone number. She answered on the second ring and apologized for not returning my earlier call. I told her I had some preliminary information. Could she come to my office?

"I'm off work for the next three days," she said. "My mother is not feeling well and I'd rather not leave her alone. Could you come to my house for lunch tomorrow? At twelve? I have the photographs of my mother's jewelry and tapestries I told you about. And when I was unpacking yesterday, I found some jewelry that belongs to Forbes. It looks custom made. Perhaps you can trace it."

"Noon will work. What's your address?"

She supplied a number on Harborview Terrace a street of well-designed condominiums in an area locally referred to as Snob Hill.

"Any ideas about the identify of "D.D." referred to in your husband's e-mail to his friend Christopher?" I asked.

"Probably some woman," she said with a bitter edge to her voice.

"The e-mail is dated last September 14. He was apparently calling from your condo in Seattle. Could you find the phone bills for that period?"

"I'll go through my files now and fax them to you. Although Forbes usually made calls on his cell phone."

"Do you know his cell phone number? And who the service provider is?"

"I have the number written down. Hold on a minute."

She returned with the number. "He had AT&T Wireless. I heard him complain about how expensive it was."

"Did you call the cell number after he disappeared?"

"Yes. All I got was a recording. I left two messages but he never called back."

"Do you know anyone named Sergei?"

A brief pause. "A school friend, I think."

"Last name?"

She didn't know. I filed Whiteley's reports and the PRI report in the case folder and stared at Forbes's cell phone number. I thought about calling the number and considered what I would say if he answered. Ask him where he was? What he'd done with his wife's investments and his mother-in-law's dowry? Ask if he'd killed Sanford Whiteley and burglarized the Whiteley apartment?

No. Not yet.

I had a better idea.

I called AT&T and requested duplicate copies of the last six months' statements on the cell phone account. The last four digits of the bogus SSN Dr. Rousseau had provided did match the phone company's records, but that cell phone number was no longer in service.

Forbes/Freddy was very good at obscuring his trail.

While I waited for the fax from my client, I downloaded my e-mail messages. The first one was from Mr. Wang, the Singapore P.I. whose talents I had enlisted to hunt down the wandering Harrison Petrovsky and secure his signatures on appropriate documents to allow the proceeds of his mother's estate to be disbursed and Harrison's share to be held until such time as Harrison saw fit to return from his nautical circumnavigation to the state of Washington. Mr. Wang did not send good news.

*Regret to advise that Ocean Dancer and
Captain Harrison Petrovsky no longer at
Golden Lotus Marina. Harbormaster informs
that vessel left yesterday evening, destination
Saigon. Sorry unable be of assistance. Invoice
for 20 hours surveillance is included below.
Respectfully, Wang Lu Wi.*

I forwarded Mr. Wang's message and bill to attorney Carolyn Smith, who was representing the estate.

The second message was the simple background
check I had requested that DataTech run on Jeremy
Rogers of Orcas Island, my Seattle client's suitor from
the upscale on-line matchmaker. I scanned the report
on-screen: Jeremy Rogers had degrees from Harvard,
UC Berkley and Stanford, with the last one being a
Doctor of Jurisprudence. He had lived in Boston, San
Francisco, and Palo Alto, California, and currently had
addresses in Bellevue, an upscale suburb of Seattle,
and Orcas Island. He had been associated with two
law firms, one in Chicago, one in Seattle. He had published numerous articles in what appeared to be schol-
arly law journals. He did not owe any taxes; he had
no police record; his credit rating was A+++; and according to DataTech, his marital status was single. Dr.
Rousseau should have been so lucky. I forwarded the
report to my client and added a personal note: *Go
for it!*

I spent the next hour with Quicken and my on-
line banker, downloading the checks I had written,
identifying deposits—of which there were far too
few—and printing out checks to pay my monthly bills:
moorage for *DragonSpray,* the landline telephone bill,
the cell phone bill, the rent for my office. A couple
of magazine subscription renewals. And that was it. I
had no mortgage payments, no car payments, and no
ugly credit card finance charges, since my credit card

charges were automatically deducted from my checking account.

I inserted the last check in its envelope, affixed postage stamps, and stacked the envelopes on the corner of the desk with a self-righteous flourish. It was eleven fifteen, and I made an executive decision not to start invoicing my clients because if there is one task I detest even more than writing reports, it is sending out invoices for times and expenses. I would do it this afternoon. Or mañana.

I was about to head downstairs when the fax of Dr. Rousseau's September phone bill came through. She had circled two numbers and added a note: *I recognize all the numbers except these two.* I knew one was a San Francisco Bay Area number, or possibly Sacramento. The other was an international number. A call to her long distance company identified the Bay Area number as a listing for the State of California, Office of the Governor. The international number was a business listing for Browne, Smythe & Goodfellow of London, England.

I tried the Sacramento listing first. A chirpy young voice informed me that I had reached Diane Duvall's office. Ms. Duvall was on another call and would receive my name and phone number as soon as she was available. I left my office and cell phone numbers and had the exhilarating sensation of beginning to fit a few minuscule pieces into a heretofore impossible puzzle: Diane Duvall's initials matched the "D.D." in Forbe's letter. That also made her "moneybags." Was she another woman who'd been seduced and divested of her life savings? Feeling I was on a roll, but still unsure of what to say to Christopher Goodfellow, I dialed the London number and listened to the phone ring fourteen times. I glanced at the clock, clicked up the timeanddate.com Web site. It was twelve thirty in Friday Harbor and eight thirty P.M. on the other side of the Atlantic.

I was to meet Jared at one. The office was warm and humid and my shoulders were stiff. I stood up, did some shoulder rolls, put the PRI report on Frederick Campbell in my bag, and locked everything else up.

Downstairs, Zelda stood up with a smug look. "God, but I'm good. I just downloaded the guest list for the Boeing party and forwarded it to the printer for the invitations. I've got a dance band lined up for them, Lily McGregor will do the flowers, and the Movable Feast people will handle the catering!"

I sat in the chair next to her desk and watched her animated face, sparkling green eyes, the sprinkle of freckles over the bridge of her nose. She pulled a sheet of paper out of the printer and waved it in front of me. "I might just start making some money from all of this."

"I'm delighted. How're you and Sheldon doing?"

"Sheldon's been reading relationship books. He says I'm afraid of intimacy."

"Is he right?"

She stared at me, unblinking. "I ever tell you I was married once?"

"No, you didn't."

"I was nineteen. He was an artist, about thirty-five. It lasted a year."

"I see."

"When he moved out, he said it was because I ruined all his underwear when I put it in with my tie-dyed shirt. Can you believe it? The dude's an artist and he gets upset over colorful underwear?"

"Did he break your heart?"

She wrinkled her nose and considered the question. "Actually, I can't remember. I think I was relieved. He had this long beard he never trimmed and it itched my face something fierce. And his friends never bathed. Anyway, Shel and I are going house-hunting this afternoon."

"You've decided to live together?" I asked, surprised.

She shrugged and began tidying up her desk. "Maybe yes, maybe no. You know I've been housesitting at Limestone Hills and that will be up in a few weeks. I get tired of moving in and out of other people's houses. Anything I can do for you before I take off?"

"Yes." I handed her the info from the Whiteley surveillance on the XJ8 license tags and pieces of information I had on the two sisters, Marianne Campbell Ashburn and Millicent Campbell Thatcher. "First of all, run the tag through the DMV database. See if you can get a VIN as well as the registration name. Secondly, get DataTech to do an international search on the two sisters. I'm off to have lunch with Jared."

"My regards to Mr. Saperstein," she called as I headed out the door.

6

All the tables in the main dining room at the Drydock were occupied. I followed the waitress past the
lunch specials board touting Copper River salmon and
into the half-filled bar. Perched on one of the red
leather–covered stools, I ordered a tall lemonade and
pulled the report on Frederick W. Campbell, the perfect British gentleman, from my bag. Impeccable family, proper parents, wonderful education, excellent
marriage . . . for as long as it lasted. And six foreign
postings, which must have been exhilarating for someone who "excelled in languages." Then, after Istanbul, nothing.

"When you have that look, my friend, I know
you're off on a new manhunt. Or womanhunt." It was
Jared Saperstein, briar pipe in mouth, brown paper–
wrapped parcel in hand. He gave me a hug and
hoisted his sturdy, five-foot-nine-inch frame onto the
stool next to mine. "Which probably means you have
a new client who's been used or abused in some fashion. Am I right?"

In a small town on a small island, one quickly learns
the value of discretion. The only people privy to details of my ongoing cases were Zelda and Jared, who
not only had never betrayed my confidences but also
often provided me with unexpected insights.

"Close," I said. "Seduced and abandoned by a British gentleman who romanced her, married her, and, aside from an apparent fondness for pseudonyms, seems unimpeachable on paper." I handed him the People Recovery report.

"As you know, in the game of investigation, nothing is what it seems, British, you say." He scanned the report, then his eyes returned to the top of the page. "Fascinating. Crème de la crème. Excellent husband material. Why did he leave her? Is your client some kind of ogre?"

Chantal Rousseau's almond-shaped green eyes, her long dark lashes, and her flirtatious exchange with Nick over the martinis came to mind. "She's not what most men would call an ogre," I admitted, narrowing my eyes.

"I see," Jared said thoughtfully. "But her husband"—he peered at the report—"Frederick Campbell, is missing?"

"Along with her investments and her mother's jewelry. My client knew him as Forbes Cameron but a former P.I. uncovered the Campbell persona. This report's fine as far as it goes, then he disappears into thin air."

"So, the game's afoot again."

"The game's afoot," Jared, an intense fan of Sir Arthur Conan Doyle, tended to regard the twenty-first-century world through the eyes and ears of Victorian London. "Any dead bodies?"

"One, unfortunately. The Seattle investigator my client hired before me."

Jared gave me a sharp look and raised his eyebrows. "Sorry for the levity," he said, and turned to the bartender. "A pint of Guinness stout, please."

"What's in your package?" I asked.

"My latest find." He untied the string and unwrapped a black leather volume. I peered over his shoulder and read the gilt lettering on the spine: *The American Review, Volume 1, 1845.* "A rare, complete volume of six issues, January to June. Contains the first appearance of Poe's 'Raven.' Along with 'Some Words with a Mummy,' and 'The Valley of Unrest.' "

I touched the soft black leather and nodded in appreciation, though I'd never heard of the last two titles. "Where did you find it?"

Jared chuckled. "Right across the harbor on Brown Island. And there are at least fifty more first editions over there just waiting to be rescued."

"What are they being rescued from, and how did you find them?"

He gave me a sheepish glance. "You'll recall my little fling with Allison Fisher last spring?"

I nodded, visualizing the tall, svelte, overdressed, not-too-bright blond bombshell of a real estate agent. "I thought you'd lost your marbles."

"It all started when a friend of mine from the Bruce Partington Society of the Fifth Estate sent me an e-mail to the effect that somebody with a Friday Harbor address who was an avid collector of Doyle and Poe had recently died. It was rumored that his widow would be disposing of the collection. I tracked the widow down, not knowing that the house was for sale. It's a fifteen-room mansion and Allison had the listing. When I mentioned that I was interested in it, all I meant was that I wanted to see the library. She assumed I had the funds to buy such a house." He grinned. "I guess I wasted her time for a while." He carefully rewrapped the black volume and retied the string.

"I wouldn't worry about it. She was last seen in hot pursuit of a wealthy skipper from Seattle. Did the widow sell her house?"

"Not yet. She's been letting me do some browsing over there." He tapped the People Recovery report. "After you exhaust all other efforts, if this rascal's history is actually the one laid out here and you can't get a lead on his movements since Istanbul, I might have some sources."

"Such as?"

"I spent a fairly long sojourn in London." Jared had retired as a freelance journalist of no small reputation and I recalled his mentioning a series he had done on Margaret Thatcher and her relationships with Ronald Reagan and Mikhail Gorbachev.

"I remember," I said, wondering what he had in mind.

"I still have some connections there. One of them is my cousin's daughter, who works in the Registry at MI-6."

"That's the British equivalent of our CIA."

"Right. And the Registry is their filing division. As you may know, MI-6's prime responsibility is to focus on espionage activities overseas. Its sister agency is MI-5, whose prime responsibility is to guard against penetrations of U.K. organizations by foreign intelligence. Like the CIA, MI-6 used to focus on the Russians, but since *glasnost* and Nine/Eleven, they're spending more funds on counterterrorism in the Middle East. Just like we are." He glanced down at the People Recovery report. "I don't know who your client is, and don't want to know, but if you run into a blank wall, I could nose around a bit."

The bartender brought the pint of Guinness. "I've been corresponding with a retired journalist in Surrey," Jared continued. "He used to live in the Mayfair area of London. Has a daughter who might be around the same age as"—he glanced at the report—"as Mr. Campbell's sisters." He smiled at the waitress, who was hovering at our elbows. "Meanwhile, how about an order of Copper River salmon?"

On my way back to the office after lunch, I stopped at Trudy's Salon and made an appointment for a trim and a manicure. The temperature was still in the low eighties but cooler than the day before. I spied Abigail Leedle dining al fresco at one of the old wrought iron

tables at Madrona Landing. Her companion was a
gentleman in a blue chambray shirt with a wonderful
shock of white hair. I assumed it was Ronald, her
geologist friend. Abby's great-grandparents were
among the original farmers and fisherman that began
to populate the islands back in the mid-1800s. When
Abby retired from teaching biology at the high school,
she turned to her second passion, which was wildlife
photography. Due to her extraordinary talent behind
the lens, coupled with the efforts of her daughter, a
university art professor at Cornell, Abby's work was
now hanging in some excellent galleries. She saw me
and waved, and I made a mental note to call and
invite her for a glass of wine while my mother was
visiting. I couldn't imagine two women more dissimilar
than Abby and Jewel Moon, but anything to keep my
mother off the mopeds.

Back at the Olde Gazette Building, the door was
locked, but a symphonic work with a lot of violins was
drifting from the speakers. Maybe Vivaldi. In my mail
cubby, I found a phone message from Angela and a
note from Zelda clipped to a printed page.

*Voilà! DMV license on Cameron. Dealer
info on the Jag attached and Washington
registration for the Jag. Ordered background
from DataTech on Millicent & Marianne.
Cheers, Z.*

I scanned the printed info, which told me that
Forbes Cameron, 180 lbs., blue eyes, DOB 04-06-63, of
197 Mariposa Street, Seattle, had a Washington State
driver's license that expired in two years. The Jag was
registered to the same address. The blue book review
on the Jag showed it had all the usual luxury sedan
goodies and currently retailed in the Seattle area for
forty thousand dollars. Rather exactly what one might
expect a successful Seattle financial advisor to be driv-

ing. Particularly so if the financial advisor was married to a successful Seattle internist.

Upstairs, my office had turned as hot as an unused garret. I made a herculean effort to raise the stuck window a few more inches and was rewarded with yet another broken fingernail. Muttering a succession of my favorite expletives, I vowed to buy a fan before the day was out and began comparing the info Zelda had compiled with the People Recovery report. The Forbes Cameron persona presented in the Washington driver's license was five years younger than the Frederick Campbell persona. My reverse street directory identified the Mariposa Street address as the location of a mail drop called Postal Options. I dialed their number, said I was calling from the State DDU in Olympia, which didn't actually exist, told the young man who answered the phone that the notice we had sent to Mr. Forbes Cameron had been returned as undeliverable. Could he please check to see if his client had a forwarding address? A long five minutes later, the young man reported that Mr. Cameron's account had been closed and there was no forwarding address.

Another dead end.

I dialed Angela's number at the sheriff's office.

"Deputy Petersen."

"Hullo, Deputy Petersen. Just checking in to see if I might buy you that drink we talked about yesterday."

"Scotia! Yes! God, do I need one. And after just two days on the job. Cutting up cadavers was a lot easier than small town law enforcement. I'm off at five. How about the outside deck at the Spinnaker around five thirty?"

"You're on. How's Matt?"

"Mostly incommunicado. Gotta go."

I hung up the phone and hoped that Matt's snit would be a short one. Being married to a commercial fisherman who spent a large portion of the year in

southeast Alaska was enough of a challenge without
the added burden of temper tantrums. Angela was far
more patient than I was with temperamental men. Or
perhaps more creative than I.

I had one new e-mail, from my mother, which made
me smile. After decades of computer phobia, she had
become an e-mail junkie and had found a free mail
program that allowed her to send messages over exotic
backgrounds. Today's epistle lay over a magenta ocean
sunset.

Scotia, I don't have anyone to leave Leonardo with.
Can I bring him with me? Do I need any dressy
clothes? Would you teach me to sail? Love, J. M.

Leonardo da Vinci was my mother's smart, well-
cared for, overly indulged white shih tzu. I considered
the impact on Calico of installing below decks not just
my mother, but also her animated shaggy dog. I could
probably get Henry to house Calico for a week. What
I was nonplussed about was the request for a sailing
lesson. I had never known my mother to voluntarily
approach anything that floated. I thought she hated
the ocean. I thought the ocean was one of the reasons
she had left my father and fled from St. Ann's Bay
when I was five. But what did I know?

I typed a reply, also over the magenta sunset.

Okay to bring Leonardo. If he can't get
along with Calico, she can bed down with
my dock neighbor. You'll have to walk him
off the docks and clean up the mess if he
poops before you get him to terra firma. As
for clothes, bring what you'd wear at home.
It's pretty much like Mendocino. We can have
a sailing lesson. DragonSpray's a rather
large boat to learn to sail, but I can teach you
some of the basics. See you on Friday.

I logged off and contemplated a week of quality

time with Jewel Moon and Leonardo. Perhaps if we stayed busy, our "issues" as Melissa called them wouldn't surface.

It was three thirty. Vivaldi had retired and the temperature was dropping. Across the street at the high school, the tennis court was empty and two young male middle schoolers in shorts nearly down to their ankles were trudging along Guard Street, skateboards over their shoulders. I stared at the phone and wondered if Diane Duvall would call back.

My calendar for the next day was blank except for lunch with Dr. Rousseau, which would give me time for a swim and some maintenance on *DragonSpray*. I reached for the Rousseau file and made a note of what I wanted to accomplish when I saw her. It probably wouldn't hurt to get better acquainted with her mother, although I had to agree with Forbes's comment in the e-mail to his friend Chris that she didn't speak much English. I tried to remember what language Nick had said Berbers speak.

On-line I found a number of sites on Berber language and culture, many of which were in three languages: French, English, and Tamazight. I learned that the Berbers live in northern Africa throughout the Mediterranean coast, the Sahara, and Sahel, where the population also includes descendants of the eighth- and eleventh-century Arab invaders, and that some twenty million Berbers speak Tamazight. I also learned about the Cultural Berber Movement and the World Tamazight Congress and the International Tamazight Commission for Human Rights. But nothing on the International Fund for Islamic Women.

My wall clock chimed off-key notes at four forty-five and I logged off the Internet, ready to hold my own at lunch the next day.

Angela was already waiting on the deck at the Spinnaker when I arrived, sipping something from a tall

glass and looking alluring and suntanned in a striped
orange and pink cotton dress with spaghetti straps.
Tan was her natural skin color, the genetic heritage
of her Cuban parentage. I wended my way through
the busy tables, noticing the appreciative glances the
three men at the next table were casting in my
friend's direction.

"It's a good thing I wasn't any later," I said in a
low voice, sliding into the chair across from her, "or
Matt would be in serious trouble."

She looked up from the newspaper she was reading.
"What do you mean?"

I rolled my eyes to the left. "The guy in the blue
shirt at the next table can't take his eyes off you."

She gave the adjoining table a sideways glance, co-
quettishly fingered one of her gold hoop earrings, and
smiled. "That's awfully good for the ego of someone
who's about to have her forty-third birthday."

"It's the dress," I said. "Probably makes you the
sexiest deputy sheriff in the history of San Juan
County."

She glanced down at the colorful smocked, elasti-
cized midriff that clung to her small, high breasts. "I
had to change. Couldn't take the uniform another
minute. It wasn't designed for eight-five degrees in
the shade."

"Neither am I. What are you drinking?"

"Strawberry lemonade. But I could be tempted by
something stronger."

I waved to the waitress with Sassoon hair who was
lounging against the back wall of the deck. Angela
switched to a glass of Eastern Washington merlot and
I ordered dry vermouth and soda. The waitress recited
the evening's specials and we agreed to consider them.

"You survived your first two days as deputy sheriff," I said.

"Barely. Two M.I.P.'s, one moving violation, one

B. and E., and a visit to Santa Maria to check on the prowler."

"What's happening on Santa Maria?"

She shrugged. "Not much, as far as I can see. A woman from California by the name of von Suder bought the old convent and three or four hundred acres that go with it. She wants to start a vineyard and a bed-and-breakfast. She said the servants claim someone's been lurking around for over a week. Things that go bump in the night. I couldn't find even a footprint."

The waitress brought our drinks and moved to the next table when we advised her we hadn't made up our minds between the halibut Delmonico and the pasta a la puttanesca. Angela took a sip of wine. At the next table, the man in the blue shirt signed the credit card voucher with a flourish, stood up, and cast a hopeful smile in Angela's direction. She ignored the look and he strolled after his friends with a disappointed face.

"Maybe the people on Santa Maria have a case of wilderness phobia," I suggested.

She nodded. "I told them that even over here there's a whole nocturnal jungle that comes alive after sundown. Raccoons, rabbits, foxes, feral cats, wandering herds of deer. And San Juan is suburbia compared to Santa Maria. I don't think anyone's lived on that property since the sisters moved out about five years ago."

"Is the owner living in the convent?"

"There's a small apartment in one wing where she's installed a propane generator. The Hispanic family who helps her out is living in one of the other wings. Husband and wife in their forties and two young men in their twenties. The wife is the cook. The men said they hadn't seen anything, but the wife thinks there are *fantasmas* in the convent." She took another sip of wine. "You should see the generator, Scotia. A 12 kW Kohler. Matt would die for it."

"Is your better half still being noncommunicative?"

"He's filling in for a skipper that quit on one of the whale watch boats. He gets up at four every morning, goes out to the Netshed for breakfast. Could be worse. I get to sleep in on the days I don't have early shift. And a few weeks with the tourists will make him appreciate me. But just in case, I've ordered the world's sexiest red lace nightie from Victoria's Secret. Satisfaction guaranteed or my money back."

Angela was endlessly creative with temperamental men.

At nine o'clock the docks at the port were still teeming with barefoot sailors in faded denim cutoffs and after-dinner strollers of every demeanor and disposition. I stopped at the port rest rooms, then made my way through the evening throng and out to G-73. There were two figures on *Pumpkin Seed*'s stern deck, one female and red-haired, the other male and balding. Calico was stretched along the rail. The female figure leaned back in her deck chair and waved a plastic champagne flute in my direction. It was Lindsey, Henry's former betrothed. Henry, beaming, had his arm around her shoulder.

"Evening, Scotia. Want to help us celebrate?"

Given the timbre of Lindsey's voice, I deduced it wasn't her first glass of bubbly. Truthfully, after a vermouth and soda at the Spinnaker and an Irish coffee at the Dry Dock for dessert I had no desire for more alcohol. But of late I'd been working on being more neighborly, so I stowed my bag on *DragonSpray* and climbed aboard *Pumpkin Seed*. "May I inquire as to the nature of the celebration?" I asked, accepting the brimming plastic flute from Lindsey.

She giggled. "I missed Calico so I came by to see

her. Henry offered me a drink. One thing led to another. And . . .'' She grinned at Henry.

"We're engaged again," he finished. "And we're
going to learn to tango."

I lifted my glass. "To the tango."

Calico stood on the rail, stretched, and leaped into
my lap. I stroked her head and decided it was an
opportune time to mention Leonardo's imminent
arrival.

"Henry, I may need you to keep Calico on *Pumpkin
Seed* all next week. My mother's arriving with her dog
on Friday."

"Not a problem. We'll see that she'd bedded down.
Won't we, toots?"

He leaned over and gave Lindsey a long kiss, followed by a longer meaningful look. I wished them
well and was headed back to *DragonSpray,* Calico at
my heels, when my cell phone chirped. The caller ID
showed a Sacramento number. Must be Diane Duvall.

"Thank you for calling back, Mrs. Duvall. My name
is Scotia MacKinnon. I'm a Washington State investigator and I'm trying to locate Forbes Cameron. Can
you help me?"

"I don't know a *Forbes* Cameron."

I caught a slight stress on the first name. "We came
across your name in some of my client's papers. Mr.
Cameron might have been using another name."

There was a long silence.

"Miss Duvall?"

"Why have you called *me*?"

"We came across your name in some of his papers
and thought you might be able to help us."

Another long silence. "It was *Will* Cameron and I
haven't heard from him for . . . a long time. I haven't
a clue as to where he might be. I hope I never see
him again."

Since Diane Duvall did not sound like a fan of my

client's missing husband, I tried a direct approach.
"Ms. Duvall, I represent Mr. Cameron's wife in a matter involving a fairly large sum of money. While she shares your sentiments concerning the gentleman, anything you could tell me that would help me find him would be appreciated.

"A fairly large sum of money." She chuckled mirthlessly. "Well, well. Was it blackmail or straight out theft?"

"Closer to the latter."

"So I wasn't the only stupid one. Look, I don't want to discuss this on the phone. You said you were in Washington. I'm going to be in Seattle this week for a conference. I could meet you there, either Thursday or Friday."

I did a fast mental review of my calendar, decided a blackmail victim was definitely worth talking to, and made an appointment to meet her at Starbuck's on Fifth Avenue on Thursday afternoon at three. I then called Puget Sound Air and booked a seat on their noon flight to Lake Union, returning at five fifteen, which would get me back in time to prepare for my mother's arrival on Friday afternoon. I hung up the phone, undressed, and mentally replayed the brief conversation with Diane Duvall, hoping Dr. Rousseau would agree that she wanted to find Forbes Cameron badly enough to pay for the hundred sixty dollar round-trip fare to Seattle.

1

Wednesday morning was Take Care of Scotia time: up at six-thirty, an orange juice–yogurt smoothie for breakfast, a four-mile walk out Shoreline Road, followed by a swim at the health club. When I got to the club a little before nine, Abigail was coming out of the print shop next door.

"Morning, Scotia." She handed me a flyer with a photograph of one of the black-and-white orca pods doing their feeding rolls completely surrounded by boats. "Whale Watching or Whale Abuse?" demanded the title in bold red letters. Reading below the photo, I was invited to an information meeting on Sunday afternoon. "I hear your mother is coming to visit. Bring her along and join us on Sunday if you have time."

"Thanks, Abby. I'll let her know. Incidentally, she'd like to meet you. Do you have time for a glass of wine sometime this weekend?"

"Let me think. There's a planning meeting on Saturday afternoon, but we could get together afterward. How about we meet around six at the Dry Dock?"

"Sounds good. You want to bring your geologist friend?"

"Ronald?" She smiled. A soft blush colored her cheeks. "I'll ask him."

The only other swimmer was a thin, bald-headed

man in yellow goggles who swam a splashy crawl stroke for thirty minutes, leaped nimbly out of the pool, and trotted off in the direction of the whirlpool. While I executed my own slower, less splashy side-stroke, I thought about Diane Duvall, the bitter tone in her voice, the reference to blackmail, the addition of the "Will Cameron" persona. I didn't like the information I was turning up.

Whether or not my client knew more about her missing husband than she'd shared with me, I was beginning to suspect this case could fall below my Circle Test cutoff. That is, anything involving individuals whom Dante would have consigned to the Fifth Circle of Hell or below: That includes serious criminals, psychopaths, or potential clients who are endangered by either of the former. Those cases were out of my league.

Between the fifteenth and twentieth laps, I decided to reserve the right to resign from the case if it got nasty. I spent ten minutes in the whirlpool, showered, and stashed my swimsuit and towel in my locker. On the way back to *DragonSpray,* I detoured to the Olde Gazette Building to check for messages and found one from Nick. He'd tried to make a floatplane reservation for me for next Tuesday but they were all sold out. Could I drive down to Seattle?

Thanks to Zelda and Sheldon's efforts, the Volvo's battery had gotten recharged after its failure on Saturday, and they'd driven it out to Nick's on Sunday. But I still didn't know what had drained the battery in the first place. I called him back and said I was thinking of taking the Volvo to the local mechanic for a checkup. "If the car's okay, I'll be happy to drive down," I said. "I have some boat supplies I need to pick up at Doc Foreman's."

"Have them check the Volvo carefully," he suggested. "There might be something going on with the alternator. I don't want you to get stranded." He paused. "Forgive my mentioning it, love, but when are you going to replace that ancient chariot?"

"One of these days, when I get time to do some research. Where shall I meet you?"

"At the condo. I should be home by six. I'll leave a key with the security guy in case I'm late. His name's Keith."

I heard a click on the line. "Another call, Scotty. See you Tuesday. Call my cell phone when you get in."

Although I'd much rather take the floatplane down to Lake Union and avoid the hassle of the ferry in midsummer, after I got the boat parts I'd have time for some girlie shopping before I went to Nick's. I wondered how he'd react to me in a red teddy from Victoria's Secret.

Chantal Rousseau's Amalfi Condominium complex overlooked Brown Island and the harbor. It was a ten-minute walk from the garage where I'd left the Volvo to her unit. I was sweating profusely as I traipsed up the flagstone walk and pressed the doorbell. A melodic bell sounded inside the condo. I waited, tapped my foot, and rang the bell again. A turquoise Subaru passed in the street, made a U-turn in the cul-de-sac, and disappeared downhill. Ten seconds or so later Dr. Rousseau appeared, attired in a well-fitting silky black V neck jersey T-shirt over black and green flowered harem pants. A filmy green scarf, the shade identical to her eyes, floated from her neck. Her perfectly pedicured feet were bare. I glanced at my sensible tan linen trousers and businesslike ivory cotton blouse. Would this woman forever make me feel underdressed and dowdy?

"Sorry," she said. "I was cutting the lemons and had to wash my hands. Please come in." She ushered me through the foyer and into a cool, spacious living room with a dark red oriental rug on the hardwood

floor. I took in the carved wooden cabinets, the embroidered silk floor cushions. A collection of jeweled
music boxes decorated a side table. The muted chords
from some stringed instrument drifted from two large
speakers. "Beautiful room," I said.

"Please sit. I will bring the information we talked
about. *Maman* is preparing our lunch. Would you like
some iced mint tea?"

I told her iced anything sounded wonderful and settled on one end of the long gold moiré sectional sofa.
The scent of cinnamon and cloves wafted from the
kitchen. In a windowed alcove I glimpsed a round
wooden table set for two. Above the table a collection
of colored glass lanterns—amber, jade green, and co-
balt—hung suspended on thick brass chains.

A set from *A Thousand and One Arabian Nights*.

With Forbes Cameron as one of the Forty Thieves?

Beside the sofa where I was seated, a cherrywood
bookcase displayed volumes of books behind glass
doors. *Nine Parts Desire, Rage Against the Veil,
Hamas: Political Thought and Practice, A Street in
Marrakesh, Holy War, Inc.* More or less what I would
have expected an Islamic French Moroccan to read. I
was starting to check out the next shelf, where I spied
Guns and Chiffon and *Women and Guns* when Chantal returned with my iced tea and arranged herself
gracefully beside me. "Were you able to identify the
two phone calls?" she asked, laying a stack of photos
on the glass coffee table.

"One was to Forbes's friend Christopher Goodfellow in London. We haven't been able to reach him."
I took a long sip of the tea. "The second was to a
woman named Diane Duvall. The one referred to as
D.D. in the e-mail. She's agreed to talk to me tomorrow in Seattle."

"The one he called 'moneybags,' " she said grimly.

I was about to tell her about the blackmail when
she abruptly reached for the photos.

"These are the photos of the jewelry and the tapestries. I found a description of the carpets in one of my father's old files."

I put the glass of tea on the table and turned my attention to the stack of photos she held. She spread out half a dozen photos and handed me a sheet of paper. It was a list of the carpets.

19th-century Middle Atlas Carpet, 11'6" × 6'1", containing diamond patterns.

Late-19th-century Zemmour carpet, 7'4 ½" × 5'8", predominately red; geometric motifs.

20th-century Mediouna carpet 12'5 ½" × 5'4", possibly of Persian influence.

"My father had the tapestries photographed when they moved to Seattle from Paris."

"I'll get color Xeroxes," I said, "and then you should put the originals in a safe-deposit box." The photos showed colorful old rugs hung on a wall. I knew virtually nothing about the value of rugs or tapestries, oriental or otherwise, and would have to find someone who did and who could suggest where a thief might fence such objects. "Did you think of filing a claim on your homeowner's insurance policy?"

"I called the insurance company. They said the tapestries and fine arts are not covered. It would have required what they call a special rider." She moved the photos of the tapestries to one side and spread out a set of large, colored prints. "My mother and father at their wedding. She is wearing the jewelry that Forbes took."

The first photo was of a girl swathed in a vivid blue cape over a long white skirt. She wore a tall, pointed headdress wrapped in bands of colored yarn and decorated with bright sequins. A face covering left only her dramatic, long-lashed, kohl-rimmed eyes revealed.

About her neck hung an ornate silver necklace with colored stones. "Wonderful photos," I said.

"Yes, the photographer was my father's friend from Rabat. A journalist. He published some of them later in an American magazine." She pointed to the necklace Raheela wore in the photo. "It is silver and glass and amber. It belonged to my mother's mother."

The other photos showed a crowded marketplace with barren mountains in the background. Some of the men wore white turbans, some wore colorful knit hats, and still others sported handsome head coverings of some woven or braided fabric. All had smiling, hopeful faces. The prospective brides were attired in the identical woven cape and ornate headdress that the young Raheela wore. I examined the photo of a couple holding hands.

"C'est moi et mon mari." That's me and my husband.

I looked up. Raheela, clad in a voluminous dark red cotton garment, but without head covering, pointed to a couple in the last photo. *"Et l'autre,"* she said, indicating the photo of two laughing young men with their arms around each other, *"c'est Guy et mon frère."*

"Guy was my father and the other is my mother's brother, my uncle Ali," Dr. Rousseau explained. "Uncle Ali worked at the consulate in Rabat. He and my father became friends. That is how my mother and my father met."

Raheela said something to her daughter that I didn't understand and then touched my hand. *"Je m'excuse, madame.* I no speak well the anglais."

"Pas de problème, Raheela," I assured her.

"Come. My mother will serve the lunch. Bring the photos. She wants you to know about the brides' fair."

Raheela declined to eat with us and insisted on serving, darting in and out of the small kitchen to the right of the dining alcove, presenting first the cucumber and lemon salad and the small phyllo pastry triangles filled with feta cheese. She interspersed the serving with glances at the photos and running comments in a language I did not understand but assumed was Tamazight.

"The annual brides' fair takes place in September," Dr. Rousseau translated. "It is also a regional market day. All the bachelors come, and all the young women who are old enough for marriage. Or who are divorced and want to get remarried."

I had assumed that a divorced Muslim woman was no longer marriageable. Dr. Rousseau noticed my look of surprise. "The Berbers are very different from the Arabs," she said. "Marriage is by mutual consent only. The marriages are arranged for the good of the community and usually the couple already know each other. At the fair, the man indicates his choice by grasping the hand of the girl he wants to marry. If she wants him, all she has to say is 'You have captured my liver.' If she does not like the man, all she has to do is break the handclasp. And if a marriage does not work, a divorce is not difficult. The Berber women are free to divorce when they want and to remarry whom they want."

"What's the significance of the liver?" I asked.

"The liver helps digestion and makes good health. So the liver, not the heart, is considered the location of true love." She glanced at her mother. Raheela nodded and added a lengthy comment.

"My mother was married before she knew my father. Her first husband died. When her brother went to work in Rabat, he really missed the family and he had Mother's picture in his room. My father fell in love with her picture. She accepted him immediately and they were married for forty-five years."

Raheela removed our salad plates and returned with a platter heaped with steaming fluffy white grains covered with slices of oranges and plump raisins. "Couscous," she announced proudly. The couscous tasted even better than it smelled and belonged to a far different culinary world than my usual midday fare of clam chowder and a piece of bread.

Raheela lingered for my smile and nod of approval and then picked up one of the wedding photos. She murmured something, then returned to the kitchen.

"My mother says the brides' fair is an old custom," Dr. Rousseau translated. "Some people think it is awful, that the girls are sold into marriage, but that is never the case. It is a very old ritual. She thinks it works better than the modern system of romantic marriage." She toyed with the couscous on her plate. "My mother is not happy that I have married twice and both marriages ended. She says if we were in Morocco and a man had treated me like Forbes did, our male relatives would have killed him." With her knife she artfully nudged the couscous onto her fork and chewed thoughtfully.

"I understand you and Crystal Cooper are involved in a relief effort for Muslim women."

She nodded. "We're working with human rights groups in all the Muslim countries where women are forced into marriages, but our focus is on the Afghan women, the ones whose families were forced to sell their daughters to the Taliban and al Qaeda fighters. It was bad enough that they usually didn't see their husbands until their wedding day, but a lot of times they didn't even speak the same language. Some of them were locked in the house all day with the curtains drawn. When bin Laden's forces fell apart, the husbands fled. Now the women don't know if they're married or if they're widows. There's no one to feed them or their children."

Raheela came in from the kitchen and stood near the table. When her daughter grew quiet, Raheela began talking, spitting out her words in anger. I looked at my client, who was nodding.

"Of all the ways the Taliban abused women," she

explained, "the worst were the kidnappings, where they would burst into houses and cull the young, beautiful women. Some were taken to Pakistan and sold to brothels that serviced the terrorist training camps. We do what we can, but the lives of these young women are ruined." She regarded the last raisin on her plate and frowned. "Crystal thinks it's all a matter of uncovering women's faces and, voilà, democracy and equality will spring up. It is a lot more complex. Many of the women, in Iran and Pakistan as well as in Afghanistan, do not really mind covering their head or face. They are very traditional and modest and feel more dignified 'observing purdah' as it is called. Keeping the *burqa* or wearing a scarf called a *chador*, like my mother was wearing at Nicholas's dinner party, is more comfortable for them. In some of the countries, the women wear it as a political statement to show their , , , their dislike for Western culture." She was silent for a moment, then pushed her plate away and changed the subject. "You said you have a report for me."

I gave her the summary of what I'd uncovered. She scanned Whiteley's surveillance report and the PRI report, frowned and muttered something unintelligible. When she finished, she laid the sheaf of papers on the table and took a deep breath. "It is worse than I expected. Forbes Cameron is an alias. You were right; he is a con man. How are you going to find him?"

I nibbled on a phyllo pastry. "Diane Duvall indicated that Forbes may have blackmailed her. Although that was not the name he was using. I'm hoping she can give me a lead."

"Blackmailed!"

"That's what she said. She may have other information. His cell phone service has been discontinued, but I will try to locate his two sisters. Do you think they'll talk to me?"

She frowned. "Forbes said that when his mother

died, the girls inherited all her money. Or most of it. Forbes got what you call a pittance. I don't know why. He was very bitter. He said once that he never wanted to see Marianne again. For some reason, he was okay with Millie inheriting."

Raheela removed our plates and brought small cut-glass bowls of lemon sherbet, a plate of aniseed cookies, and small cups of strong coffee. We finished the meal in silence and I was about to leave when Dr. Rousseau gave a small exclamation. "The cuff links! I almost forgot. Excuse me."

She returned immediately and handed me a small, dark blue velvet pouch with a thin black drawstring. I emptied the contents into my hand: a pair of chunky gold cuff links monogrammed with the initials "F.W.C." in an intricate, old-fashioned script. They were heavy, probably custom made. "Did you ever see him wear these?" I asked.

She shook her head.

I tucked the velvet pouch in my bag and told her I'd be in touch as soon as I had more information. As I moved toward the door, Raheela padded briskly across the thick carpet and pressed a small glass jar into my hand.

"Pour vous, madame. Confiture d'oranges." I thanked her for the marmalade and for the lunch and turned to leave when I felt her small hand grasp my arm tightly. *"Le mari de ma fille, il est mauvais,"* she whispered fiercely, her green eyes blazing with hatred. *"Je l'ai maudit. Il va mourir."*

My daughter's husband is evil. I have cursed him. He is going to die.

Involuntarily I shivered, pulled my arm away, and let myself out into the warm summer afternoon.

8

Raheela's fierce words followed me all the way down the hill to the auto repair shop and I speculated on exactly what Dr. Rousseau's motives might be in wanting to locate Forbes Cameron. Not that I had much hope that I was going to find "Freddy" if he didn't want to be found.

The Volvo was waiting outside the shop. The mechanic had added water, cleaned the cables, recharged the battery, checked the alternator, and found nothing amiss. Relieved, I paid the cashier, drove down Spring Street and parked in front of Martinelli's Jewelry and Fine Arts. Mrs. Martinelli was in the front of the store showing diamond rings to a couple that looked too young to be contemplating marriage. I found Mr. Martinelli with his head of thick gray hair bent over a workbench back in the repair department. He emptied the blue velvet pouch I handed him, stared at the monogrammed cuff links, and shook his head. "Not like anything we sell," he said. "Probably made by some hippie somewhere. Most likely cost an arm and a leg, but it's sloppy workmanship." He returned the two pieces to the pouch with disdain. I pulled out the wedding photos of Raheela in her silver and amber bride's necklace.

Mr. Martinelli gave a short whistle. "Now that's beautiful stuff. You trying to sell it?"

"It was stolen from a client of mine. Where would a thief peddle something like this?"

He shrugged. "Places that specialize in estate sales, antique jewelry stores. Probably wouldn't get very much if he pawned it." He turned slowly around on his chair and stared at a row of dusty books behind his desk. He pulled out a large red volume and began turning pages, running down the columns of fine print with a gnarled index finger. "There are two or three stores on the West Coast that buy antique jewelry and pay pretty good for it." He wrote several names and phone numbers on a sheet of Martinelli stationery and handed it to me. "Try these. I hope your client gets her jewelry back."

I returned to the car, drove it back up to the port lot, and returned to the Olde Gazette Building. An operatic aria that I failed to identify filled the first floor. Zelda once did a stint for a Seattle FM station. Her knowledge of classical symphonies and opera far exceeded mine. There was no sign of her or her lab Dakota.

Upstairs the stifling heat reminded me that I'd forgotten to buy a fan yesterday. I laid out the items Dr. Rousseau had given me: photos of her parent's wedding, photos of the missing tapestries and jewelry, the monogrammed cuff links. Downstairs the door opened and Dakota's toenails scrabbled across the plank floor. The door slammed and a minute or so later I heard the sound of popcorn kernels tumbling into the hot air popper.

I examined the monogrammed cuff links with the ornate initials twisted around a lion's head and considered the infinitesimally small possibility of identifying the "hippie" designer who had cast them. I checked the photo of Forbes on their wedding day. The requisite three-eighths of an inch of white French cuff was showing but no jewelry was visible. I replaced the

photo in the file. It was four o'clock. I wanted to get
to the hardware store before my four-thirty appointment at Trudy's. I gathered up the photos of the missing dowry and the list of estate brokers and antique
jewelers Martinelli had provided, hopeful of cajoling
Zelda into calling them. I stared at the cuff links,
started to put them in my desk, then took them downstairs as well.

"Hi, boss. Popcorn's ready. Sorry it's late today.
Shel and I went to look at an old house out in the
valley. Really funky but a lot better than the condo
he thought we should rent last weekend."

I laid the two cuff links on her desk. She frowned
and reached for them. "Where'd you get these?"

"Inadvertently left behind when Forbes Cameron
pulled his Houdini act. Or maybe it wasn't so inadver-
tent. They don't look like what a Fortune 500 financial
advisor would wear."

"They're Cuzcos. Maybe some dame gave them to
him."

"What's a Cuzco?"

"It's a him. He casts jewelry. His name's not really
Cuzco, it's Nathan Tate. That's what he calls himself
because he claims he's using the same process to cast
gold that the Incas did. We shared a house right after
I moved to the island."

"You mean he's here? On San Juan Island?"

"Yeah. Or, actually, he's almost got his *own* little
island. He lives out near Jefferson Beach and you can
only get to his studio at low tide. At high tide you
wade or use a rowboat. That's why I moved out." She
turned the cuff link over. "See this little twisty "C"
here? That's his signature. You want I should call
him?"

"Does he keep records of who buys his stuff?"

"You better believe it. He's even got it computerized. He gets very attached to his creations. Once he

refused to sell a ring to a woman because he didn't like the shoes she was wearing." She chortled. "He didn't think she would give the ring a good home."

"I'd like to talk to him."

She dialed a number, spoke affectionately to whoever answered, and said a friend of hers needed help. She handed me the phone.

I identified myself and explained that in connection with an investigation I had come across a pair of cuff links he had designed. I described the cuff links and the monogram and asked if he could tell me who had ordered them.

"That would have been a while ago," he said. "I don't do much monogrammed stuff, but I could check. Look, I'm in the middle of a project right now. Where can I reach you this evening?"

I gave him my home phone and my cell phone numbers.

"Sheldon's picking me up in about an hour and we're going to look at something out near the gravel pit," Zelda said. "Any sleuthing you want done?"

I handed her the lists of antique jewelers and estate dealers and the photos of the tapestries. "This is the stuff Freddy absconded with. See if you have any luck tracking these down. You still have the list of Seattle pawn shops we contacted after the diamond heist over on Orcas?"

"Sure do. And an old buddy of mine at Microsoft just forwarded a new site called Hidden Assets. They recover missing stuff. If these lists don't do the trick, I'll check out the site."

"Also, see what you can find on the death of Gwendolyn Campbell, daughter of Sir Frances Godfrey, back in '85 in London. There was a burglar involved."

"Anything else?"

I handed her the Post-it note with the number for Goodfellow et al. "This is a bit touchy," I said slowly. "It's too late today, but tomorrow morning, make up a cover story and call Christopher Goodfellow's office. See if you can get anything out of a secretary about Goodfellow or Freddy. It's a fishing expedition. Whatever you do, don't tell Goodfellow we're looking for his chum. And you might also try to hack your way into Forbes Cameron's e-mail. It could tell us a lot."

The hardware store was out of fans but had them on order. Coming out of the store I ran into Angela, also in search of a cooling device. She invited me to dinner at her house and I accepted. I hurried over to Second Street for my hair trim and manicure and was back on *DragonSpray* at six o'clock for a change into tank top, shorts, and sandals.

It was six thirty when I turned off Pear Point Road and onto the long private drive that wound for half a mile through Oregon grape and salal down to the edge of Griffin Bay. The house Matt had inherited from his mother was a sprawling, weathered two-story brown-shingled structure in need of considerable maintenance. The only new elements Matt had added after he married Angela was the expansive wraparound cedar deck and a Wolf cooking range she'd talked him into a year ago.

I parked the Volvo behind the two-car garage, admired the lush tomato plants and the herb garden surrounded by the deer-proof fence. Away from the concrete pavement of town, it was ten degrees cooler. The black earth under the trees gave off a damp, woodsy smell. I found Angela reclining in a weathered Adirondack chair on the deck, bare brown feet propped up on top of the deck railing, sipping what looked like a gin and tonic. "There's beer and wine in the fridge," she offered without getting up, "and hard stuff in the liquor cabinet. I'm trying to stay cool by not moving. Help yourself."

I found dry vermouth, added ice and club soda, and toted it out to the deck along with my cell phone. I

pulled up the other Adirondack chair and we gazed
out at the tranquil blue expanse of Griffin Bay and
beyond to San Juan Channel that stretched southwest
to Cattle Pass, the narrow rock-studded passage that
separates San Juan from Lopez Island. Along that passage numerous sailors over the years had come to grief
or narrowly avoided it. One of the more memorable
near misses featured a Washington State ferry boat
pilot who had smoked a bit of B. C. Bud, the Canadian marijuana, before taking the helm and deciding
to vary the usual route from Friday Harbor to Sydney,
B. C., by running through the pass. He had nearly run
aground on Goose Island with 250 passengers on
board.

"Where's Matt this evening?" I asked.

"He'll be late. By the time they get the last group
of whale watchers unloaded and the boats ready for
the next day, it's at least seven o'clock."

"Are you two talking yet?"

"He's beginning to thaw out. But you know, I really
don't give a rat's toenail! He can't throw me out in
the street. Though right about now he's probably mad
as a hornet that he put my name on the deed for
this house."

I remembered the quibbling that had transpired
after they got married. Quibbling about how the house
had been built by his great-grandfather and about how
he had already lost half his assets when his first wife
divorced him. But ultimately he had acquiesced to
adding her name to the title. From what Dr. Rousseau
had said, the title to her Seattle condominium had also
been held jointly, and Freddy in his Forbes Cameron
persona could have walked away with half the equity,
if he had so chosen, although in the mutual-power-of-
attorney clause he had found an easier tool for theft.

I eyed the cell phone, wondering when I'd hear back
from Nathan Tate about who had ordered the monogrammed cuff links. It was a tenuous connection, but

no more tenuous than hoping for something from Diane Duvall or trying to trace the tapestries and jewelry. Angela finished off her G & T and returned to the kitchen to answer the phone. Above the deck a bald eagle circled and circled again, huge wings outspread, powerful eyes searching for the careless rabbit or wandering feline. The sun still rode high in the sky to the west. In July, thanks to living at forty-eight degrees north latitude, daylight lasts until well after ten p.m.

Angela padded back to the deck.

"Matt?"

She nodded, stirred her drink with one finger, took a long sip. "How'd you survive when your first husband—I forget his name—just up and left? How'd you stay sane?"

I watched her lounge against the deck railing and wondered if there was more trouble brewing between the Petersens than could be repaired by red lingerie. "His name was Simon," I said slowly, answering her question. "I was finishing my senior year at San Francisco State. Melissa was four. When Simon didn't come back from his dive expedition to the Seychelles, I thought I was going to die." I took a long swallow of the vermouth, recalling how long I'd been in denial that he had, indeed, left us for good. "The only thing that kept me going was Melissa. She had to be fed and taken to day care and picked up from day care and fed again and read to and put to bed. And after she was asleep, I had homework to do. On Saturday nights, Melissa stayed with my neighbor and I tended bar at a raunchy saloon on Geary Avenue. I put one foot ahead of the other. I graduated with honors. I enrolled in the Police Academy and got hired by S.D.P.D. Then one lovely fresh spring morning I made the surprising discovery that I didn't feel anything for Simon any more." I took a deep breath.

"I married Matt for all the right reasons," Angela

said, "but I know and he knows I can't simply be the wife of an old island fisherman. However good my intentions were, I found I have to have meaningful work."

"You gave it a good try. Going from UCLA professor of forensic medicine to a stay-at-home housewife on a remote island was quite a jump." Of course, the stay-at-home job description required accompanying Matt to southeast Alaska for six months of commercial fishing, which she did only once. For a long time, I didn't know why she hadn't returned to Alaska the following year. Recently she had confided they'd almost lost the boat in a storm. Or at least Angela thought they'd almost lost it; Matt had referred to it as "a little blow."

"Now I don't even try to be the perfect wife," she went on. "Matt's started preparing his own breakfast or going out to the Netshed if I leave early. A year ago, he'd have gone on a hunger strike." She looked at me over the rim of her glass. "Isn't it dazzling the things we try to talk ourselves into?"

I nodded and reached for my chirping cell phone. It was Nathan Tate. Angela disappeared in the direction of the kitchen muttering about spinach ravioli.

"I found the records you wanted," Nathan reported. "The cuff links were ordered by Kimberly Korda for her fiancé a little over a year ago. I don't know his name. Kim is from Orcas but she was living in Ventura, in Southern California then. I heard she's moved back here with her kids. She's working at the Doe Bay Realty Office. Does that help?"

"Tremendously," I assured him, and dialed directory assistance. There was no listing for a Kimberly Korda on Orcas Island. A call to Doe Bay Realty got me the answering machine. I left my name and number and joined Angela in the kitchen. She was stirring something creamy in a pan. A pot of water steamed on the Wolf range.

"Good news or bad?" she asked.

"Not sure yet."

"You on a serious case?"

"Could be. What can I do?"

"There's a bag of washed greens in the fridge," she said. "Freshly picked tomatoes on the counter."

I tore the romaine lettuce into bite-sized pieces and sliced the ripe tomato into wedges, recalling similar evenings in San Diego a long time ago: Angela unwinding from a grueling—and from my perspective gruesome—day as the P. D. Medical Examiner, me recovering from one or another case of domestic abuse.

"What's the news from Mendocino?" she asked.

"Giovanni is off to climb mountains in Italy with his cousin and Jewel Moon is arriving on Friday for a week. Merde! Today is Wednesday and I've got to go to Seattle tomorrow, which means I have to clean up the boat tonight."

"I seem to remember your mother isn't too fond of boats. You want to park her here? There's plenty of room. Clean sheets in both the guest rooms. Does she drive?"

"Does my mother drive? She's crisscrossed the country at least ten times and could have stood in for either Tom Wolfe or Jack Kerouac."

"Then I'll plan on it," Angela said. I thanked her profusely and added a hug. She drained the pasta, transferred it to two plates, and ladled the cream sauce over it. "Let's take this into the living room," she suggested. "I came across an old Marcello Mastroianni video when I was cleaning yesterday. *Divorce Italian Style.*"

We settled in to watch the movie. Matt arrived home as the final credits were rolling. By the time I got back to town, the hands on the court house clock pointed to 10:18. I turned down First Street to Spring Street, which was as crowded as Las Olas Boulevard during Fort Lauderdale spring break, and slowed the Volvo to a crawl as two unsteady twenty-year-olds assisted their even more inebriated pal off the curb in front of George's and down the middle of the street toward the waiting white ferry boat.

According to the big digital sign outside the Bank of the Islands, the weather was still a sultry eighty-five degrees, the wind southeast at three. I left the car in the port parking lot, stopped at the rest rooms, and ambled down the wide main dock. A thin crescent of new moon floated over the harbor. Out on G dock, *Pumpkin Seed* lay white and tranquil in the moonlight and no tortoiseshell feline rose from beneath *Dragon-Spray*'s canvas dodger to greet me.

With the hatch boards back in place, I made a cup of Sleepytime tea and donned the gauzy cotton pj's Zelda had left on my desk after one of her raids on the thrift shop. Just before I turned out the light, a small fresh breeze drifted through the porthole. I turned on Fox News, which was reporting a swarm of earthquakes in the San Francisco Bay area and the upcoming Pacific Rim Trade Conference to take place at the Westin Hotel in Seattle, beginning tomorrow. Seattle P.D. would furnish extra security since some demonstrations were expected. I turned off the TV and crawled gratefully under the comforter to toss restlessly until midnight, wondering if Diane Duvall's visit to Seattle had anything to do with the trade conference . . . reviewing what I hoped to learn from her . . . wondering how Kimberly Korda and the monogrammed cuff links fit into the equation. Would Kimberly have her own tale of woe? More importantly, why had a British intelligence agent turned into a con man? And where was he now?

9

I partially awakened a little after six from a troubling dream of veiled women snaking their way through a barren mountain valley to the accompaniment of a wailing flute. A soft shape moved along my right knee. Calico had returned. Eyes closed, I reached a hand from under the comforter and stroked her silky body, pondering my conversation with Dr. Rousseau and her mother yesterday. Given the opportunity, I had no doubt that Raheela would cheerfully tear Forbes Cameron limb from limb. And I'd wager her daughter wouldn't lift a finger to stop her.

DragonSpray rolled against her lines. A fender creaked against the dock. I hoped Kimberly Korda would call back. Just as I was about to drift back into sleep I remembered today was the day of my courtroom testimony on the foster child case *and* I was flying to Seattle to meet Diane Duvall.

Attired in a beige suit and taupe shoes with sensible heels, at seven thirty I headed uphill to the bakery where I got in line behind a pretty elfinlike woman in blue jeans and a white shirt with a mop of curly brown hair. When she turned away from the counter, I recognized Bronwyn O'Banion, the writer bride. I wondered if her preoccupied demeanor was the result of wedding complications or historical romance plot twists. With a glass of freshly squeezed orange juice, a whole grain pecan muffin, and coffee, I claimed the rickety empty table next to the window and the news vending machines. The latest good news in *U.S.A. Today* included the announcement that energy department scientists were poised to begin work on a new "bunker-buster" nuclear weapon intended to deter rogue states from stockpiling weapons of mass destruction. And down in the Seattle suburb of Renton a housewife was on trial for having hired five teenagers, including her own daughter, to murder a business associate.

"Don't spend too much time on that rag. It'll destroy your neurons." Jared Saperstein put down a cup of black coffee and lowered his sturdy body into the chair across from me.

"Which the *Friday Gazette* is guaranteed not to do?" I asked.

"No guarantees. But the *Gazette*'s philosophy of news is the same as Joe Friday's: just the facts, ma'am. And I have a few facts on the new case you're working on."

I folded my newspaper. "Terrific. Let's hear them."

Jared took a sip of coffee and pulled a sheet of paper and his reading glasses from his briefcase. "I e-mailed my niece Silvia, the one who works in Registry for MI-6, to see if she could dig up anything on your Frederick Campbell. She wrote back that the scuttlebutt is that Campbell may have been given a pink slip insofar as his diplomatic duties are concerned. No one has heard a word about him in two years. She doesn't have a security clearance that would allow her near his file." He peered at a page of scribbled notes. "There's some other stuff here. I don't know if it will help you."

"What is it?"

"Without compromising you or your client, I queried my friend in Surrey. His family used to live in Mayfair, is well connected socially and all that. Since

I suspected they might be of the same social class, I inquired if he or his daughters knew the two Campbell sisters."

"And?"

"It turns out his daughter knew the one named Millicent . . . or Millie. Belonged to the same tennis club. He says Millie is still living in London, goes by the name Millie Thatcher. No relation to the Iron Lady. She's divorced and owns a fancy dog grooming salon called Your Pampered Poodle." He frowned at the paper and gave me a grin. "My handwriting gets worse by the hour. Anyway, he also remembered a lot of ugly rumors floating about when Frederick's wife was killed."

"What kind of rumors?"

"He was pretty vague but something to the effect that the wife's death might not have been the result of a burglary gone wrong."

I nodded, watching his face, hoping Zelda would turn up something on Gwendolyn's death.

Jared handed me the paper with his notes. "There's a phone number for Your Pampered Poodle. If it's helpful, you owe me lunch." His cell phone chirped from his pocket. "This is going to be from the widow on Brown Island. It could take a while."

"Thanks for the info, Jared," I said. "See you later." It was 8:10. I tucked his notes into my briefcase and headed for the old brick courthouse for the custody hearing, wondering why Jared was having early morning conversations with the widow on Brown Island.

For no reason I've ever explained to myself, a little red flag goes up whenever it appears Jared might get seriously involved with someone. Without analyzing it, I know it has to do with the fact that if Nick and I ever split up, I think Jared would be happy to replace him in a heartbeat. There'd been a short time last spring when I thought that was going to happen.

Nick's wife had come to Seattle, gotten a DUI, and moved into Nick's condo. The worst-case scenario occurred when she OD'd on antidepressants and Nick "just couldn't leave her alone." A week later, Jared had asked me to accompany him to San Francisco for a meeting of the Baker Street Irregulars and I'd accepted. But by the time we'd arrived at the Hilton, I knew my heart was still back in Seattle.

My testimony was the last one presented and I had less than an hour before I had to leave to catch the floatplane to Seattle. I raced back to the office to check my messages and pick up the Rousseau file. New Millennium was ominously silent. Zelda—hair uncoiffed, clad in a man's white shirt about ten sizes too big for her over a pair of old white cutoffs—sat hunched over her workstation in a manner guaranteed to wreak havoc with her lumbar region. Dakota was snoozing with his eyes open on the red futon in the corner. Both ignored my cordial greeting. I poured a cup of coffee, added a few drops of the nonfat milk. In my cubby I found two pink message slips, several sheets of a typed report, and a note from Zelda clipped to something titled "Sweetheart Swindlers, Fortune Hunters, Con Men, and Million Dollar Studs."

"You taking clients in California these days?" Zelda's voice halted my move toward the stairs.

"California?"

"Yeah, somebody from the governor's office called. She changed your meeting in Seattle."

I glanced at the two message slips. One was from Kimberly Korda, the real estate agent over on Orcas; the second was from Diane Duvall: could we meet at one thirty instead of three?

"She may have information on Forbes Campbell," I said.

"Another one of his abandoned princesses?"

"That's what I hope to find out."

"I came in early this morning. I may have something on that Berber wedding necklace in a little bit. I put some info on the tapestries in your cubby."

"Thanks." I glanced at Zelda's uncombed hair and naked face. Her daily personal hygiene and clothing selection were always an indication of her state of mind. "Everything okay?" I asked.

"No," she muttered without turning around. "Sheldon Wainwright is a jerk. I never want to see him again."

"I'm sorry to hear that," I said. I truly was. Sheldon was stable and dependable. And Zelda needed stable and dependable.

"Anything from DataTech on the two Campbell sisters or the Gwendolyn Godfrey murder?"

"Not yet."

Annoyed, I gave her hunched shoulders another glance, decided not to chide her or offer maternal suggestions, and went upstairs. I returned Diane Duvall's call first. Her assistant said Ms. Duvall had changed her flight plans. I confirmed one thirty, which would leave me ample time to make the five-fifteen flight back to the island.

Kimberly Korda answered on the first ring with a perky "Good morning, Doe Bay Realty, Kimberly speaking." I identified myself, then said I was doing a background investigation on Forbes Cameron and understood that she had commissioned a pair of monogrammed cuff links for the gentleman.

"The cuff links were for Forrest," she said slowly, the perkiness gone from her voice. "My ex-husband, Forrest Clark."

"Ms. Korda, I represent a woman who's trying to locate the man who had these cuff links. He may have used several names. Could you tell me where you met your husband?"

"I met him in Santa Barbara. But this is not a good

time to talk. I'm on the floor all morning. I have a
closing this afternoon. Could you come over here on
Monday?"

"What about this weekend?"

"I've got an open house on Saturday and Sunday."

I pulled the Washington State ferry schedule from
my top desk drawer and scanned the eastbound sail-
ings. "I could be in Orcas at one twenty. How will I
find your office?"

"You might want to walk on. There's an art festival all next week in East Sound and the ferry will
be overloaded. How about I meet you at the Wildflower Café above the ferry dock, and then you can
catch the next ferry back. I have a showing at
three."

I consulted my schedule again, which told me that
the next ferry back would be two thirty. Not a lot
of time.

"Look for somebody tall and skinny with long
brown hair going gray and glasses," she said. Apparently Kimberly belonged to that coterie of island
women who refused to color their hair. The description was a far remove from Chantal Rousseau's curvy
dark elegance. Freddy was eclectic in his choice of
brides.

I hung up the phone, added the Forrest Clark persona to the Rousseau file, read Zelda's typed report
on Raheela's tapestries. None of the estate dealers
whose names Mr. Martinelli had given me admitted
to purchasing anything resembling the missing items
in the past six months. The one in Orange County
would, however, be interested in acquiring the items,
should they turn up. None of the dealers, nor any of
the antique-jewelry stores, had anything resembling
the silver and amber bride's necklace. Zelda's hand-
written note on the bottom of the report provided the
only wisp of optimism:

*My friend at Hidden Assets has some ideas on
the necklace. He'll call back. Z
    P.S. I called Browne, Smythe and Goodfel-
low. Goodfellow is away until next week,
but I had an interesting chat with the "bird"
who answered the phone. I'll tell you about
it. Z.*

Wondering why the hell she hadn't told me about
the conversation when I came in, I glanced at the
last sheet.

*A freebie report from me. Looks like Freddy's
in good company. Depressing, huh? Z.*

Sweetheart Swindlers, Fortune Hunters, Con Men, and Million Dollar Studs

Porfirio Rubirosa, the "Big Dame Hunter" M.O.:
had four wives including daughter of the president of the Dominican Republic; film actress Dan-
ielle Darrieux; tobacco heiress Doris Duke (richest
woman in the world).

Karl Carrol, the "Casanova con man" M.O.: makes
his living out of cheating vulnerable women out
of their life savings or forcing them to borrow
money. Stole $330,000 from his victims in 18
months; has a gambling habit. He encouraged
one victim to steal the deed to her mother's flat
so she could borrow money for him.

**Tommy Adams, the "Serial Sweetheart Swindler"
(known to have at least six aliases). M.O.:** targets
older women, romances them, convinces them
he's wealthy, borrows large sums of money, disappears; wanted on felony charges and securities
fraud. Police tracked him from California to

Texas to Ohio. Will face up to 8 years in prison if convicted. Previously convicted of burglary and attempted grand theft. In one scam a 70-year-old woman lost more than $150,000 in six months.

Allen McArthur, alias Ashur McAvey. M.O.: meets women through "lovelorn" columns and defrauded numerous women simultaneously by acquiring "temporary loans" from his "fiancée" until his funds were available.

The list was more than depressing. The women who had been swindled would never recover emotionally or financially, and the swindlers would serve minimum sentences and start their confidence games all over again.

I tossed the list in the file, locked up and went downstairs to talk to Zelda about the call to London. To my chagrin, she and Dakota were gone.

There are no tickets and no departure gates for flights on Puget Sound Air. The pilots tie the float-planes up on the breakwater, check your name against the reservation list, and stow your luggage behind the last seat in the cabin or in the nose of the plane. I was the last passenger on the plane, and after a passenger briefing—my flight was a seven-passenger de Haviland Beaver—the pilot passed out earplugs in place of peanuts and we were off, taxiing across the choppy waters of the harbor and into the clear air over Shaw Island. Flying low across the sun-drenched postcard landscape, our route took us over Rosario Strait and Fidalgo Island and down the inland waterway of Puget Sound.

We touched down on Seattle's Lake Union at 12:52, and at 1:15 I was en route in a Yellow Cab to my appointment. The traffic moved slowly and we crept past the Westlake Shopping Center and the soaring Westin Hotel, where a demonstration seemed to be in progress. Led by a man with wild red hair in what looked like a Civil War uniform and a pregnant woman with a blond Afro, a group of protestors with placards thronged the hotel. The taxi dropped me on Fifth Avenue and I got a number to call for my return trip.

It was an off-the-shelf Starbuck's with the order counter at the front and small bistro tables filling the rest of the space. The only woman sitting alone had long white hair and a high-cheekboned face like my grandmother Jessica's. Her tattered red sweatshirt said "Get it while you can." Apparently Diane Duvall had been delayed. Or had changed her mind about meeting me.

I approached the counter and did *not* order a fresh macadamia nut cookie. Confining my midafternoon indulgence to a tall single café mocha with nonfat milk and no whipped cream, I self-righteously seated myself at the only vacant table located next to the woman in the red shirt. She looked up, gave me a friendly nod, and returned to reading a dog-eared paperback copy of Henry Miller's *Tropic of Cancer*. Ten minutes later, an auburn-haired woman wearing large dark glasses came briskly through the door. She hesitated at the pastry counter, scanned the room, met my eyes. I waved and she waved back. She was wearing the businesswoman's requisite black: straight-legged pants, a well-cut black cardigan sweater-jacket over a white turtleneck jersey, black shoes with sensible heels. Her auburn hair was styled in a smooth page boy cut that just touched her collar. She stood at the order counter and taped one foot impatiently on the tile floor. The espresso machine hissed, the concoction was stirred, the hot steamed milk was added. She pulled several bills from her black leather bag and carried her coffee to my table. I reached inside my canvas bag, pressed the Record button on the tape recorder, then stood up and extended my hand.

"Scotia MacKinnon. Thank you for meeting me."

"Diane Duvall." She gave my hand a brief clasp and sat down. Up close I could see the fine lines on her face, the ones that appear some time around the fifth decade. Her large eyes were hazel with long, lightly mascaraed lashes and well-defined brows. "Thanks for meeting me early. When I got here from Sacramento, I had to sneak in and out of the Westin through that mob of demonstrators without being recognized. What a nightmare!"

"What are they protesting?"

"Our conference on Pacific Rim shipping. God knows why. All we're trying to do is get the various port officials to talk to each other and lure more container ship traffic to the West Coast. You'd think we were proposing to conscript their infant daughters." She added something white to her coffee, stirred it, took a sip, and set the mug on the table with a small clatter. Her third finger left hand was adorned with a plain gold band accompanied by a wide circlet of small diamonds. The ring a devoted husband gives for a milestone anniversary. "I really didn't have time to meet you, but when you said some other woman had lost money because of Will Cameron, I knew I had to make time. What's going on? You mentioned a client?"

I handed her my business card. She read the card and smiled. "I didn't realize you lived in Friday Harbor. That's where my husband and I are planning to retire." She and ten thousand others.

I showed her the photo of Forbes Cameron. "Is this the man you knew as Will Cameron?"

She nodded. "That's the bastard. Pretty SOB, isn't he?"

"I have a client who's trying to locate him. His

name may actually be Frederick Campbell. We found
your telephone number on my client's phone bill. I
thought you might be able to help me locate him.
Could you tell me how and when you met Will Cameron and why he was blackmailing you?"

She glanced around the café before replying. As if
on cue, the white-haired woman at the next table
stowed her belongings in her blue canvas bag. She
stood up, nodded in our direction, and made her way
to the door. Diane took another sip of coffee, blotted
her mouth with a paper napkin. "I met Will in San
Diego at a political fund-raiser in June 2001. The reason he was blackmailing me was that I did something
indiscreet. Bastard that he is, he gambled that I'd
rather pay than expose him and risk having my career
and marriage ruined."

"I don't need the details, but was the indiscretion
personal or political?"

"Personal. The fund-raiser in San Diego was a five-
hundred-dollar-a-plate dinner to reelect the governor.
After—" She stopped, glanced down at my card, then
directly into my eyes. "Ms. MacKinnon, I am telling
you this in total confidence. Is that agreed?"

I thought of the microcassette recorder silently running in my bag. "Absolutely. I will not share it with
my client if that is your wish."

"That is absolutely my wish." She chewed her lower
lip for a second or so. "I can't remember who Forbes
was with, but somebody introduced us. I was going
through a difficult time in my marriage. My husband's
teenage daughter had been living with us for six
months. My husband is an attorney. He was up for a
judgeship and had gone off to Singapore on a political
junket with the Lieutenant Governor. We'd had a big
fight about leaving his daughter alone. I was considering a divorce. It was heaven on earth to meet an unat-
tached, terribly attractive, terribly intelligent man like
Will. Even if he was a little younger than I was. I

was infatuated. After the fund-raiser, we spent a week together on Coronado Island."

She paused and her eyes became unfocused for a minute.

"He said he wanted to spend the rest of his life with me," she continued. "I believed him. We agreed I would go home and tell my husband I wanted a divorce, and he'd call me in a week." She took a gulp of her coffee. "When I got back home, my stepdaughter had left for the East Coast to live with her mother. My husband came home and was terribly apologetic." She fingered the diamond ring with her left thumb. "To make a sordid story as brief as possible, my husband and I had a reconciliation and I felt like shit. I was terribly ashamed of my fling with Will, or whatever the hell his name is. I just wanted to forget the whole thing and prayed that he would do the same."

"Let me guess: Forgetting wasn't on Will's agenda."

She shook her head and sighed deeply. "What a mess. *What a goddamn mess!* A week later, he phoned me at work. I told him I couldn't see him again. He was furious and called me some very ungentlemanly names. Not exactly Sunday school words. Then he asked what it was worth to me to keep our week on Coronado a secret." She paused, raised the coffee cup. Her hand was shaking. "I was so shocked I could barely talk to him. All I could think was how incredibly *stupid* I'd been."

"Could it have been a setup?"

"Maybe. I'd been on a TV panel show the week before. There were a lot of call-in's and the fund-raiser was mentioned." She paused, thoughtful. She stared into space, then sighed. "When I told him about the reconciliation with my husband, he said he'd give me a week to think things over. Exactly seven days later, he called back. He wanted five thousand dollars a month or he would contact my husband and make sure the press found out about where the special assistant to the governor and the wife of a prominent San Francisco attorney had spent her spring break." She stared bleakly at the table. "When I first met Will, he asked a lot of questions. About me, my family, my husband. I was flattered. I talked too much."

"And you started paying him?"

"I had no choice. I was desperate. At that point, I'd have died rather than have my husband find out. And my career would have been ruined. I told my husband I needed to send money to my mother."

"This went on for how long?"

"A year."

"Five thousand a month is sixty thousand dollars."

"Yes."

"What happened after a year?"

"My mother died. My brother Mike came over from London. He works for *Time* magazine in their London bureau. After the memorial service, I fell apart. I told Mike about Will. He was furious. He told me to stop sending money and if the guy made any trouble, we'd go after him for extortion. I was terrified, but I stopped sending the money. Will called and asked what happened to the monthly payment. I told him I had no more money and if he kept harassing me, I would prosecute him."

"And?"

"He said, 'You will pay, one way or the other. It's just a matter of time.' And if I ever told anyone about the blackmail or went to the police, I would be very sorry."

"Did you hear from him again?"

She shook her head. "I still look over my shoulder and break out in a cold sweat when the phone rings in the evening."

"Did you tell your husband about Will?"

"I'm too much of a coward. I think he would forgive me, but my boss is holier-than-thou."

"What did Will tell you about his background?"

"He was born in Scotland. Father was a veterinarian. Worked with polo ponies or race horses. I can't remember which. I think the family must have had some money because he went to boarding school and then to Cambridge."

"Did he mention his immigration status?"

"He said he was a U.S. resident."

"Employment?"

"An investment consultant. Or, as he described it, 'A private banker for the carriage trade.' She reached into her bag and handed me a white business card with navy blue printing. *"Strome Investments,"* the card said. *"Professional investment services for the preferred client."* The address was on Wilshire Boulevard in Los Angeles. "The address and phone number don't exist," she said. "I had my assistant check it." She turned the card over, glanced at the numbers written on the back, and handed it to me. "This was the cell phone number he gave me."

"Is it current?"

"I've no idea. He's the last person on the planet I want to talk to."

"What did he tell you he did before he came to the U.S.?"

"The British Foreign Service. He headed up offices in Moscow and then somewhere in North Africa."

"He ever mention Istanbul?"

"I don't think so. I was intrigued by the foreign service work, but he didn't want to talk about it. Said he couldn't stand the politics."

"What about family or friends?"

"Both his parents were dead. He had two sisters. One in London and one in Australia. Or maybe it was New Zealand. And a wife who died." She reached for her bag. "This part is interesting." She pulled out a sheet of paper and raised her left eyebrow quizzically. "After you called this week and gave me the other name—Frederick Campbell—I sent an e-mail to Mike and asked him to see if he could uncover anything. I got this today." She scanned the paper and handed it to me.

I checked the Times and the Mirror archives for anything on a Frederick Campbell. What came up was a Gwendolyn Godfrey Campbell who was murdered in 1984 by a burglar she apparently surprised in her flat. She was survived by her husband, Frederick W. Campbell, who was living in Sophia, Bulgaria, her parents, Sir Francis and Lady Henrietta Godfrey of London, and a brother, Willis Godfrey, also of London. Father was a prominent banker, mother was the daughter of an earl. Two days later there's a follow-up article in the Mirror *that says her parents didn't believe the burglar story. They hired a private investigator and tried to get New Scotland Yard involved. A final story by the same columnist six months later says neither NSY nor the investigator ever found anything. Both parents died a year later in a boating accident in Scotland.*

I glanced up. "A boating accident. How convenient."
She nodded. "Keep reading. It gets better."

Gwendolyn's brother, Willis Godfrey, is an attorney. A year after Gwendolyn's death, Godfrey got into a brawl with your friend Frederick at a private London men's club and it made the papers. I called this Godfrey yesterday. He hates Campbell. Said he never believed the bit about the burglar and wants to reopen the case. Seems like a nice bloke, as they say over here, and he's willing to talk to the private investigator you mentioned.

Mike had included an address and phone number for Willis Godfrey and closed with best wishes to his sister and her husband.

"May I keep this?"

"Yes, it's for you."

I tucked it into my bag and asked if Will had ever mentioned anyone named Sergei.

"Not that I remember."

"Does 'Mundolito' mean anything to you?"

She started to shake her head, then stopped. "Mundolito," she repeated slowly, frowning. "Yes," she said slowly. "He was talking about a friend of his who breeds horses. I think he said something like, 'And he took a first at Mundolito.' "

"Any idea where or what Mundolito is?"

Another shake of her head.

"The friend's name?"

"Sorry."

A group of people surged in the door, and I recognized the red-haired man in the Civil War uniform I'd seen in front of the Westin. Diane looked over her shoulder and shrank down in her chair. The group milled about the order counter, their backs to us. She checked her watch and stood up, her back to the protestors. "I've got two meetings before dinner and I'd like to get out of here before I'm recognized."

"Call me if you think of anything, and thanks for making time for me."

"No problem. I hope you find the SOB." She stood up, put on her dark glasses, started to leave, and then turned back. "Tell your client to be careful. Will is a very smart cookie. When he wants something, he doesn't care *what* or *who* gets in his way. He told me a story about waiting seven years to get revenge once." She shivered. "There's something . . . *menacing* about him." She made her way quickly toward an illuminated Exit sign at the rear of the café, head averted.

It was nearly two thirty. Through the large front

window that overlooked Fifth Street I spied an empty taxi half a block away. I stuffed the file into my briefcase and made my own exit, speculating on what Diane's warning meant for my client.

10

I spent the next two hours shopping and made it back to the floatplane terminal on Lake Union by five, checked in for my flight, and was about to listen to my recorded conversation with Diane Duvall when my cell phone rang. It was Melissa.

"Hi, Mumsy. Where are you? I called your office."

"I'm in Seattle."

"With Nick?"

"No, I'm about to fly back to Friday Harbor."

"Oh." There was a pause and then came the reason for the call. "I think I'm in love."

"With Justin?"

"Yeah. I think either he's going to try to get a job teaching in California or I might transfer to Montana."

"All this after just a week?"

"*Mother,* when you're in love, you *know* it. Time doesn't matter."

I watched through the big window overlooking the lake as a Puget Sound plane successfully landed and maneuvered around a sailboat trying to hoist a sail. "That is true. Tell me about Justin. Where's he from? How old is he?"

"He's lived in a lot of places. New York, Texas, Florida. His dad was in the military. He went to school at MSU in Missoula. He's got a master's in English and he's an instructor there. I'm thinking of switching to English. And before you say anything, I *know* I'll be a senior in September. But I was looking at the statement on my trust account before school was out. I think there's still enough money for two more years. And I can't exactly figure out what I'm going to do with a degree in political science."

Albert, my third husband, had set up a small trust account for Melissa before he left on a fateful cruise to the South Pacific from which he did not return. I refrained from pointing out that she'd had four years to figure out what to do with the degree.

"It's your money, Melissa. And I imagine a degree in English with a teaching credential is more marketable than a degree in political science."

"Yeah, that's what I thought. Oh, I might as well tell you. Justin is divorced."

"I see. How long was he married?"

A pause, then, "Five years. He has two kids. They're coming to the ranch next week."

"How old are the children?"

There was no answer. "Melissa? Melissa?"

I didn't know whether her cell phone or mine had suddenly lost contact with the mother tower. I called her back. "Guess I lost you."

"Yeah, I guess."

"You were telling me about his children."

"Okay! One's ten and the other's fourteen."

I swallowed. "How old is Justin?"

"He's thirty-eight. And before you say anything, I don't think chronological age is important."

"How long has he been divorced?"

There was a brief silence. "They've been separated for ten years. She's Catholic and she doesn't believe in divorce. But they never see each other."

"I see."

"No, you *don't*. I can't believe how you always focus on *negative* things. God! I'll talk to you later." The connection was dead again.

My flight was called and as I followed the pilot down the dock, I tried to determine how I felt about my twenty-three-year-old daughter being in love with a not-divorced man with two children—an *older* not-divorced man—and whether I was most bothered by the marital status, the children, or the age.

The pilot made a stop at East Sound on Orcas Island where a couple in vacation attire deplaned and ten minutes later we were taxiing among the anchored sailboats in Friday Harbor. I was back on G dock by six thirty. Once Calico was fed and watered, I changed out of my city clothes into T-shirt and shorts. I had one phone message waiting, from Zelda. I played it while I fixed a vermouth and soda.

"Hi, boss. I wanted you to know that the DataTech background on Freddy's two sisters came in. It's pretty sparse, but it's in your cubby. I also just received the old article on the Gwendolyn Godfrey murder. It took umpteen e-mails to the *Times of London* archivist. Sorry I was such a grouch this morning."

I took my drink and climbed into the cockpit. The evening was calm, the temperature around seventy-five degrees, the water flat. A large brown and white seagull swooped over *DragonSpray*'s mast and settled onto the spreaders of the blue-hulled ketch moored next to me in slip 75. The boat belonged to a family from Chicago. They usually came out before the Fourth of July, took the boat north for two months of cruising in the Gulf Islands, and brought her back to the slip for another ten months. I hadn't seen them this year.

I sipped the vermouth and thought about Diane Duvall and the high price she'd paid for her week in paradise with the terribly handsome, terribly intelligent, slightly younger British investment advisor she'd happened to meet at the fund-raiser. When "Will" became "Forbes" and set about romancing Dr. Rousseau, he'd changed his M.O. slightly—marriage instead

of an adulterous affair, power of attorney in place of
blackmail—but the pattern was the same: meet the
mark among the "right people," gain her confidence
and trust, promise love and devotion, lead her to expect a luxurious life, and divest her of her assets. I
finished my drink, went below, prepared some
chicken stir-fry, and decided to go for a walk before
bed and pick up the DataTech reports Zelda had left
for me.

When I got back to the boat it was 10:05. I made a
cup of tea and read the report on Millicent Campbell
Thatcher. As Zelda had said, it was brief. She was
born in Edinburgh, Scotland, fifty-two years ago, parents Peter Campbell and Elizabeth Fleming. Married
at eighteen to Timothy Thatcher, divorced at twenty-
eight, no children. Currently proprietor of Your Pampered Poodle, 14 Anne Boleyn Street, telephone 5848-
3761. The report on Marianne Campbell Ashburn was
even briefer and contained only an address and phone
number in Alice Springs, Australia. I would call them
both in the morning. I donned my pj's, brewed another cup of tea, and turned on the remote in the
main salon. The local ten o'clock news was already
in progress.

"We return now to the Westin Hotel where the Special Deployment Unit of the Seattle Police Department is attempting to contain the large crowd of
demonstrators that stormed the entrance to the hotel
about six thirty this evening. The hotel is the site of
the Pacific Rim Trade Conference where the opening
ceremony was scheduled to begin at seven thirty. The
latest news from the scene is that the ceremony has
been postponed. Around fifty of the demonstrators
have been arrested. We go now to the Westin Hotel
on Fifth Street."

The Asian anchorwoman was replaced by an on-site
Hispanic male standing in front of the hotel. The
straggle of protestors I'd seen that afternoon had

grown to a mob of several hundred angry, screaming
individuals either attacking or defending themselves
from (it was difficult to determine which) the hel-
meted police officers. I stared at the screen, looking
for the man in the Civil War uniform and any of the
other protestors I'd seen at Starbuck's that afternoon.
After several minutes, the anchorwoman was back.

"The organizers of the Trade Conference are puzzled by the protest. They say the conference is not
related to the World Trade Organization that caused
the riots here in '99, and have refused to reschedule
it. Beginning tomorrow—" she paused and picked up
the sheet of paper a young blond woman had placed
in front of her. The anchor's face turned grim. "This
just in from the Westin Hotel. One of the conference
participants, a woman from California, has been shot
to death. Her body was found on the sidewalk in front
of the Westin about an hour ago. We will have further
details as soon as the family has been notified."

The two women exchanged glances, raised their eyebrows, and moved on to the next news topic.

A woman from California has been shot.

Goose bumps rose on my arms. No doubt many
women from California besides Diane Duvall were attending the Pacific Rim Conference. But I remembered the threat Diane had received from Will: *You
will pay, one way or the other. It's just a matter of
time.* Shivering despite the heat, I muted the TV,
checked the lock on the companionway hatch and
washed my face. I returned to the main salon and
switched to CNN, where there was a three-minute cov-
erage of the Seattle conference and another report on
the death of the unidentified female from California.

I paced the narrow cabin, brushed my teeth, returned to the main salon and surfed from one news
channel to another. Fox News had interrupted regular
programming for the P.R.T.C. incident and a little before midnight, the weary, tousled blonde at the Westin

reported that the protestors had grown to at least a thousand and the Seattle police were badly outnumbered. When the visual switched back to the anchorwoman, my worst fears were confirmed. "The woman who was shot earlier this evening near the entrance to the Westin Hotel in downtown Seattle has been identified as Diane Duvall of Sacramento, California. Ms. Duvall was a special assistant to the governor of California. The governor has expressed shock and sorrow at his assistant's death. Ms. Duvall's family could not be reached for comment."

I swallowed the bile that rose in my throat. The woman I'd talked to less than twenty-four hours ago was dead. Murdered. Why? By whom?

Suddenly claustrophobic, I unlocked the hatch covers and climbed up into the cockpit. Huddled near *DragonSpray*'s stern, I stared into the darkness, vainly trying to convince myself that Frederick Campbell had no way of knowing his former "moneybags" had talked.

PART 2

11

At the Seven Swans Bed and Breakfast Michael Far-raday turned off the jet of hot water, opened the steamy glass shower door, and reached for a dark blue bath sheet. As he dried his body, he glanced out the window. It was a little after five A.M. A blanket of soft white mist hovered over the bucolic pond where five trum-peter swans hung out a good part of every day. On an island like this—two or three thousand people, winding country roads, one small town with one main street— a daily reality check was imperative. To remind himself the only reason he was in Friday Harbor was to hunt down the rogue agent Frederick Campbell, code named Polo.

God knew the hunt had been far-reaching. Too bad he wasn't collecting frequent flier miles in his own name. Istanbul, North Africa, Honolulu, Sydney. That sheep ranch in the middle of nowhere and the uncoop-erative she-cat of a sister. It had been two years—with three other assignments in between—and what had kept him going was his unshakable conviction that eventu-ally Freddy had to make a mistake. Any mistake, how-ever minuscule, and Farraday would be on him in a second.

A mistake or some little piece of serendipity.

Twice he'd been close. First in Miami, when he'd spotted his quarry at the polo match with the brunette *whose real estate developer daddy was responsible for draining half of the Everglades. By the next sunrise, Freddy was gone. It had taken three months to pick up the track in Los Angeles. A track that he reluctantly owed to John Baxter, retired FBI agent.*

The second time was in Santa Barbara where, to Farraday's infinite chagrin he, Farraday, had been made by the overripe, flashily dressed female Freddy was schmoozing at the Santa Barbara Biltmore. Not because the woman had been smart enough to realize who and what Farraday was, but because she misinterpreted a fleeting glance and probably told Freddy she had another admirer. Baxter had thrown a hissy fit that night. Farraday's only satisfaction was watching the female deal with the check when she returned from the Ladies to find her handsome suitor had "been called away."

John Baxter was two years out of the FBI, father of the unfortunate Moira who'd paid the supreme price for her Turkish dalliance with the British agent she suspected of double dealing. Baxter's son, John, Jr., headed up the FBI office in Seattle.

The serendipity had come in June: The Seattle office had received an anonymous tip that a French-Moroccan doctor named Rousseau was funneling money to Islamic terrorists through a phony charity called the International Fund for Muslim Women. The doctor had checked out clean and had blamed the tip on her ex-husband whose description—a Scottish-born British diplomat who spoke French and Arabic and had been posted to Moscow, Latin America, and the Middle East—had sent up a red flag to John Jr. Even more interesting, Dr. Rousseau, who had just moved to San Juan Island, had hired a Seattle P.I. to track her ex. Before Baxter or Farraday could get to the P.I., he was murdered and more red flags went up. It was a long shot, but Farraday had decided to stake out Friday Harbor in the likely event that the doctor became bait *for the elusive British diplomat whose photo matched the image of Frederick Campbell that MI-6 had supplied.*

So far Freddy had not shown up. Farraday was anticipating another dead end when Baxter called yesterday, en route to Friday Harbor with a new plan. They'd arranged to meet for breakfast.

Farraday slipped on white cotton boxer shorts and a short-sleeved tan sports shirt. He thought about Baxter, whom he disliked immensely. Baxter was humorless, uncultured, poorly dressed, and overly aggressive. But Baxter was a man on a mission of vengeance and had resources far beyond what Farraday, through MI-6, could have tapped into. Farraday pulled on khaki Dockers and zipped them up to his trim midsection, which was growing trimmer from the last five days of daily runs out to the Cattle Point Lighthouse. The brown leather moccasins were actually running shoes in disguise.

The day would be too warm for a jacket and Farraday slid the PPK into the holster in the right-side pocket of the Dockers, clipped a cell phone to his belt, glanced around the cozy room, and locked the door behind him.

Baxter was at a back corner table, wolfing down fried eggs and sausage when Farraday arrived at the Dry Dock. Baxter nodded, made no apology for not waiting for his colleague, and continued eating while Farraday ordered.

"They're going to bring her in again," Baxter said, mopping up the egg yolk with a piece of white toast. "Looks like she's funding arms and training for a new police force in Kabul."

"Rousseau?" Farraday added two spoons of sugar to his coffee.

"Yeah, they think the police training is a front. That the police will be trained to unseat the new government."

"Time frame?"

"Saturday night. She's having a big charity ball. Lots of bigwigs. They'll pick her up after." Baxter drained his mug and set it down with a clatter. "Lousy coffee. Stupid one-horse town."

Farraday's bowl of cornflakes and glass of orange juice arrived. He began slicing a banana over the cornflakes and refrained from responding.

"You find out anything about the local P.I.?" Baxter asked.

"Scotia MacKinnon, former San Francisco private security officer, former San Diego P.D. detective. Has an office in the Old Gazette Building on Guard Street, shares an office with an events arranger and a naturopathic physician. Rousseau came to her office on Monday. MacKinnon had lunch with the publisher of one of the local newspapers on Tuesday. She spent an hour with Rousseau at the doctor's condo on Wednesday. Thursday she flew down to Seattle on Puget Sound Air, was home last night. I left a message with your son about the Seattle trip in case he wanted to pick her up. She lives alone on a sailboat in the harbor."

"A boat?" Baxter wrinkled his nose in distaste. "Johnny put a tail on her in Seattle," he said between bites of sausage. "She met with a dame for coffee, then flew back here. No ID on the dame. You talk to her?"

Farraday shook his head. "Not yet. Anything on who did Whiteley, the Seattle P.I.?"

"Naw, the police put it down to a drug deal gone bad so they don't have to spend any time on it."

"Did you talk to the wife?"

Baxter shook his head. "She didn't return Johnny's calls. Now the phone's disconnected. Not a trace of the Jag Rousseau says he was driving. Probably dumped it like he did the Beamer in L.A."

"Any luck with the e-mail address you got from the woman in Florida?"

"Spent a week on it, can't break the password. Guy's

*a wily bastard." Baxter shook his head. "God, but I
hate his guts."*

*Farraday finished his cereal and coffee. "What's
your plan?"*

*"We're going to put the screws to the P.I. here. If
she's been on the case a week, she's gotta know something. Shouldn't be too hard to convince her to share.
We better get to her while she's still alive." He pushed
his chair back and stood up. "You get me a room?"*

*Farraday nodded. "We're at the Seven Swans. It's a
B&B."*

*"I can hardly wait," Baxter said with a sneer, head-
ing for the door.*

12

Sometime during the night the wind rose. I'd crawled into bed about 2:00 and for several hours I'd been semi-aware of a loose halyard chiming against *DragonSpray*'s mast. When the noise joined forces with encroaching daylight, I opened my eyes. It was 5:05 A.M. on Friday morning. Assuming no one would be on the docks at that hour, I padded up the companionway and across the deck without putting anything over my pajamas. The sun peeking over the neighboring islands to the east illuminated the soft blanket of white mist that hovered over the harbor. I fastened the offending halyard to the stays with a bungee cord and crouched for a minute on the cabin top, caught up in the morning. A great blue heron stood motionless on the dock at the University of Washington marine labs. Immediately to the southeast lay tiny Brown Island, dark and still and heavily wooded. In one of the houses on that small island lived the widow with the first editions Jared coveted. I wondered if the widow had anything besides first editions to offer.

My peripheral vision registered a quick movement behind me. I whirled around. It was Calico on the top companionway step, yawning and washing her face. We both went below. I gave her an early breakfast, locked up the companionway, and crawled back in bed. Eyes closed, I hoped for sleep, which did not come. Half an hour later, I pulled the comforter off the bed and went into the main salon to watch the early news, hoping that Diane Duvall's murderer had been identified or at least that a suspect was in custody. The National Guard was being brought in to contain the protestors. There was no mention of a suspect.

I remembered how Diane shrank down in her chair when the protestors came into Starbuck's. Obviously she hadn't wanted to be recognized. Had she been threatened by one of them? Was she the accidental victim of a protestor who'd gone berserk? Could her death possibly be linked to Frederick Campbell? If so, why now? Why in Seattle and not in Sacramento? How could he have known she was in the city? I wondered if Diane's brother Mike had been informed about his sister's death before he learned it on CNN.

It was 6:07. If my mental arithmetic was correct, it would be 2:07 P.M. in London. I pulled a pair of sweats over my pj's and poured a glass of orange juice. I found the folded e-mail message in the side pocket of my bag and read it again: *Gwendolyn's brother, Willis Godfrey, is an attorney. Two years after Gwendolyn's death, Godfrey got into a fracas with your friend Frederick at a private London club . . . I called Godfrey yesterday. He hates Campbell . . . wants to reopen the case. Said he'd talk to the private investigator you mentioned.*

I found my notebook and a pen, located the portable phone on the shelf above my bunk, and punched in the international code and phone number Mike had included in the e-mail. A woman with a crisp voice answered. I asked for Willis Godfrey. He came to the phone immediately.

"Mr. Godfrey, my name is Scotia MacKinnon. I'm the private investigator that Michael Duvall mentioned to you recently. I'm investigating a securities fraud in the state of Washington involving a man by the name of Frederick Campbell."

"Duvall? Ah, yes, the chap from *Time* magazine. Securities fraud, you say? Freddy Campbell? The bloody blighter never changes, does he?"

"I understand your sister was married to Campbell."

"Unfortunately, yes. Very headstrong girl, Gwennie. We told her he was on the rebound. He'd just been dumped by a Texas millionaire's daughter because of his fondness for the casinos. I told Gwennie that Campbell just wanted her for her inheritance."

"I also understand you believe her death may not have been accidental."

"Positive of it. We talked the Yard into investigating, but they couldn't put their hands on a thing. Her missing jewelry was never recovered. If Gwennie hadn't died when she did, she would've divorced him and he wouldn't have inherited her portion of our mother's estate. But the man is smart and slippery. Had a perfect alibi. Twenty people saw him at an embassy cocktail party in Bulgaria the evening she was murdered. No way to prove different."

"Did he inherit Gwendolyn's money?"

"The whole pot of it. He talked her into making a will as soon as she got pregnant."

"Did she have a baby?"

"Had a miscarriage after she got back to London. Broke her heart."

"Do you know why she was divorcing him?"

"After her death I reread the letters she'd sent me while they were in Bulgaria. I didn't find anything definitive, but she did mention that he was often away until late at night and that he was always short of money. He wanted her to pay his debts. I gather they had several fights about the matter. After she came back, she hinted that he had threatened her. Our poor

Gwennie." His voice broke, there was a pause, and he collected himself. "I regret I can't give you anything concrete, Ms. MacKinnon. I'm sure the blighter had something to do with Gwennie's death, but there's no way to prove it."

"You mentioned his fondness for casinos. Was Campbell a gambler?"

He chuckled mirthlessly. "Oh, my, yes. Tried to keep up with that chum of his, Goodfellow. Thick as thieves, the two were, and they both had quite the reputation at the gaming tables. Not just here but also in France. Goodfellow could afford to lose a fortune at blackjack every night, but Campbell couldn't. That's what the debts were about that he wanted Gwennie to pay. Gambling debts. And there was a third fellow, a foreigner. Can't recall his name."

"Would it have been Sergei?"

"Sergei? Yes, yes, that's it. Sergei . . . Sergei Feodorovich. The three were chums at school, Gwennie said. She thought he was a ne'er-do-well. Claimed to be a descendant of the Russian imperial family."

"Do you know where I could find Sergei?"

"No idea."

"Mr. Duvall mentioned that you and Campbell had some sort of . . . misunderstanding after your sister's death?"

"Misunderstanding? Ah, the fracas at the club. That was no misunderstanding. He came prancing in with another woman on his arm. I would have sworn the necklace she was wearing belonged to my mother. I'd have taken his head off if my friends hadn't restrained me." I heard a woman's voice in the background.

"Ms. MacKinnon, I'm afraid you'll have to excuse me. A client has just arrived."

"One last thing, Mr. Godfrey. I want to be absolutely sure that the man I'm looking for is Frederick Campbell. If I faxed you a photo of my client's husband, would you let me know it it's the man your sister was married to?"

"Of course." He gave me his fax number, I thanked him for his time, and I replaced the phone in the cradle. Another facet had been added to my quarry: *Freddy was a compulsive gambler.* No wonder he needed a wealthy companion, or a series of them. And the mysterious Sergei had acquired a surname.

I was about to put the Rousseau file back in my briefcase when I remembered Jared's note on Freddy's sister Millie, the dog breeder.

A man whose voice sounded more Cockney than Cambridge answered. I heard yapping and buzzing noises in the background. I asked for Millicent Thatcher. Several seconds later the buzzing ceased.

"Millie here," said a bright voice.

"Ms. Thatcher, my name is Scotia MacKinnon. I'm calling from the Seattle, Washington branch of Fargo West Bank. We've been reviewing a number of old accounts and found a dormant one with a considerable balance in the name of Frederick Campbell. Both your name and a Mr. Goodfellow's were listed on the account card and we thought one of you might be able to help us locate him."

A tinkling laugh drifted through the fiber-optic cable. "Freddy must be getting forgetful in his old age if he's letting money lie around. If you can hold for a minute, I'll check my address book."

I waited, listening to a faint hum and faraway *whoosh*ing on the line. There was a murmur of voices, then a deep-throated bark, and Millicent was back. "The last address I have is PO Box 18, Goleta, California."

"Is that a recent address, Ms. Thatcher?"

"The last one I have, luv."

There was a moment of silence, more murmuring in the background. "Lionel suggests that you try Chris Goodfellow's sister in Seattle. Annie Goodfellow. Except it's Taylor-Bickford now. Annie Taylor-Bickford. She's sure to know where he is."

I refrained from responding that if Annie knew where Freddy was, she hadn't shared it with Sanford Whiteley, even if she had unwittingly blown Freddy's cover.

"There's another name that's come up," I said. "Sergei Feodorovich. Would you know him?"

"Sergei? My dear Sergei?" A peal of laughter. "I'd better know him. We've been cohabitating, as you Yanks call it, for quite a time now." She paused. "Why do you want Sergei?"

More circles within circles. "I understand he's a chum of Freddy's. Without being presumptuous, have you or Sergei spoken with your brother recently?"

Another peal of laughter. "Oh, heavens, no. Freddy never calls. I don't know about Sergei, but the last time I actually spoke to the boy was about five years ago. He was in . . . let me remember . . . I believe he was in Moscow. Or maybe it was someplace in South America. He's such a gypsy." A bell tinkled in the background and the bark-and-yap chorus resumed. "I really must go, luv. Good luck with Freddy. If you find him, tell him to ring us." A final peal of laughter and the connection ended.

I hung up, wondering if Millicent's laughter was authentic. I considered the Goleta address and called directory information. Not to my surprise, there was no listing for Frederick Campbell or Forbes Cameron or Will Cameron or Forrest Clark. Nor was there any answer at the sheep ranch in Australia.

I looked over the notes I'd taken while talking to Willis Godfrey and found a number in the San Juan Islands phone directory for Nadine Norse, a psychologist. I'd met Dr. Norse while investigating the child custody matter I'd testified on yesterday. Given the earliness of the hour, I expected a message machine, but she answered on the second ring. I told her I was working on a case involving someone with a possible gambling addiction and admitted my ignorance of the subject. She said she had about ten minutes before her first client arrived.

"Is pathological gambling similar to chemical dependency?" I asked.

"There are some similarities. Both pathological gambling and chemical dependency are progressive diseases. Both involve the inability to stop or control the behavior and may include denial, severe depression, and mood swings. We call pathological gambling "the hidden disease." It's difficult to identify: no falling down drunkenness, no needle tracks, no smell of alcohol. One of the first clues is often the tremendous financial problems that become evident, at least to the addict's family."

"What percent of gamblers are addicts?"

"Around five percent."

"What is the gambler actually addicted to? Winning money?"

"The addiction is to action, not to the money per se. For a gambler, the act of gambling is similar to being high on cocaine for the cocaine addict. And gambling is as seductive and destructive as cocaine. By the time pathological gamblers come to a counselor for treatment, they're usually in devastating financial straits." She was silent for a minute. "Apparently, as long as they're gambling, it's a consistent high. Nothing else matches the adrenaline rush. Neither sex nor alcohol is as consistent."

"Is there a genetic or biological basis for addiction to gambling?"

"There's a theory that some pathological gamblers have lower levels of norepinephrine than normal gamblers. That's the chemical that is secreted when someone is thrilled and excited or under stress or arousal. It's been hypothesized that pathological gamblers engage in the activity of gaming to increase their levels of norepinephrine.''

Norepinephrine is one of the chemicals released in the brain when you fall in love. Along with dopamine and something called PEA, it creates a state of euphoria. If what Nadine said was true, each bout of gambling would be like falling in love all over again.

"Would a gambler commit acts of violence to get money to gamble?"

She laughed. "Scotia, some gamblers become thieves; some sell their blood. They will destroy everything in their life to get the funds to gamble and pay for their losses. As you know, gambling debts are taken very seriously by those to whom the money is owed. I'm sure you've heard of enforcers.'' She paused. "I recently read a case study of a woman who gambled away more than eighty thousand dollars in one year. When her husband cut off her money, she stabbed him to death.''

Life was going full bore when I got to the Olde Gazette Building that morning: Pavarotti on surround sound, Dakota chomping on a rawhide bone, Zelda on the phone haranguing someone about a dance band named Aquarius. On edge over Diane's death, I prepared my morning coffee and pulled four phone messages from my mail cubby. One from Jared Saperstein, two from Dr. Rousseau, one from my customs friend, Meredith Martin. They all wanted a callback.

Zelda slammed the phone back in the cradle and flashed me a grin over her shoulder. "I got them for five hundred dollars less than we budgeted for.''

"What's a good dance band cost these days?" I asked, not really caring.

"These guys wanted five thousand dollars, but I told them I had several events coming up and talked them into a discount. By the way, Dr. Rousseau called twice," she said, tidying up her desk. "She didn't sound happy the last time. You find out anything from your California connection, the woman who was getting blackmailed?"

"Yes," I said slowly. "I may have a lead through her brother. But Diane Duvall is dead."

"Dead!" She whirled around to face me.

I nodded. "She was attending a trade conference in Seattle. There was a big protest and—"

"—and she was the woman who was shot outside the hotel! Are you shitting me? Is there any connection to Dr. Rousseau?"

"I don't know," I said slowly. "The police were badly outnumbered. I would imagine some of the protestors were carrying. Could have been a matter of wrong place, wrong time. I'll call Dr. Rousseau." I tried to collect myself, but all I could see were Diane's frightened eyes when she left Starbuck's yesterday.

"Scotia, are you okay?"

"I'll be fine. By the way, your note yesterday said you might have a resource on the stolen tapestries and jewelry."

"Yikes! I forgot to tell you." She fumbled through the papers and magazines on her desk. "I talked to Hidden Assets. They'd be happy to look for the missing tapestries and jewelry. Their fee is fifteen hundred dollars or fifteen percent of the value of the recovered property, whichever is greater." She handed me the Post-it note. "Whadya think?"

"I'll run it by the doctor."

Upstairs, I opened the window and turned on the desk lamp. Zelda's coffee tasted bitter that morning. I stared blindly at the phone message slips for several minutes, processing Diane Duvall's death, recalling her last words: "There's something . . . menacing about him. Tell your client to be careful."

The number Dr. Rousseau had left was the clinic. She was with a patient. I left my name and number and called Jared at the *Gazette*. He'd received a new e-mail from his niece Silvia, who worked at MI-6.

"She suggests you check out the *Crustacean* Web site. There's a reference to Campbell."

"Crustacean as in shellfish?"

"*Crustacean* is a watchdog London on-line weekly that reports all the news no other publisher would dare print about what's going on at Whitehall. Particularly the security agencies in Whitehall. Silvia's boyfriend is the assistant editor. He's just posted a new story alleging that two years ago, a double agent deal in Turkey went sour and an MI-6 agent by the name of Frederick Campbell went AWOL."

"I'll check the site."

"Want to have dinner on Saturday? I just bought a new rice steamer I'd like to try out."

"Jared, I *have* to solve this case. There's been another death."

"Not your client?"

"No, it was a woman Freddy was blackmailing, you may have seen it on the news. Diane Duvall, the California governor's assistant."

"Good grief, the woman who was killed at the Westin. But the police think she was one of the protestors. You think there's a connection to your case?"

"I hope to God there's not. Let me get back to you about Saturday."

I clicked up Netscape, then typed in www.crustacean.com and waited as the colorful Web site, bordered by various and sundry types of shellfish, filled the monitor screen. The on-line magazine's masthead proclaimed it "the only periodical that will tell you what's really happening in allied security." A sidebar listed previous articles: "The Rise of American Fascism," "Who Was Really Behind the Twin Towers?" "Oliver North's Link to Chandra Levy," "The SIS-CIA Attempt to Oust Saddam Hussein," I scrolled down to the table of contents for the current summer issue and found what Jared had been pointing me to: "The Disappearance of Freddy Campbell: MI-6's Most Wanted?" I clicked on the title and waited impatiently as the file for the article loaded and filled the screen.

In much the same way that anti-Castro Cuban refugees who fled Havana back in the '60s prayed for the day when Fidel would be overthrown and they could go home again, for several years there was a growing group of Iraqi dissidents who had fled their homeland and sought refuge in Istanbul. It should come as no surprise to anyone that our own Secret Intelligence Service—along with the CIA—was funding these dissidents and planning how best to infiltrate them into Iraq when the time was ripe to overthrow Saddam Hussein.

But the twist in the scenario, hotly denied by both MI-5 and MI-6, involves an MI-6 agent code-named Polo. According to sources here and in Istanbul, Polo, born Frederick W. Campbell, along with two other MI-6 agents, was dispatched to the city on the Golden Horn more than two years ago. Assignment: work with the dissidents and bring them into the Allied fold. This assignment he apparently carried out with aplomb. But then Polo appears to have diverged slightly from the original assignment—whether for money or in support of political beliefs is unknown, although this writer suspects the former—and apparently began selling information to Saddam's agents in Istanbul. Information on the very people Her Majesty's funds were supposedly supporting and recruiting. A very dirty trick, Freddy.

However, the dirtiest of the tricks occurred on February 22, 2000, a cold wet night so nasty that even the roasted-fish venders around the Galata Bridge had packed up their hibachis and headed home. In a third-floor room of the Kemal Hotel, four blocks away, three high-ranking Iraqi dissidents were waiting for a meeting with Polo when the door burst open and the room was riddled with automatic-weapon fire. Two of the dissidents were killed, while a third managed to leap from a back window onto the awning of a kebab restaurant below and was rescued by the Turkish police. After checking out the survivor's story and taking the man to headquarters for questioning, the police, well aware of both the residences and activities of the MI-6 agents, went to Polo's residence hotel in Beyoglu and found another dead body, that of Moira St. Martin, a U.S. Embassy employee who, we understand, was Polo's mistress. St. Martin was shot once through the heart with a 25-caliber bullet. No personal effects were found in the apartment. Three days later, at a residence across the Bosphorus in Uskadar, police discovered the bodies of two other MI-6 agents, a man and a woman. The apartment in which they were found lay in a shambles.

More than two years have elapsed and no one has seen Freddy. Not the Turkish secret police. Not Freddy's sister in London or his sister in Australia. Not MI-6. Our question of the day: Did Polo meet the same fate as his mistress and MI-6 colleagues? Or is the man a double agent? Is SIS leaving no stone unturned to find him? We'll put our money on the latter. We'd also be willing to wager, no

*matter how MI-6 may deny it, that the hunt
for Freddy will be what the KGB brethren term
a 'wet operation.'*

A wet operation. What the CIA call an "executive
action." Assassination.

I stared at the screen, a cold sweat forming on my
forehead. If Sanford Whiteley was correct in tying
Forbes Cameron to Frederick Campbell, then I was
way out of my league. I pulled the photo Dr. Rousseau had given me from the file and was preparing
the cover sheet to fax it to Willis Godfrey when I
heard the downstairs door open and close. Dakota
barked, there was a murmur of voices, then the stairs
creaked. I looked up.

Jewel Moon stood in the doorway, resplendent in
an ankle-length tie-dyed lime green and blue cotton
dress and Birkenstocks.

Panicked, I looked at her, at the photo in my hand,
at the computer screen. *I'd forgotten she was coming.*

"Mother!"

She stepped into the room and I stood up and returned her hug. Her long hair, the same undefinable
shade between blond and brown as mine, had more
threads of gray than when I'd last seen her. And her
face had a few more lines.

"I know I'm a little early, dear, but I got lonely, so
I left at six yesterday morning. I got to Anacortes last
night, too late to take the ferry. How are you? How
was your trip to Seattle?"

I didn't remember telling her I was going to Seattle
and I wasn't about to discuss Diane Duvall's death.
She settled into the wicker chair.

"It was foggy along the coast," she said, not noticing
I hadn't answered her question. "But the drive across
the mountains was wonderful. There was a lot of traffic on I-5 and everything was a mess in Seattle. Did
you see how the police treated those poor protestors?

I was going to stop and join the demonstration, but the streets were blocked off. And that poor woman from California. I hope her husband sues the city of Seattle!"

My mother's politics have always been to the left of left. My earliest lessons in civil rights came from being dragged to Vietnam protests after I came to San Francisco's Haight Ashbury to live with her and Giovanni. I was saved from the task of defending the city of Seattle by my phone. It was Chantal Rousseau. What had I learned from Diane Duvall? Had I made any progress in locating Forbes, or her mother's jewelry and tapestries?

I asked her to hold, covered the phone with my hand. Aside from issues of confidentiality, Jewel Moon liked to think that while I might occasionally stumble over a dead body or hunt down a missing person, my life resembled Miss Marple's. "Mother, would you excuse me? This is apt to be a rather tedious conversation. Why don't you get a cup of coffee? There's a basket of magazines and newspapers downstairs. Oh, ask Zelda for the book on sailing. I'll be down as soon as I finish."

"That's a good idea. Then I need to take Leonardo for a walk and take a nap."

I had also forgotten that Jewel Moon was bringing Leonardo. I sent up a prayer for the largesse of Angela, who had offered her guest bedroom, and returned to my client.

"I apologize for not getting back to you yesterday, Dr. Rousseau. I left early to go to Seattle for an interview with Diane Duvall."

"What did you learn?" Her voice was impatient.

"She said that a man she knew as Will Cameron blackmailed her for over sixty thousand dollars."

"What did he blackmail her for?"

"I'm afraid I can't divulge that." I hesitated. "Dr. Rousseau, have you seen the news this morning?"

"No. I came in to work early. Why?"

"Diane Duvall was killed in Seattle during the riots at the Westin Hotel last night."

"Killed! What do you mean killed?"

"She was shot. The police are investigating it."

"That is terrible. You don't think it has anything to do with Forbes, do you?"

"I certainly hope not. Mike Duvall, Diane's brother who works in London, has tracked down the brother of Forbes's first wife."

"Gwendolyn?"

"Gwendolyn Godfrey. I have a copy of the news article on her death and I spoke with her brother this morning. He doesn't believe Gwendolyn's death was an accident. I also learned that your husband may be a gambler. Were you aware of that?"

There was a long pause. "On our honeymoon, we went on a cruise in the Mediterranean. The ship stopped at Monaco and we went to a casino one evening. He played roulette. He won for a while, then he started losing. Maybe twenty or thirty thousand dollars. It seemed like a lot of money to me, but I thought he was very rich. He . . . what do you say, he shrugged it off."

"Did he ever borrow money from you or ask you to pay any debts?"

"Just the money I put down on the condo while he was waiting for funds to be transferred from an offshore account. What about my mother's jewelry? Have you been able to find it?"

I summarized the contacts Zelda had made in attempting to locate both the jewelry and the tapestries and told her about the property-recovery firm called Hidden Assets and their fee.

"I will need to think about that. Could you please send me a report on your conversation with Ms. Duvall? And the article on Gwendolyn?"

I glanced through the notes I'd added to the file

last week. I wanted time to review the tape recording of my interview with Diane Duvall, to think about my conversation with Willis Godfrey this morning, and to process the contents of the *Crustacean* article. "I'll try to get to it today. Shall I mail it or do you want to pick it up?"

"I'm leaving for Seattle today. Call me when you get it done."

"There's one other bit of information, Dr. Rousseau."

"Yes?"

"There's some information on your husband on a Web site. I'll make a copy of it and send it with the report." I gave her the Web address. "Your ex-husband may be a dangerous man, Dr. Rousseau. *Please* be careful and be sure you keep your doors and windows locked at home. And tell your mother to be careful."

"Forbes may be a lying son of a bitch, but he will not hurt me," she said, and hung up.

13

A lying son of a bitch.

An obsessive gambler.

A double agent.

What now? Call MI-6 and inform them I was on the trail of one of their agents? Call the CIA? Call the sheriff? Sheriff Bishop was already of the opinion that law enforcement on San Juan Island would be far easier if not for me. It didn't take much imagination to figure out what his response would be if I suggested our new doctor's life—or mine—might be threatened by a psychopathic foreign agent.

From downstairs, I heard Abigail's voice. I fingered the other phone message, from Meredith Martin, and dialed her number at the U.S. Customs Office.

She answered in an officious voice that gave way to plaintive. "Oh, God, Scotia, I don't know what to do. I had a terrible fight with Mark and Becca's run away from home. I really need some advice. Could we have lunch?"

"Meredith, my mother's here and I've got a case that's turning deadly. Can you hold off for a week or so?"

"I don't know if we'll still be together." Her voice broke slightly and I remembered my own stepparenting travails after I married Pete. I flipped through my calendar and stopped at Sunday. "How about I arrange something for my mother to do on Sunday and we have a late breakfast? Say eleven at the Dry Dock? They're doing a nice Sunday brunch."

"I'll be there."

I faxed the photo of Forbes/Freddy to Willis Godfrey, made a note on my calendar to prepare an interim report for Dr. Rousseau, and headed downstairs.

Abigail was updating Zelda and Jewel Moon on the latest in her whale crusade, and after confirming our drinks date for tomorrow afternoon, I followed Jewel Moon's little Jetta out to Griffin Bay and installed her in Angela's guest room, as per instructions from Angela, who was at work. I left with a promise to call Jewel Moon later to discuss dinner and sailing plans. As I backed out of the driveway, she and Leonardo were headed for Jefferson Beach.

When I returned to the office a little after twelve, New Millennium was empty and quiet. Zelda's desktop was covered with wedding magazines to which she had added *The Bride's Little Book of Cakes and Toasts*. An engraved wedding invitation lay on the desk, the requisite embossed wedding bell decorating the outside.

I fingered the pristine whiteness of the invitation, touched the heavy embossing. For a brief moment, I felt a sense of loss, of emptiness. Although I've been married three times, I've never had a formal wedding. When I married Simon, neither of us had any money. My mother and Giovanni were in Italy and Simon's parents were on the East Coast. On the spur of the moment, we drove to Reno, Nevada, and were married by a justice of the peace. Pete and I were married in a small wedding chapel in Mazatlán with only the *juez* and his sentimental wife for witnesses. My marriage to Albert was a private civil service, followed by a party at the St. Francis Yacht Club where most of the attendees were Albert's sailing and golf buddies.

"Hi, boss." The door banged against the wall and

Zelda and Dakota burst into the office. "Nice invitation, huh? Cost a small fortune." She tossed her bag under her desk. "You see my note?"

"You called Goodfellow's office?"

"Yes! I took a cue from that e-mail Freddy sent to his chum and I presented myself as a reporter with *Polo International*." She pulled out a notebook half buried under the wedding magazines and began flipping pages. "I said I was doing an article on barristers who play polo. The secretary was out of the office for some local holiday. I talked to the temp, a real Chatty Cathy. She's a wannabe actress when she's not answering phones. Says Christopher is quite the handsome bloke. She thought I was one of his 'birds.' She says he plays polo with Prince Charles. It was a long shot, but I said I thought Mr. Goodfellow's friend—I wasn't sure if his name was Cameron or Campbell—was also a polo player and did she know how I could reach him. She went through the address files and found a phone number for an F. Cameron in Florida and a Seattle address, 43 Carlyle Place. She says Goodfellow'll be back next week. How come I don't ever meet a nice bloke like Goodfellow instead of jerks like Sheldon?"

"Did you call the Florida number?"

"No longer in service. It was a cell number. AT&T. I did a reverse phone search on Carlyle Place, called the Rose and Thistle and got an impolite brush-off."

"Any luck cracking Freddy's e-mail?"

"Not yet."

I thanked her, poured a cup of coffee, and went upstairs, disheartened by the lack of new leads. Damn, but the man was good at covering his tracks! There was a fax in the tray from Willis Godfrey: *That's the blighter. Hope you catch up with him.*

I leafed through the Rousseau file again, looking for any lead I'd missed. Except for Kimberly Korda, the only person I hadn't talked to was Marianne Ash-

burn, Freddy's sister who was married to the sheep
rancher in Australia. I found the phone number and
checked the time. It should be early evening down
under. A woman answered on the fourth ring. A TV
or radio news program filled the background. I identified myself and said that I was searching for her
brother Frederick. I wondered if she knew where I
could find him.

"What is it this time? Roulette? Greyhound racing?
Baccarat?" The voice was educated, British, and
caustic."

"I have a client who is trying to find him."

There was silence, then: "I haven't seen Freddy
for . . . several years. My brother is a thief and a liar.
Everything he touches turns to . . . well, you know
what it turns to. I hope you find him and I hope this
time he gets what he deserves. My husband threatened
to shoot him if he ever came back."

"Could I inquire as to the nature of your conflict
with Freddy?"

More silence. Somewhere a door slammed and I
heard a strong masculine voice. "It's a personal matter, Ms. MacKinnon. I have to go now."

Freddy's gambling had come up with Willis. Dr.
Rousseau said that he had gambled and lost considerable sums of money on their honeymoon. Apparently
the same fondness for games of chance, or the debts
incurred by games of chance, had torn a rift between
him and his sister.

I have a whiteboard on my wall that I use to create
sociograms when I need to clarify intertwined relationships in a complex case like this one. In the center I
drew a circle and wrote in Frederick Campbell and
his aliases. I then connected each of the people who
were related to Freddy with a line: Gwendolyn Godfrey, the first wife who had been murdered by a burglar. Chantal Rousseau and her mother Raheela.
Kimberley Korda, the real estate agent who had or-

dered the monogrammed cuff links. Sanford Whiteley, the Seattle P.I. who'd been shot. Christopher Goodfellow, the London barrister. Charles and Annie Taylor-Bickford. The two sisters, Millicent and Marianne. My drawing resembled the tentacles of a giant octopus. The *who* of the case was clear. What I needed was the *when* and *where* of it all, and some way to predict Freddy's next move.

I needed a time line.

With the exception of Gwendolyn Godfrey's murder in 1985, the PRI report covered Freddy up to his Istanbul posting, so I began with the date of February 22, 2001 from the *Crustacean* article. I went over my notes in the file, my conversations with Dr. Rousseau, Diane Duvall, Kimberly Korda, Willis Godfrey, and the two sisters. I finished at four thirty and read over the chronology.

February 22, 2001	Incident in Istanbul: double or triple cross with Iraqis, MI-6, CIA, six people die, including Moira St. Martin, his American mistress (U.S. Embassy employee); St. Martin killed with 25-caliber bullet.
June 2001	Will Cameron/Los Angeles. Meets and seduces Diane Duvall; threatens exposure; she pays $5,000/month for a year.
? ? ? ?	As Forrest Clark, meets Kimberley Korda in Santa Barbara.
? ? ? ?	Marries Korda. Where?
? ? ? ? ? ? ? ? ?	Divorces Korda. Where?
June 2002	As Forbes Cameron, Seattle, WA. Meets Chantal Rousseau at private party.
	Crystal Cooper knew him from a charity function where he was ac-

	companied by an English couple. (Taylor-Bickfords?)
October 2002	Marries Chantal Rousseau in Seattle with prenup and mutual power of attorney.
May 2003	Produces bogus Cameron/Rousseau "divorce" papers & disappears, ostensibly to Scotland.
June 2003	Rousseau discovers her investments have been sold. Hires Seattle P.I. Sanford Whiteley to track down Cameron.
	Freddy dines with Taylor-Bickfords at Sorrento Hotel; Whiteley calls T-B residence re: bogus monogrammed handkerchief;
	Sanford Whiteley murdered in Pioneer Square;
	Whiteley apartment burglarized.
July 2003	SJ MacKinnon takes over investigation.
	SJM phone contact with Diane Duvall.
	SJM phone contact with Kimberley Korda
	SJM meeting with Duvall in Seattle; Duvall shot dead.

As I stared at the last line, my phone rang. It was Lieutenant Stein from the Seattle P.D.

"Ms. MacKinnon, I'm investigating the death of Diane Duvall. We found your name and phone number in her pocket diary and your card in her briefcase. What is your relationship to her?" His voice was brisk and businesslike.

"I met Diane Duvall for the first time on Thursday," I said, choosing my word carefully. "She was a former acquaintance of the ex-husband of a client of mine. I was trying to find out if she had any information as to his whereabouts. I just learned about her death. Do the police have any suspects?''

"Who's your client?" he asked.

"Chantal Rousseau. She's a doctor who lives in Friday Harbor."

"Where can I find her?"

I supplied the phone number at the clinic.

"One of the protestors who was arrested was carrying a weapon of the same caliber as the weapon that killed Duvall. What's your client's ex-husband's name?"

I hesitated, wanting to be cooperative, but anticipating how convoluted the conversation would become if I started explaining about the aliases and ex-wives and Her Majesty's Secret Service.

"Hello? Ms. MacKinnon? Are you still there?"

"His name is Forbes Cameron. I don't have a current address or phone number for him. That's why Dr. Rousseau hired me. To find him."

"What's she want to find him for?"

"She didn't like the property settlement." It had a grain of truth.

"What's the last known address for this Cameron?"

I gave him the address at the Rose and Thistle. "He's also used the name Will Cameron and Frederick Campbell."

"You know any reason why this guy would want to kill Ms. Duvall?"

I hesitated, wanting to honor my promise to Diane, wanting even more to know if Freddy had anything to do with her death. "She told me Will Cameron was blackmailing her."

'For what?"

"A personal indiscretion, I believe. I don't have the details." So I was hedging.

I assured Lieutenant Stein I would be around if he

had more questions and hung up, relieved that bigger guns than mine were after Freddy. I called Angela again. She had just gotten home and was having an iced tea with Jewel Moon. They were talking about my teenage years in San Francisco. My mother came to the phone and reported that she hadn't gotten her nap because she'd taken Leonardo to Jefferson Beach for a walk and had met a woman named Rainbow who was a psychic. She'd spent the afternoon having a deep reading. Jewel Moon hoped it was all right with me, but she'd accepted an invitation to attend a late afternoon concert with Rainbow, then she was going to bed early to read the book on sailing. What did we have planned for tomorrow?

"We're meeting Abigail and Ronald at the Spinnaker at six thirty," I said, immensely relieved I didn't have to provide evening entertainment. "The rest of the day is open. If there's any wind, we could go sailing in the afternoon. Would you like to do something in the morning?"

"I'd like to sleep late. Could we take a picnic lunch on the boat?"

"Sure. I'll make some sandwiches. What time would you like to go?"

She promised to call me after she got organized.

Suddenly immensely tired, I decided to call it a day. Dr. Rousseau's report would have to wait. I stopped at the post office for my personal mail and at the Corner Grocery for cat food and a bag of fresh green beans. In need of some light entertainment, I rented *My Big Fat Greek Wedding* and headed out to G-73.

I opened all the portholes, took a package of frozen chicken breasts out of the freezer, and turned on the news. The anchorwoman was describing a terrorist attack in the Middle East and I started reading the news trailers. The third one caught my eye: SUSPECT IN CUSTODY IN SEATTLE CONFERENCE SHOOTING. I flipped through the other news channels, hop-

ing for an update. Nothing. Suspecting that Lieutenant
Stein, who was investigating the murder, would not
share any information with a private citizen, I
thumbed through my address book for Bernie Morgan's number.

"Morgan, Homicide."

"Bernie, Scotia MacKinnon. I know you're not on
the case, but I just saw on the news that you have a
suspect in custody in the Duvall shooting. Could you
tell me who it is?"

"Why do you want to know?" His normally friendly
voice was less so.

"Lieutenant Stein called me yesterday. I told him I
had talked to Diane Duvall the afternoon she was
killed. It's in connection with the missing person case
I talked to you about on Tuesday. The one where the
P.I. was murdered."

"Hold on. I can't give out the name of the suspect,
but I can give you what's been released."

"Which is?"

" 'White Caucasian male, 5'8", 150 lbs., red hair,
age 47, unemployed. No permit for a concealed
weapon, same caliber as the bullet that killed Duvall.'
He has a record of getting arrested at demonstrations,
including the '99 WTO fracas. Wears a Civil War uniform. Got violent when he got his mug shot taken and
had to give up the hat. Scotia, if you know anything
about this guy, you should be talking to Stein, not me.
Shall I transfer you?"

"Please."

"By the way, that P.I. who got shot? Whiteley?
Looks like there was a neighborhood drug deal that
went sour and he was in the wrong place at the wrong
time. I hear there's two suspects in custody."

"Thanks, Bernie." About two minutes later, Stein
answered.

"Lieutenant Stein, this is Scotia MacKinnon in Friday Harbor. We spoke yesterday. I understand you

have arrested one of the protestors in relation to the Duvall shooting."

"We have. Do you have any information about him?"

"A group of demonstrators came into Starbuck's while I was talking to Duvall on Thursday. One of them was wearing a Civil War uniform. Diane obviously didn't want to be seen by them, but she didn't mention anything specific."

"I think we've got our boy, but thanks for your—"

"Lieutenant Stein, what is the name of the suspect?"

"It's just been released to the press. Raymond Prout, no known address."

"Thanks." I hung up and put on the videotape I'd rented. As I watched Nia Vardálos and her family eat, meddle, gossip, and argue, I felt as if a huge burden had been lifted from my shoulders. Frederick Cameron had not killed Sanford Whiteley or Diane Duvall.

14

I slept in until eight on Saturday. The weather had cooled considerably overnight and a reasonable wind was blowing out in San Juan Channel. I checked the marine weather radio: winds of ten to fifteen knots were predicted for the Strait of Georgia with zero percent chance of precipitation. Jewel Moon called a little after nine. She'd just returned from walking Leonardo and was waiting for a call from Giovanni. We agreed to meet at the Olde Gazette Building at noon. I made tuna fish salad, put together two sandwiches, and tidied up the galley, then climbed topside to remove the mainsail cover. As I uncoiled the lines, I took a hard look at the winches, gathered the tube of winch lube and some rags and the special little tool to lift the ring off the self-tailing winches. It took the better part of an hour for the lube and reassembly and it was almost eleven by the time I stowed the rags and tools, locked up *DragonSpray* and headed for the office for e-mail and messages.

Waves of energy were bouncing off the walls of New Millennium, to the accompaniment of *Les Noces de Figaro*. Bronwyn O'Banion, her face looking like a thundercloud, was leaning against the counter in front of the coffee machine. She held a cell phone over her right ear and her tone of voice was anything but sweet.

"I don't give a *damn* whether you want to wear the

lavender gown or not, Chloe. It's what you're bloody well going to wear or don't even bother coming out of your room on Saturday. And if you don't intend to put in an appearance, get your bags packed and yourself ready to go back to Detroit to live with your father. I've had enough of your histrionics for one week. Or for a lifetime, for that matter."

A brief silence ensued. Bronwyn rolled her eyes toward Zelda, shook her head, and retreated outside. I emptied my cubby. Zelda watched her client pacing on the sidewalk in front of the building, and scowled.

"Dare I inquire how the details are . . . uh, progressing?" I asked. I couldn't imagine arranging a formal outdoor wedding for one hundred guests, let alone a wedding in which the bride was a celebrity writer and the national media were to be in attendance.

Zelda's gaze dropped to the scribbled list in front of her. "One hundred and ten RSVP's. The matron of honor is flying in from Chicago and hasn't tried on her dress since it was ordered. The white tent for the garden has been delayed but will arrive tomorrow, God and the ferry system willing." She ticked off items on the list. "Everything's reasonably under control except for Chloe." She nodded outside, where Bronwyn's pacing had become more agitated. "Bronwyn's thirteen-year-old daughter, who's supposed to be a bridesmaid. Hates the fiancé, detests the lavender satin bridesmaid dress because it makes her look fat, would rather die than wear lavender shoes, and is threatening to boycott the wedding."

I sidled toward the stairs. "You ever consider going back to doing computer graphics for a living?"

Zelda frowned and did not respond.

I had phone messages from Jared and Kimberly Korda. I called Kimberly first. She thought she had a buyer for one of her listings and the Sunday open house had been canceled. Would I like to come over to Orcas Sunday instead of Monday? We made an

appointment for three and I wrote it in my calendar
right below the "brunch with Meredith" notation at
eleven. Jared's message was brief: "Dinner at my
place on Sunday?" I'd forgotten to get back to him
and I did want his take on the authenticity of the
Crustacean article. I called back and accepted for six
thirty, musing that my fears of an empty weekend
without Nick were proving to be groundless.

I checked for e-mail and found one from Melissa:
*Would it be okay if Justin and I came to Friday Harbor
right after Labor Day? Could we take* DragonSpray
and do a little cruise? I replied that she was on the
calendar and that I looked forward to getting to know
Justin. The door downstairs opened and closed, followed by a murmur of voices, then a burst of Zelda's laughter.

My mother appeared at the office exactly as the clock
sounded its single off-key note. By the time we'd picked
up our bottles of lemonade and made our way through
the crowd on the main dock and out to G-73, it was
one forty-five. Last night's wind had calmed to what
I estimated was a comfortable ten to twelve knots.
Not exactly a gale, but enough to move *DragonSpray*.
I'd left the cell phone on the boat. There was one
missed message from Nick. "Scotty, I may have to go
to Mexico for a couple of weeks and there are some
issues I need to work out with Nicole. Give me a call."
I saved the message, pulled a San Juan Channel chart
out of the nav table, and slammed the cover down,
assuming the message meant he wasn't going to be
available on Tuesday.

Nicole's "issues"—dating an unemployed musician
and living with him against her mother's wishes, and
her ongoing attempts to sabotage her father's relationship with me and reunite her parents—weren't new. I
wondered angrily if they would ever be solved. Particularly the latter one.

"What's wrong, Scotia?"

I shook my head. "Nothing, Mother."

"Scotia?"

"Yes?"

"I don't want us to fight today."

'Why would we fight?"

"Well, it just seems like . . . like sometimes you're angry with me. That you've never forgiven me for all those years ago."

She was right. I hadn't. But that was a biggie and I didn't want to go there. "Sorry, Mother, I'm working on a difficult case."

And my lover keeps forcing me to reorganize my social calendar.

I found my polarized sunglasses and sunscreen, pulled two life vests out of a locker, and handed one to Jewel Moon. "Let's go up on deck and get the boat ready for sailing."

"One more thing, dear."

"What?"

"I don't want to get seasick. Do you have something I can take?"

I reached into the cabinet over the stove and pulled out the small tin I kept handy for guests with a tendency toward *mal de mer*. "This is candied ginger. Chew a couple of pieces. I think Christopher Columbus used it for his crew. And in case that doesn't work, there's one other little device." I crawled into the aft berth and found the sea bands in the cabinet. "Put one of these on each wrist. No one knows precisely why, but they seem to prevent seasickness." I watched her slide the bands on and realized how fragile her arms had become. I gave her a quick hug. "And stop worrying. We're going to have a great sail."

I sometimes forget what an intelligent woman my mother is. Perhaps because the intelligence often hides behind psychic readings and crystals and intergalactic channeling. Not only had she read the first three chapters of the sailing fundamentals book, she'd also been reading Angela and Matt's copy of *Chapman Piloting*, knew port from starboard, and was comfortable with the fact that sailboats have lines and not ropes. She wanted to know whether *DragonSpray* had a full keel or a spade keel.

"She's got a full keel, which makes her stable in rough seas and a great offshore boat, but not so great in the light air we get here in the summer. We're lucky to actually have some wind today."

By two thirty we were off the dock and outside the breakwater. The anemometer indicated twelve knots of wind, and the temperature was up in the low seventies, a lovely and unusual summertime combination. I brought *DragonSpray* into the wind and talked Jewel Moon through the hoisting of the mainsail and the unfurling of the headsail.

She pulled on the jib sheet. The sail snapped out and began flapping in the wind. "Hey, this is a lot easier than the book described!"

I smiled and watched her cranking in on the winch handle. "That's because the previous owners got tired of going up on the foredeck to hank on the sail and hoist it in rolling seas, so they installed roller furling." I helped her trim the sail until it was a few inches off the stays, tweaked the mainsheet a few inches, cut the engine, and began steering a course toward Lopez Island. Off to our left, the bell on Reid Rock clanged a warning. On our right, two white plastic power boats raced in toward the harbor. I altered course slightly so that the wake from the two boats would pass under the starboard quarter instead of hitting us on the beam and brought up our sandwiches and lemonades. When we finished eating, I stowed the trash below and asked Jewel Moon if she wanted to put on sunscreen before she took the wheel.

Her jaw went slack. "You mean . . . I'm going to sail it?"

"Yes, ma'am." She went below and returned wearing a floppy hat. "Pick out something over there on Lopez Island," I said, pointing to the southeast. "A tree or a building or something, then steer for it. When you're close to land, like we are here, it's easier than using the compass." The wind shifted slightly. When Jewel Moon asked about the traveler, I provided a brief discourse on the block-and-tackle device attached to a carriage below the boom that moved from side to side and allowed me to control the angle of the boom to the centerline of the boat. We sailed in silence and I watched a small smile grow on Jewel Moon's face. Half an hour later, we were off Upright Head and I talked her through the tacking procedure. "Right now the wind is coming over our port side." I gestured to the left. "You're going to turn the bow of the boat through the eye of the wind and then you'll be on a starboard tack. When you're ready, say 'Ready about' and I'll release the sheet on starboard and pull it in on port."

She raised her eyebrows, took a deep breath, and uttered the appropriate command. I released the starboard sheet, watched the boat come slowly through the wind, and trimmed the flapping headsail in on the port side. She had overtacked a bit. I corrected it with a small turn of the wheel and we were headed back across the channel. We sailed silently and my mind was about to drift back to the *Crustacean* article with its deadly tale.

"I had an interesting reading with Rainbow yesterday," Jewel Moon said, gazing aloft at the wind indicator.

"The woman you met on the beach?"

She nodded. "She said I'm trying to go on to a new level. But there's a lot of old stuff holding me back."

"What kind of old stuff?" I asked, not really wanting to know.

"The stuff that happened when you came to live in San Francisco."

I felt my jaw clench hard. So that's what the earlier comments were about. I stared straight ahead and refrained from answering. I had gone to live in San Francisco's Haight Ashbury district with Jewel Moon and her boyfriend, Giovanni, when I was fourteen because I had no where else to go. My grandmother Jessica had raised me after my mother's disappearance. When I was ten, my father and grandfather, both fishermen, were lost in a terrible winter storm. Then a few days after my fourteenth birthday, I had found my grandmother dead in her chair when I returned from school. "An aneurism," the doctor said. "She probably died instantly. Painlessly." For two days I wandered around the big house in my inconsolable grief until my great-aunt Susan took me to stay in her dark little apartment on the other side of Cape Breton Island. I refused to eat or go to school and my grandmother's attorney tracked down my mother. The day a sullen, badly-dressed Cape Breton teenager got off the plane at the San Francisco airport was not a joyous one for any of us.

I wondered what Jewel Moon wanted of me now.

To apologize for being a "difficult adolescent" who never did fit in with my San Francisco peers?

To beg forgiveness for my bitter fights with Giovanni, who thought I had become "a spoiled American brat?"

"I don't want to dredge up the past, Scotia," my mother went on. "Mostly I want to tell you how terribly hard it was for me to leave you when you were so little."

"Hard, Mother? *Hard?* You didn't even say goodbye! All you did was leave a letter for Dad! You didn't write to us for six months!" My peripheral vision picked up something large and white from the north. I swung around. One of the Washington State ferries was bearing down on us. I made a quick mental calculation that confirmed we wouldn't make it across the channel in time and took the wheel from Jewel Moon. "We're going to need to do a quick tack here, Mother, and then as soon as the ferry passes, we'll tack back. Just follow my instructions."

I turned the wheel to starboard, Jewel Moon released the port side sheet, *DragonSpray* moved through the wind, and we came over on the new tack. I helped her winch in the sheet, and watched the big ferry move past our stern. The wind had picked up. I adjusted the traveler. Jewel Moon climbed up to the high side of the boat and we sailed on in awkward silence, staring straight ahead. I knew Jewel Moon was watching my angry face. And I knew I was too furious to talk.

"Scotia, dear," she began tentatively, "please listen to what I have to say. I was very young when I met your father. And probably very silly. It was summer on Cape Breton Island. The Gaelic dance festival was wonderful and I thought your father was the love of my life. I know I did a wrong thing when I married a fisherman, but I did it for the right reasons. I did it for what I thought was love."

"That sure didn't last long, did it?" I made no attempt to hide my bitterness.

"No, it didn't. I knew it was a mistake the first winter. I was pregnant with you and sick most of the time. Your grandmother never approved of me. Your father was out fishing all the time. The other young wives didn't like me. I was miserable. When you were born, I was a terrible mother to you. It got worse every day. I didn't know how to take care of a baby, which your grandmother was very quick to point out. I was horribly depressed."

Her voice trembled. I stole a glance at her. She looked pale. "After you left," I said slowly, "it was so *embarrassing,* trying to explain to my friends why I had no mother. Sometimes I just wished you had died."

She winced. "One day I spent a whole afternoon walking along the cliff, thinking about throwing myself off. That's when I knew I had to leave. I thought about taking you with me. Please believe that I *wanted* to take you with me. But I didn't know where I was going. I knew your grandmother would do a better job of raising you than I. She adored you. It was a terrible decision to make, but staying there might have been worse."

I frowned, wondering if I could let go of all the years of resentment.

"For nine years, I thought about you every day. I did a lot of drifting. Those weren't very stable times for people my age. I don't know what would have happened to me if I hadn't met Giovanni."

The wind shifted; the headsail luffed and flopped. I corrected the wheel.

"I regret not finishing college and finding a profession," my mother said. "When your grandmother died, I was happy you were coming to live with us. I thought I could make everything up to you. But you never liked Giovanni. I know you think he's just a rich Italian dilettante. That he doesn't have any talent. That's partly true. But he gave me stability when I really needed it, Scotia. So did his family, even though they're kind of eccentric. We've been together for over thirty years. And I am *so* sorry for all the bad times we had in San Francisco."

Something in her voice held me. It didn't erase the abandonment, but for the first time, I glimpsed what she must have gone through when she realized she had to leave St. Ann's Bay. Had I been unjust all these years? Had I failed to grow up myself? What would I have done if I had found myself in the same predicament? Very slowly I moved my hand from the wheel and put it on her shoulder.

"You did the best you could at the time, Mother." She leaned her face against my hand, then looked around and sat up with a smile. "Scotia, the boat's barely moving. What's happening?"

'The wind has died, is what's happening. Time for what they call the "iron genny." I turned the ignition switch and pressed the starter button, and the engine turned over. "Let's lower the sails and get back to the dock. We have to prepare for your next Friday Harbor engagement."

Abigail and her friend Ronald had their heads together over drinks when Jewel Moon and I arrived. Abigail's tanned and weathered face held a pink blush that I doubted came from anything she had purchased at the drugstore. Part of me was dreading the meeting since to my way of thinking, there could hardly be two more dissimilar characters than Abigail—a retired seventy-three-year-old high school biology teacher married for fifty-two years to an Old Island Family—and Jewel Moon—a precocious, sixty-something New Age California bohemian. To my surprise, despite their widely different histories, Jewel Moon and Abigail were soon conversing like long-lost sisters while I learned that Ronald was a third cousin of Abby's departed husband. When Ronald wasn't chasing tectonic plates, he lived in Campbell River up on Vancouver Island. He was taking a recess from his research and writing to charter a boat and planned to take Abigail cruising up to Princess Louisa Inlet on the B. C. mainland.

By seven thirty Abby and my mother were on their third glasses of Australian semillon blanc and working out the agenda for the next day's Save the Whales meeting. Ronald and I exchanged a look and ordered up deep-fried zucchini sticks and cheese quesadillas. Ronald was drinking lemonade. I didn't know whether he was a teetotaler or had been appointed the designated driver for the evening. To my relief, around eight o'clock he herded the two women out of the restaurant in a courtly fashion and offered to drop Jewel Moon at Angela's on the way back to Abby's house. Delighted that Jewel Moon had found a kindred spirit and that I didn't have to worry about her getting a DUI, I thanked Ronald and watched the two women stroll up the hill arm in arm.

I crossed Front Street, stopped at the Corner Grocery to buy the ingredients for Angela's eggplant caviar recipe that I intended to bring to dinner at Jared's, and trotted along the path to the port. It was a little after eight thirty when I got back to G-73. Henry, Lindsey, and another couple I didn't know were laughing over a shared platter of something that looked Mexican on *Pumpkin Seed*'s poop deck. I declined offers to join the party and opened up the boat. Too tired to trek up to the Port building, I took a sponge bath in *DragonSpray*'s less than spacious head. While drying off, I remembered Nick's message. I pulled on my pj's and listened to it again. "Scotty, I may have to go to Mexico for a couple of weeks and there are some issues I need to work out with Nicole. Give me a call."

I supposed the message meant our Tuesday night was off. Depressed, I climbed into bed, me under the white comforter, Calico on top, and we both fell asleep halfway through a rerun of *Casablanca* on my tiny TV.

15

I didn't hear from my mother on Sunday morning. I roasted an eggplant and made the eggplant appetizer to take to Jared's. A little after eleven I locked up *DragonSpray* and walked up to the Dry Dock to have lunch with Meredith, mentally preparing for my interview with Kimberly Korda. Meredith was seated at a table near the window. My usually meticulously dressed friend looked harassed: lipstick worn away, long blond hair mussed, one side of a white collar sticking out from under her navy blue U.S. Customs uniform.

"You look like you've had better days. Dirtbag smugglers or problems at home?" I asked.

"I had to come in early this morning to deal with a recalcitrant ferry passenger who didn't want his car searched. *And* problems at home. Or as my mother would say, 'Marry in haste, repent at leisure.'"

"That bad?"

She nodded. "It started last Thursday. Becca had a sailing class at Jefferson Beach. When I went to pick her up she wasn't there. She showed up at home three hours later. Claims she left me a message, which she didn't. I grounded her Friday night."

Becca was her thirteen-year-old stepdaughter. "That must have made for a lot of laughs around the old homestead."

"It was only the beginning." The petite, brown-eyed waitress in a skimpy white shirt and navy blue shorts approached our table. I scanned the brunch menu, ordered the Eggs Benedict with orange juice instead of a mimosa. Meredith duplicated my order and continued her tale of domestic woe. "On Saturday morning, a plastic baggie fell out of Becca's backpack. A nice little stash of B. C. Bud." She pounded a rueful smile. "Given the stuff people try to smuggle past me every day, it wasn't exactly hard to identify."

"What did Mark say?" Across the room I saw Bronwyn O'Banion come into the restaurant accompanied by a gray-haired woman in a pink and white flowered dress, an older version of herself, and a tallish man in sunglasses with dark hair and a beard that I assumed was her fiancé. Bronwyn had received considerable local publicity after her novel was optioned for a movie by Julia Roberts and several diners watched the threesome as they crossed the room to the new atrium addition. The waitress brought our orange juice and Meredith continued her story.

". . . didn't think it was a big deal. He says all the kids use it. He used to smoke pot in high school. I said it was an illegal drug and she'd promised us she wouldn't use drugs, and the grounding should be extended to Saturday night. Mark said I was right in theory, but now we'd have to stick around instead of going to our friends' for dinner."

"To which you replied . . ."

"That's the price of parenting and raising kids." She sighed a tremendous sigh. "He went off and drank beer with one of his buddies and didn't get home until 2:30 A.M. On Sunday morning, Becca announced she was leaving home and going to live with her mother. What do you think I should do?"

"I think you and Mark should run, not walk, to the nearest family counselor. If you want to get her through the Friday Harbor labyrinth of drugs and alcohol—"

My cell phone rang. It was Zelda. "You might want to go rescue your mother."

"She was going to Abigail's meeting. What's happening?"

"After the meeting, Abby marched the save-the-whales demonstrators over to Madrona Circle to save the 100-year-old tree the Tracy family wants to cut down to put in an open-air ATM kiosk."

"I think I know where this is going."

"Abigail claims the tree isn't on the Tracy's property. It's on property that her grandfather owned and never deeded away. Joe Tracy owns Paradise Whale Watch Tours. This morning Abby and your mother and a bunch of high school kids picketed the Paradise Tour dock and half the passengers canceled their reservations. Abby even persuaded one of the Seattle news channels to send a helicopter." The waitress brought our eggs Benedict. I took a deep breath and rolled my eyes at Meredith. My mother had found her niche.

"You might want to get your mother out of there. The apes with the chain saws are not real patient with environmentalists."

And I'd worried about my mother and Abigail having nothing in common. "I'll check it out. Thanks for the call."

"Crisis at the office?" Meredith asked.

I shook my head and glanced at my watch. It was a little after noon. "Abigail has expanded her agenda and my mother's with her."

Meredith was summoned back to the Customs office as we were paying our bill. I hurried up to Madrona Circle, a crescent shaped alley that runs between Blair Avenue and Blackberry Court, where the Save the Madrona protest had attracted what looked like a hundred people, a mixture of locals and summer tourists. Two enterprising young girls had set up a lemonade stand. A number of video cameras were at work. I spotted a *Friday Gazette* reporter with a still camera next to Abby's friend Ronald, who was also snapping away with his Nikkon. A helicopter circled overhead while a large yellow bulldozer whose driver appeared to be having a bad day blocked the entrance to Madrona Circle. Three burly men in orange vests and dirty white hard hats conferred in front of the earthmover. A collie mutt pursued an Irish setter around the lemonade stand.

In the center of the melee, shackled to the huge spreading madrona tree with what looked like a rusty logging chain, were four or five shaggy young men and several scantily-clad nubile young women. Plus Abigail, my mother, and—enveloped in something long, purple, and diaphanous—my client's mother, Raheela Tabbal! Unsure whether to laugh or weep, I must have briefly closed my eyes when I felt a tap on my shoulder. It was Ronald.

"I tried to talk Abby out of it, Scotia, but it wasn't any use."

I nodded, noting that none of San Juan Island's finest seemed to be in attendance. "I'm sure you did, Ronald. Trying to talk Abby out of something she intends to do is like reasoning with a tornado." I glanced up at the circling helicopter. Raheela peered over the top of her veil while Abby engaged in a less than amiable conversation with a sweating, stocky, blond woman in a black suit and high heels. It was Elizabeth Dunn, Friday Harbor's newest attorney. Behind Ms. Dunn stood two men, one tall with gray-white hair and dark glasses, the other shorter and wearing a baseball cap. The shorter, handsomer man gave me a long glance, then looked away. I realized I'd seen him at George's sometime the past week. They weren't locals or tourists, so they had to be reporters. Jewel Moon was going to make the evening news.

"Your mother's waving," Ronald said. "Maybe we should go talk to her." I didn't figure anything would be gained by chatting with Jewel Moon, who looked like a six-year-old at a circus, but what the hell? I followed Ronald's tall, gaunt figure through the crowd just in time to catch the end of Abby's interchange with Ms. Dunn.

". . . not going to accomplish anything with these histrionics, Ms. Leedle."

"Wanna bet? Stealing is stealing, Ms. Dunn. The Tracy's don't own the land this tree is on and they'll have to take me out before they take out the tree. However, if Joe wants to consider treating the whales a little more humanely, we might be able to work something out." Abigail turned away from the perspiring Ms. Dunn and struck a pose for the *Gazette* photographer. As she turned back, I saw the leonine, white-haired James Smith, Friday Harbor's oldest practicing attorney-at-law, shouldering his way through the crowd. He carried a blue-jacketed document in his hand. "Ms. Dunn, it gives me great pleasure to serve you with this restraining order. I suggest you read it immediately and ask your clients to vacate Ms. Leedle's premises." He smiled broadly.

Ms. Dunn glared at James Smith and the blue-jacketed document being thrust at her chest. Reluctantly she reached for the paper, opened it, and read it. Her shoulders drooped, her mouth pursed, and without a glance at Abigail and her associates, she made her way through the crowd to the burly fellows in hard hats. After a short conference, the hard hats shook their heads and moved over to the bulldozer. The earthmover soon made a large turnaround, needlessly tearing up the green sod, and approached the flatbed truck parked behind it.

Abigail unshackled her triumphant minions. I watched Jewel Moon approaching with Raheela, whose lined, mahogany-colored face was exposed to the afternoon sun. "Wasn't it wonderful, Scotia?" she said. "If we hadn't done that, the poor tree would be lying on the grass right now. And maybe we can save the whales as well." I smiled at Raheela and gave Jewel Moon a hug. "You were fantastic. What's next on your political agenda?"

My mother sighed. "Ronald is going to take us to lunch and then he's going to drop me at Angela's. I'll take Leonardo to the beach and maybe take a nap. This protesting seems harder than it used to be. I'll call you tomorrow."

I bade the group adieu and walked down Blair toward my office. I wanted to pick up the Rousseau file to review on the ferry to Orcas. The *Gazette* photographer had disappeared and the two girls were dismantling the lemonade stand. As I waited at the corner on Guard Street for the traffic to clear, the white-haired man and his companion in the baseball cap stopped beside me. They gave me a once-over, the shorter one nodded, and they crossed the street to a turquoise Subaru.

The two-ten ferry to Orcas Island was overloaded. Not a single additional car could be squeezed on, but that didn't affect me since I was a walk-on. Accompanied by twenty or thirty cyclists clad in colorful spandex, water bottles clipped to their cycles, I walked onto the car deck of the *Hiyu* and climbed the stairway to the outside upper deck. I tucked myself onto a white wooden bench in the shade where I had a view of the line of cars snaking into the ferry and of the hillside above. The town of Friday Harbor is an eclectic mix of architectural styles: some old but renovated according to the guidelines of the San Juan Historical Society, some not; some new but of no particular design; some flat-out decrepit.

The ferry engines revved and the vessel reversed past the tall pilings, backed to port, and began creeping through the harbor, which was teeming with private and commercial vessels. Beyond the university docks the ferry turned left into San Juan Channel, glided past Shaw Island, and ten minutes later, made a wide right turn into Wasp Passage, the twisting waterway that meanders past tiny Crane Island and joins with Harney Channel to divide the San Juans from east to west. I pulled the Rousseau file from my briefcase, glanced at the time line, and tried to summarize what I knew for sure about Frederick Campbell a.k.a. Forbes Cameron, Will Cameron, and Forrest Clark—even though I knew there was no "for-sure" about Freddy, and there were far too many question marks on the time line. Was Kimberly Korda his second wife? Were there other wives? Other blackmail victims? Were they still alive? Where had he gone after he left Chantal? Was he even now devising the seduction of some naive, well-heeled woman under some fresh disguise? How the bloody hell was I going to find him?

We docked at Orcas Landing at two forty-five. I disembarked with the cyclists, who probably had little idea that most of the roads on the island were hilly and narrow with nary a bicycle lane to be found. The Wildflower Café occupied the open-air deck and first floor of the Harney Hotel, a white four-story, Victorian-era lodge that overlooked the water. The café was crowded, but I had no trouble identifying Kimberly Korda at one of the tables on the deck. Her hair was shoulder length, light brown changing naturally to gray as she had said. She stood up and waved without smiling and I threaded my way among the tables. Her pale pink linen dress was simply styled and draped easily over her slender, girlish body. I returned her brisk handshake and sat down. "Thanks for meeting me, Ms. Korda."

She nodded. "It was partly out of curiosity," she said. "And please call me Kim."

There was a tall pitcher of lemonade and two glasses on the table. I pulled my tape recorder from my rucksack. "Okay if I record this?"

Her blue-green eyes widened in surprise. "Is this . . . a police investigation?"

"As I told you on the phone, I'm a private investigator. I have a client who is trying to find the man you know as Forrest." I pulled the photo of Frederick out of the bag. "This man."

"That's him." She gazed at the picture with sad eyes.

I dumped the two cuff links out of the blue velvet pouch onto the table. "Do you recognize these?"

She touched the gold jewelry and gave a small lopsided smile. "They were my wedding gift to Forrest. He loved monogrammed stuff. Nathan Tate and I went to high school together in Friday Harbor, so I thought of him." She looked at me and frowned. "How did you get them?"

"My client gave them to me, and my assistant recognized them as the work of an island jeweler. Would you tell me when and where you met the man you ordered these for?"

She picked up the cuff links, laid them in her left hand, and closed her fingers over them. "I met Forrest two years ago in Santa Barbara—in July. At our church. The minister introduced us. It was love at first sight. Forbes was an investment analyst in Santa Barbara. I'd never seen such a beautiful man. And *nice*. He took me to dinner every Sunday after church. For the next three months, we spent all our time together. He was a real gentleman, not rushing me, not hitting on me like a lot of men do." Her face grew sad. "I'm not a glamorous woman, Ms. MacKinnon. I'd never had anyone treat me like that. You know, roses, little gifts, midnight suppers and picnics on the beach. He took me to Maui for our honeymoon." She hesitated, sighed, and continued. "He was wonderful with the kids. My daughter wanted to learn to ride horses and he found a trainer for her. He taught my son to play tennis." She paused for a minute, her face bleak. "Real estate was really hot. I'd just sold a three-million-dollar waterfront estate and I had both the commission on the sale and cash from my divorce settlement. Forbes suggested I put part of the cash into a new house and the rest he would invest for me. When he asked me to marry him, I thought I'd died and gone to heaven."

I asked about family. "Talking about his family made him sad," she said. "His parents were both dead, but sometimes he talked to his sister in London. I've forgotten her name."

"Any medical problems?"

She thought for a minute, looked at her hands, and shook her head. "He was kind of a health nut. Always taking vitamins."

"Did you have a prenuptial agreement?"

"Yes. Forbes said it was to protect me."

"Did it have a power-of-attorney clause?"

She nodded. "That's how he was able to sell my stocks before the market went down. The bad part was that when we divorced, I had to sell the new house and he got half of the equity. And he said all his investments had been lost in the crash."

Kimberly Korda seemed blissfully unaware that she had been scammed.

"Do you have a copy of your final divorce decree?"

She frowned and reached for her bag under the table. "That's a funny thing. After I talked to you, I looked through my records. I couldn't find it. All I found was the prenuptial and the property settlement I signed after we filed for divorce." She pulled a sheaf of papers from the bag and handed them to me. "I was really upset over the divorce. I probably misplaced the decree."

The law firm shown on the top of the documents was Lockerbie and Skye, the same as on Dr. Rousseau's documents. The contents were similar to the Rousseau-Cameron petition, except that this one was filed in California. And I noticed that Clarke was spelled with an "e."

"This petition says you were married less than a year."

She closed her eyes briefly. When she opened them, two tears drifted down her cheeks. She wiped them away with one hand. "We lived together for four months. And then we filed for divorce about one month later. Actually, Forbes did all the paperwork."

"Why did you get a divorce?"

"After two or three months, Forrest started getting depressed. He would stay away for several days or part of a weekend. Sometimes he wasn't home at all on the weekends. He said he needed to travel to see his investment clients. I didn't believe him and at first I thought it was another woman. Then I thought it was an alcohol problem, but he hardly ever drank anything. He finally said he'd never gotten over his first wife. She died a very tragic death. I really felt sorry for him. I wanted us to go to counseling, but he said he'd done that and it hadn't helped."

"Did Forrest gamble?"

She smiled indulgently. "Oh, he played roulette on one of those on-line sites. I don't think he ever won or lost very much, but it made him happy."

"When did you last see him?"

"Over a year ago."

"Did you ever meet any of his friends?"

"We had dinner once with a couple from England. Annie and John. Annie was the sister of one of Forrest's friends in England."

"Do you keep in touch with them?"

She shook her head. "I don't think Annie liked me. Forrest was always rather . . . private about his correspondence and stuff. I was busy with the kids and selling real estate. I just let him take care of our social life."

She combed her fingers through her hair. "After the divorce, I dated an attorney. I showed him the prenuptial. He said he couldn't believe I'd been brainless enough to sign it because it gave Forrest discretionary power over my assets. Fortunately, the only thing I hadn't declared was my family's house up here. For some reason I never told Forrest about it. A year ago, I gave up the So Cal rat-race and moved back. I'll never have what I had when I met Forrest, but at least it's a roof over our heads and the kids like the school here." She tilted her head to one side. "Why are you trying to find him?"

"You're not the first woman Forrest Clark has conned, Kim."

"What do you mean? I know he got married again and he used a different name. My sister in San Francisco sent me this." She pulled a newspaper clipping from the pocket of her dress and handed it to me.

The clipping was the "Vows" section of the *San Francisco Chronicle,* from March of a year ago. The lead item, taking up three columns, covered the nuptials of Hannah von Suder and Fletcher Curtis under the caption, "Wine Country Chatelaine Weds English Banker." I peered at the large, informal photo of the couple with their guests, a huge stone fireplace in the background. The man had a mustache, his hair was darker than in the photo my client had supplied, but the glint in his eyes and his self-confident smile were the same. The laughing woman on his arm was short and plump with a squarish face and short, straight dark hair under a shoulder-length veil. She clutched a bouquet of white flowers in one hand and held his arm possessively with the other.

"It really hurt me that he remarried so soon after leaving me," Kim said. "Is she your client?"

"No," I said. "She's not." She watched me scan the text below the photo. The couple had been married on Saturday, the second of March, in the Lady of Our Sorrows Chapel in St. Helena, California. Following the nuptials, a reception had been held at the von Suder Cellars in St. Helena. The bride, who would continue to use her name professionally as manager of the Cellars, was the daughter of Helga and Henry von Suder. She had a B.S. degree from the University of California–Davis in oenology and an M.B.A. from Stanford University. The bridegroom, who had been educated at Cambridge University, was a mortgage banker with offices in Los Angeles and San Francisco. The couple had met six weeks earlier at a charity wine-tasting that the Cellars had hosted to benefit children with cerebral palsy. They planned to divide their time between a residence on the winery property in St. Helena and a home in San Francisco.

"If she's not your client, then he's been married *twice* since he divorced me?"

"Unless you find a final decree, Kim, it's quite possible that there really was no divorce. Did you ever talk to anyone at Lockerbie and Skye?"

She shook her head. "I couldn't think of any reason to. I could tell it was over. I finally figured out Forrest wasn't going to change his mind." She frowned at the documents on the table. "So I might not be divorced?" Something seemed to happen to her face. First she smiled, then she looked at the von Suder–Curtis wedding announcement and her face crumbled. I thought she would cry. Then, very slowly her chin came up and a small smile played around her lips. "It's all right. I know I was stupid. But you know what? It was wonderful while it lasted. No man ever treated me like that. Probably no one ever will again."

"You might want to consult an attorney," I said, reluctant to point out that Forrest Clark was probably a bigamist as well as a swindler. I tucked the clipping into my bag, turned off the tape recorder and saw the ferry from Anacortes make a swing in toward the dock. I handed her a card. "If you think of anything that will help me find him—any names, phone numbers, forgotten documents—call me." We stood up and made our way to the door and down the steps. "Kim, it's possible that the man you know as Forrest may be dangerous."

She looked startled. "Dangerous? Forrest?"

"Yes. Is there a place where you and the children could stay until we find him?"

"Actually, my vacation starts next week. I'm taking the kids to Disneyland and then they're going to their father's in L.A. for the rest of the summer." She frowned. "But I can't believe that Forrest . . ." Her voice trailed off. She shrugged and walked away down the hill toward the parking lot.

I headed in the opposite direction to the ferry, feeling as if I had just told a child that there was no Santa Claus. In some situations ignorance might be bliss. In the case of Frederick Campbell, ignorance might be fatal.

16

"This is Henry von Suder." The voice was old and tired.

"Mr. von Suder, my name is Scotia MacKinnon. I'm a private investigator and I'm trying to get in touch with your son-in-law—" I consulted the clipping again. "—Fletcher Curtis."

"He is not my son-in-law."

"Please don't hang up, Mr. von Suder."

"Why do you want to find Curtis?"

"It's a personal matter. Do you know where he is?"

"Hopefully, very far away. He ruined my daughter's life."

"May I speak to your daughter?"

"She doesn't live here any more."

"Do you know where I can find her?"

A pause. "She moved up north."

"Where up north?"

"To Washington."

"Where in Washington?"

"I don't know."

"Do you have a phone number for her?"

"No. I do not want to talk to her." The line began buzzing.

Merde! Even if I called listings for every area code in the state of Washington, there was no guarantee I would find her. And if she didn't want to be found, she would have an unlisted number. I called directory assistance for Seattle and got nothing. Ditto for Tacoma, Olympia, Everett, and Bellingham. *Merde encore!*

It was almost six o'clock and I hadn't heard from my mother all day. Hopefully no news was good news. Frustrated by the constant dead ends in my investigation, feeling rushed and overscheduled, I grabbed my shower bag and headed for the Port building. The hot water did little to loosen my tight shoulder muscles. Back on the boat I put on a David Lanz CD and opened the hanging locker in my cabin. It was too hot for blue jeans and I wasn't in the mood for a skirt or dress. I found an old but still classy pair of white linen pants and a blue chambray shirt, added turquoise earrings, and a found a pair of Mexican sandals in the bottom of the locker. My hair was still damp from the shower. I combed it out and gave it a quick shake to style it, reflecting that it looked better than it had right after Trudy trimmed it. With the addition of two flicks of mascara and a touch of mauve lipstick, I was ready for dinner.

Goldie, Jared's yellow Lab, announced my arrival before I knocked. Jared was relaxed and casual in a faded blue print Hawaiian shirt, tan Bermuda shorts and bare feet. Ordinarily I don't think of Jared as sexy, but seeing his well-muscled bare legs for the first time made me wonder if I'd overlooked something. He gave me a hug. The stress of rushing from one crisis to another must have shown on my face. He raised his eyebrows, gave me a kiss on the cheek, and took the canvas bag with the eggplant appetizer.

I followed him into the kitchen, which smelled of sautéing onions, and pulled up a stool to the big wooden island where our dinner was in preparation. A large white ceiling fan moved the hot air around. Goldie circled twice around the island, then flung her-

self down on the braided rug, head between her paws.
"I'm working on a cold ale," he said. "Would you like
your usual?"

"Actually, the ale sounds better."

"Why did I know you were going to say that?" He
took a bottle of Full Sail from the fridge, poured it
into a mug and handed it to me, then transferred the
eggplant from my plastic container to a glass bowl and
set out some melba crackers. "I forgot to ask how
spicy you like your curry," he said.

"On the mild side of spicy. Can I help with
anything?"

"It's all under control." He gave me an impish look.
"I see your mother is enjoying her visit to Friday
Harbor."

"What do you mean?"

"My reporter covered a couple of demonstrations
today. You may have heard about them. And he got
an interesting photo of Abigail and a woman in a
burqa and an attractive older woman in a pink skirt
chained to a tree. Unless you tell me not to, we'll run
the photo on the front page next Friday."

"The attractive woman in the pink skirt was my
mother," I said dryly. "That's what I get for introduc-
ing her to Abigail. And she'll love the publicity." I
rubbed my shoulder muscles.

"Does that sore shoulder have anything to do with
your current investigation?"

"It's a combination of my mother, a friend's domestic crisis, and my frustration with the investigation.
This afternoon I met with Kimberly Korda, a real estate agent over on Orcas. Another of Freddy's abandoned wives."

"How did you find *her*?" Brows knitted, he filled a
pot with water and put it on the stove.

How *had* I found Kimberly? I shook my head, trying to reconstruct my conversation with her. Her
meeting with Forrest down in Santa Barbara . . . her

daughter who rode horseback . . . the honeymoon on Maui . . . the monogrammed cuff links . . .

"The cuff links! That's it! My client found a pair of gold monogrammed cuff links with the initials "F.W.C." that Forbes left behind when he moved out. For a minute there, I thought I'd lost it."

"And the cuff links led you to this Kimberly?"

"By stroke of sheer random luck, Zelda recognized them as being the work of an island jeweler. The jeweler went to high school with Kimberly before she moved down to California. She ordered the cuff links as a wedding gift for the man she knew as Forrest Clark."

"The world gets smaller every day." He spooned a dollop of eggplant onto a cracker. "Did this Korda person have any leads for you?"

"Somebody in California sent Kimberly Korda a newspaper article about the wedding of a California wine heiress. She recognized her ex—under the name Fletcher Curtis—in the photo. The wedding would have taken place before Freddy met my client by a few months. I tracked the new bride to a Sonoma winery. Her father says she's moved to Washington and he doesn't know where."

"I would say you've met your match, dear lady. Or as Holmes would more accurately put it, your mettle is being tested."

"In spades. Sometimes it all seems preposterous. Not the phony weddings and divorces and the sweetheart cons, but that the man behind all of them is the same individual described in the background report on Frederick Campbell. And the MI-6 agent described in the *Crustacean* article. A British agent who may have caused the deaths of five people in Istanbul! Do you think that article is for real?"

Jared added rice to the steaming pot before replying. "They may not have all the facts correct, but I would hazard a guess that there's more than a grain of truth in it. *Crustacean* has been so uncannily on the money in the past that Whitehall's had them investigated a couple of times. By the way, did you hear the suspect in the Duvall shooting at the Westin was released?"

"Where did you hear that?"

"It was on the news just before you got here. Seems the gun the protestor was carrying was such an antique it would never have fired. And they can't make any connection between him and Duvall except that she happened to be leaving the hotel when the protest turned ugly. Did you learn anything from her?"

"Diane Duvall identified Frederick Campbell as the man who called himself Will Cameron, the man who blackmailed her. Anyway, when Duvall stopped paying him, he told her she'd be sorry. Or words to that effect."

"Freddy sounds like someone who doesn't like women much. Did you ever talk to either of the sisters?"

"Millicent said she hadn't heard from him in five years. She gave me an address in California that's history. Marianne, the sister in Australia, called her brother a liar and a thief and said her husband would shoot him on sight. I would guess Freddy is not hanging out in Australia. The most informative conversation was with Willis Godfrey, the brother of Freddy's first wife, Gwendolyn. He hates Freddy and said Freddy was fond of hitting the casinos. That he lost a lot of money he couldn't afford to lose, and that he inherited a bundle when Gwendolyn was murdered. Dr. Rousseau said Forbes gambled on their honeymoon and lost a considerable sum of money. Kimberly says Forrest may have been gambling on-line."

"On-line gambling—or gaming, as it's called—is a multibillion-dollar industry. Two point four billion last year, to be exact, with estimates that it will grow to ten billion over the next five years."

"How does that work in states where gambling is illegal?"

"Betting on-line is illegal under the federal Wire Act, although that's being challenged in a federal appeals court. A lot of the gaming Web sites are run by offshore operators. The players are supposed to register with a non-U.S. address, which has to match credit card info. In reality, all you need is a credit card. Legislators everywhere are rushing to pass laws to control the gaming, but as one of the white-haired worthies said, 'It's like trying to lock the barn after the horse is already out.' "

"Well, at the end of the day, it doesn't matter how Freddy does his gambling. What matters is where he is and whether he's going to target my client next. What makes me crazy is that all I can do is sit on my hands until he makes a move."

"Do you have a chronology for your villain's little romances?"

"Diane Duvall met him in June 2001 in San Diego. Kimberly apparently fell into his net and married him three months after that. He married Hannah last spring and my client in the fall."

"No real divorces?"

"I've yet to see a divorce decree. I would guess Freddy prepared all the papers himself. The law firm for all of them is Lockerbie and Skye."

"Lovely Scottish destinations." Jared turned down the heat under the rice and excused himself to make a phone call. I wandered into the living room. The focal point of the room was the huge stone fireplace with deep, well-worn, overstuffed chairs in front. Floor-to-ceiling shelves of books covered the walls on either side of the hearth. The shelf of Rex Stout first editions seemed to have acquired one or two new Nero Wolfe capers. One was an advance reading copy of the 1934 first edition of *Black Orchids*. Below Nero Wolfe was a shelf of books on British military intelli-

gence: *MI-6, Open Secret, My Five Cambridge Friends.*
Enigma was there, the novel of the World War II
British code breakers that had been made into a
movie. Stacked on a small wooden table in front of
the bookshelves was an old copy of *The Thin Man*
and an oversize leather-bound edition of *The Maltese
Falcon.* I picked up the *Falcon* volume and turned the
pages. It appeared to be a scene-by-scene presentation
of the classic film with hundreds of blown-up photos.

"You've found my new indulgence." Jared peered
over my shoulder as I turned the pages.

"This is fabulous, Jared. Did it come from the library on Brown Island?"

"Yes. There are a few other gems over there that
I'm lusting after, but we're still negotiating a price."

I glanced at him, wondering if any of the lust was
directed toward the widow, but I refrained from in-
quiring. I also wondered how Jared earned enough
money from publishing a small town newspaper to ac-
quire rare first editions. Thinking about my failure to
find Frederick Campbell, my gaze wandered back to
the shelf of military intelligence. Jared's gaze followed
mine and he pulled *Spycatcher* from the shelf.

"As you probably know, this is the book the British
government went to great lengths to keep from being
published," he said.

"Wright was a key figure in British Intelligence, as
I recall."

"MI-5. For nearly a quarter of a century. He had
moved to Australia when he decided to write the book.
The Brits sued him down there to keep him from writing it. They lost." He replaced *Spycatcher* and pointed
to *A Spy's Revenge.* "I met Hall, the chap who wrote
this one, in London. He covered the trial in Sydney."

"If you don't mind my asking, what exactly were
you doing in London, Jared?"

"Trying to write enough pages every day to pay the
rent and buy steak and kidney pie." He grinned. "In

the early eighties I was working for the *Washington Post*. My wife at the time was English. She was working for the British Embassy when I met her. She waited until after we were married to tell me she hated D.C. and wanted to go home. I tried to finagle an assignment to the London bureau, but it didn't happen. So to keep her happy, we moved to London and I went freelance."

"And she stayed happy?"

He shook his head and moved to the table. "Not for long. Our flat didn't meet her expectations and since I was freelancing, I had to go where the stories were. That meant Belfast and Bangkok and Teheran. She refused to travel with me and one cold, drizzly night I came home and found she'd moved out of the flat."

"I'm sorry."

"Don't be," he said tersely. "She did me a favor. She got a divorce and married a bureaucrat and they had three kids. All's well that ends well." He pulled *Open Secret* from the shelf. "Here. Since you've become a San Juan Island spycatcher, this is one you might like." He handed me the hardbound volume with the photograph of an attractive woman on the front. "Good lady, Stella. First woman DG of MI-5. You'll love the descriptions of her visit to Russia in '91. Gorby had asked that some people from the security service be sent to talk to the KGB about what it would mean to work in a democracy. It was the middle of winter. Her descriptions of Moscow are wonderful. Cold, dark snowy nights, lamplit rooms behind heavy curtains. Pure cloak and dagger. And somewhere in there she describes how Vernon Kell, the first DG of MI-5, recruited his male agents."

"How was that?"

"They had to be able to make notes on their shirtcuffs while riding on horseback."

"And the female agents?"

"He liked his girls to have good legs." He gave me a grin and a once-over. "You would have made the top of the list. Anyhow, the rice is ready. You've done everything you can do for the moment. Let's put the gambling spook on hold for an hour or so and enjoy the curry. I'll turn on the big fan over the table and you can pretend you're in Rangoon."

The second cup of after-dinner chamomile tea that Jared insisted on brewing for my "stressful investigation" finally relaxed my shoulder muscles. Around eleven thirty he gave me a ride down to the port. I could tell his bad knee was aching and I declined his offer to walk me out to G-73. I saw no one near the Port administration building. The main dock was quiet and mostly deserted, except for an embracing couple near the fish vendor's shack.

Pumpkin Seed lay dark and silent in the summer darkness. Calico uncurled herself from under Henry's canvas dodger and carped about my late return. I followed her down the companionway and locked up from below.

Two new voice-mail messages awaited: Jewel Moon advising that she had had an exhausting day and was going to sleep in on Monday, perhaps coming into town for lunch; and Nick wondering why he hadn't heard from me. It was too late to call him back. I washed my face and crawled into bed, recalling what Jared had said about the suspect in Diane Duvall's shooting having been released.

Did that mean I was back where I was two days ago? That the payment Freddy had referred to was payment in blood?

In spite of Jared's tea, I spent what felt like most of the night helplessly observing Abigail and my mother and the burqa-clad tribeswoman chanting and circling a steaming cauldron that was giving off as much heat as a furnace. The chanting ended, the three disappeared momentarily, then reappeared dragging a man bound up like a trussed pig. The man was Captain Joe Tracy of Paradise Tours. Sweat poured off my face. I screamed and screamed again, but none of the three paid the slightest attention, their exertions focused on hoisting the squealing offender into the boiling cauldron. Through a lake of molten lava, I slogged toward the murderous trio, felt a sharp pain in my right leg, and found myself sitting up in bed, dripping with sweat, tongue glued to the roof of my mouth.

The phone was ringing. It was still dark. A damp, salty breeze blew through the open hatch cover above my head. Confused, I was unable to find the light switch above my pillow. The phone rang again. Shivering, terrorized by a call in the middle of the night, I fumbled under my pillows and managed to grab it on the third ring.

"Hello?"

For several seconds I couldn't understand the soft, whispery voice.

"I'm sorry, I can barely hear you. Please speak louder."

"My daughter Hannah. She lives on Santa Maria Island." The voice was still whispering.

I shook my head, trying to wake up. "Hannah? Santa Maria Island? Mrs. von Suder?"

"Yes. I must be quiet. I don't want to wake her father. I want to give you her telephone number. He doesn't know I'm calling you."

"Hold on, please. Let me get something to write with." I found the lamp and a pen and paper on the shelf above the bed. "Tell me her number."

She whispered the number. I repeated it back to her.

"She is a good girl. It was not her fault."

"*What* was not her fault, Mrs. von Suder? Why is her father angry with her?"

She did not answer. The line was dead.

Hannah von Suder was living on Santa Maria Island, not more than ten or twelve miles from San Juan Island. I examined the number on the scrap of paper and squinted at the phosphorescent digits on the clock. It was 3:35 A.M. I would call the number in the morning. The wind made me shiver. I closed the hatch cover above my bed, turned out the light, and stared into the dark, my mind racing.

Why had Hannah von Suder left her family winery and moved to Santa Maria Island?

What "wasn't her fault"?

When I spoke with Henry von Suder before going up to Jared's, he had said, "He is not my son-in-law. He ruined my daughter's life."

DragonSpray rocked in the wind and moved against her lines. At four thirty a loose line began tapping gently against the mast. I visualized my calendar for Monday. Except for calling Hannah von Suder and following up on whatever I learned, I didn't have anything scheduled and could spend some time with Jewel Moon.

At 5:07 the first flapping line was joined by a second. At five thirty, I gave up, pulled on sweats, and went out for a morning walk. I got to the Netshed at six thirty as Peg O'Reilly pulled a pan of fresh cinnamon rolls from her oven. But even the smell of yeast and cinnamon could not wipe out my feeling that each new piece of information I added to the portrait of Frederick Campbell pushed all of Freddy's wives one step closer to death.

17

Hannah von Suder's voice when I reached her on Monday morning at the Santa Maria Winery was firm and authoritative. It was hard to imagine her being related to the tentative, whispery voice I'd heard in the middle of the night. I identified myself and asked for her help in locating Fletcher Curtis.

"No, I'm sorry, I don't have time. I've got three fields to disk before Friday."

"Do you have any idea where I might find Mr. Curtis?"

Silence, then, "How do I know you are who you say you are?"

"I'm in the yellow pages. My Washington State private investigator's license number is listed there. I'd appreciate hearing from you as soon as possible. You could also call an attorney here in Friday Harbor, Carolyn Smith, for a reference."

"I'll do that." The line went dead.

She wasn't the first person to distrust a private investigator.

The scent of freshly brewed coffee drifted up the stairs. While I waited for her call back, I busied myself with typing up the main points of my conversation with Kimberly Korda and filled in several of the blank spaces on the time line of Freddy's activities. Downstairs the door opened and closed and something

heavy hit the floor. It had been five days since I'd
heard from Dr. Rousseau. I called her home number.
Dr. Rousseau was not in and they did not know when
she would be. I called her home number. Raheela
answered.

"Do you know where Chantal is? I need to talk to
her, Raheela. *Je dois lui parler.*"

"Elle est allée à Seattle. Une réunion."

Gone to Seattle for a meeting? I frowned. "Is there
a telephone number where I can reach her? *Un num-
éro de téléphone*?"

There was a long pause, then, *"Je ne sais pas,
madame."*

She didn't know. "When she will return?"

"Peut-être demain."

Maybe tomorrow? Puzzled, I thanked her and hung
up, wondering why Raheela didn't know where her
daughter was or how to reach her. I would just have
to wait until tomorrow. While I was trying to sort it
out, Nick called. "Scotty, I've been worried about
you."

"Sorry, Nick. I've been tied up in this investigation.
You're going out of town?"

"I have to leave Wednesday evening for L.A., then
Mexico. Might have to be gone for two weeks. I'll tell
you about it. But I still want to get together with you.
Are we on for tomorrow night?"

My fretting had been for nothing. I glanced at my
calendar and noticed a dentist appointment I had this
morning at ten. Tomorrow and Wednesday were open.
My mother had said she was going to stay a week and
unless Angela threw her out, she would probably be
okay with my leaving her for a night. "I can be there
tomorrow afternoon about five," I said. I did not ask
what had happened with the "Nicole issues."

"Call me when you get to Seattle," Nick said. "I'll
leave a key with Keith, the security guy, in case I get
held up."

It was nine twenty. I went downstairs for a cup of coffee. "I can't do it," Zelda said, without turning away from her computer.

"Can't do what?" I reached for the least stained cup in the plastic dish drainer, in no mood for any histrionics.

The inscription on the cup—"The only difference between a rut and a grave is the depth"—was not particularly uplifting.

"Move in with Sheldon."

"I'm confused," I said. "I thought you guys weren't talking."

"We made up. But I still can't live with him. If I did, I'd be doing the right thing for the wrong reason."

"The wrong reason being what?"

"I don't love him."

"I see." I frowned and added nonfat milk to the coffee. For quite some time Zelda's main focus in life had been to find a life partner. Her forays into chat rooms, Internet matchmaking, and cyberspace introductions had turned up a married Scottish laird, a teenaged Lothario in Munich, a retired KGB agent in Vancouver. I'd been privy to a running critique on each potential mate relative to virility, intelligence, and geographical desirability, but at no point had I heard the four-letter word beginning with "L." "I see," I said again. "Well, that is certainly a . . . reason. On the other hand, right now you need a roof over your head. In addition to being downright handsome, Sheldon is actually a very decent guy."

"Sheldon Wainwright is also prissy and passive-aggressive," she snapped, "and his politics are way to the right of Attila the Hun."

I leaned against the counter, listened for the phone, sipped my coffee. "You could do worse," I said finally.

"I'm too much of a romantic. I need to be in love before I can live with a man. Even if it doesn't last." She typed a short e-mail message, clicked on "Send" and scowled at her monitor. "Jean Pierre is arriving on Friday."

One of Zelda's earliest event-arranging assignments had been a lavish birthday party aboard a yacht piloted by a handsome Frenchman from Martinique. During the Gatsby-like festivities, Zelda had taken umbrage at Jean Pierre's attentions to one of the guests. "A blond twit in fuck-me shoes" were, I think, her exact words, and she had abruptly backed out of an invitation to cruise to Alaska with Jean Pierre. "Jean Pierre? What happened to the half-naked tart he was lusting over?"

She released a deep sigh. "In hindsight, I think I overreacted. You know, as in guys will be guys. I mean, he *said* all he was doing was checking out the Celtic cross on her left breast. I shouldn't have gone ballistic. By the by, I was working late last evening and two men came by looking for you. One was a corporate type. Short hair, jacket and tie, brown wingtips. The other one had more style. But definitely not locals."

"I don't know any corporate types."

"I got the impression they'll be back. Maybe some rich new clients. Oh, yeah, Jewel Moon called. She wants to have lunch with you today. Okay if I take her to a Corona meeting tonight? We're going to see *Die Another Day* and then grab a burger at George's."

I flashed on last night's dream and laughed. "Sure, just keep her and Abigail away from boiling cauldrons."

"Boiling cauldrons? Did I miss something?"

"Never mind." I shook my head and moved toward the stairs, stress and fatigue mixed with mild hysteria. "I'm a little spacey this morning. By the way, did you ever try to breach Freddy's e-mail security? The address he used in the e-mail to his chum Christopher?"

She shook her head. "Yes, but still no luck. I'll be

done here in a few minutes. If I could go through his dossier, I might be able to break the password."

I brought down the file. "I'm off to the dentist, back in an hour. If my mother calls, ask her to come by here at noon."

Zelda was hunched over her computer monitor when I returned a little after eleven thirty and I did not disturb her. Ten minutes later, Hannah von Suder called.

"All right," she said, "I guess you're legit. I talked to one of your deputies over there. Why do you want to find Fletcher?"

"It involves some missing property."

I heard a mirthless laugh. "*Property* as in investments and real estate?"

"Close. Do you know where he is?"

"The last address I had was in San Francisco. An apartment on Telegraph Hill. He's gone now. Who's he swindled this time?"

"A client of mine. How long were you married to Fletcher?"

She didn't answer right away. "How do you know I was married to him?" she asked finally.

"I have a newspaper clipping. Are you still married to him?"

"If I am, then I lost half of my interest in the Cellars for nothing. We were married for three months."

"Where did you live?"

"In one of the houses on the estate. We could have used his apartment in San Francisco, but I needed to stay close to the winery."

"Do you remember names of any of his friends or family?"

"He'd just moved up from So Cal, so he didn't have any old friends. We hung out with some couples in the valley that I knew. His parents had passed away. He had two sisters, but I never met them."

"What did he do for fun? Golf? Tennis? Racquet-ball?"

"We both played golf. And he was a good swimmer. Swam every morning. He once mentioned horses. I think his father was a vet."

"Any medical problems?"

"Not that I knew about."

"Why did you divorce him?"

"I didn't have a choice. I think his words were, 'It was a bit of a mistake, old girl.' "

"Did you have a prenuptial agreement?"

"Of course. His list of assets was substantial. My mistake was in not verifying them. We agreed to share everything fifty-fifty in case of a divorce, which I never anticipated. When we did the property settlement, fifty percent of my assets was a little under a million dollars. Fifty percent of his turned out to be zero. He said he'd had a 'bad investment year.' The only thing that matched the list of assets was the Jag. And that was leased."

"Was there a mutual power-of-attorney in your agreement?"

"There was, but my attorney advised me not to sign it. The only thing I did right in the whole stupid affair."

"Did you consider taking legal action?"

There was a long silence. "Our attorney filed a suit against him for fraud. Misrepresentation of assets. Then one day my father had an accident in his car. The car rolled twice. My father nearly lost a leg. He'll spend the rest of his life in a wheelchair. The insurance company had a mechanic check it over. They said the brakes had been tampered with. I got the message."

"What brought you to Santa Maria?"

"After my father threw me out, I came up to Orcas to visit a college friend and lick my wounds. I heard about the convent property being for sale. My friend loaned me the money. I'm going to turn the property into a vineyard and a bed-and-breakfast."

So Hannah von Suder was the new owner of the convent. "Are you living there alone?"

"Yes, except for a Guatemalan family my mother sent up to help me."

"Have you heard from Fletcher since the divorce?"

"Not a word. If I ever saw him, I'd probably kill him."

"Do you have a copy of the final divorce decree?"

"In California it's called a dissolution. I probably do. I'll look for it. And would you like to know my suggestion for your client? Tell her to quit while she's ahead. Fletcher is a nasty piece of work underneath that pretty Cambridge accent. I've gotta go."

"Ms. von Suder, I understand you made a report of a prowler on your property last week. Do you think there was someone on the property?"

"Not really. Cecilia, who works for me, thinks there are ghosts in the convent. It was probably some animal."

"Please take all the security measures you possibly can. I would agree with your evaluation of Fletcher. He is a nasty piece of work. And possibly dangerous."

I should have said more. I should have suggested she leave the island until we caught up with Freddy. I didn't and it may have changed everything. Or maybe not.

I refilled my coffee cup and updated the sociogram on my whiteboard. After I put an "X" through Gwendolyn, Moira St. Martin, the two MI-6 agents in Istanbul, Whiteley, and Diane Duvall, it resembled a deadly game of tic-tac-toe.

When the two men came through my door I knew they weren't corporate types. FBI, I thought instantly, realizing I'd mistaken them for reporters at the Save the Madrona demonstration on Sunday. I was half right.

The taller one was close to his late fifties with a gray-white brush cut, pale blue eyes and nearly lashless eyes. Despite the heat, he wore a white shirt and thin sixties-era dark tie under a brown blazer with tan trousers and brown wing tips. He showed an ID that identified him as John Kenneth Baxter of the Federal Bureau of Investigation. There was no date on the ID. Without a phone call, I had no way of verifying its authenticity.

John introduced his shorter, far handsomer, dark-haired companion as Michael Farraday. Farraday's blue blazer was faultlessly tailored and I would bet it did not come from the Men's Wearhouse.

I leaned back in my chair, feigning calm. Even though Farraday hadn't opened his mouth, I was ninety percent sure he was a Brit. It was possible that MI-6 had enlisted the help of their American cousins in hunting for their treacherous agent, but I would have thought it would have been CIA, not the feebs.

Without waiting for an invitation, Baxter lowered himself into the wicker chair in front of my desk and nodded to Farraday to take the other chair. "We understand you have a client who hired you to locate a man name Frederick Campbell," Baxter said. "And he may have other aliases."

"How do you know my client?" I knew the question was futile, but I asked it anyway.

"Mr. Farraday and I are working on an investigation involving Mr. Campbell. We'd appreciate your cooperation."

"What is the nature of your investigation?"

The tiniest of frowns appeared between Baxter's pale eyebrows. "We are not at liberty to reveal that. It involves a matter of international security. What information do you have on Mr. Campbell?" He glanced at my desktop. I wondered if he was planning to search it and what recourse I would have if he tried to. Should I call an attorney? Would I be allowed to?

"U.S. security or British security?" I said, stalling for I wasn't sure what.

Baxter's frown morphed into a scowl. He leaned forward and placed both hands flat on the top of my desk. "Ms. MacKinnon, please do not insult us with your phony professionalism. Your client, Dr. Rousseau, has been detained under suspicion of funding terrorist groups. She was or is married to a man named Forbes Cameron, which we know is an alias. We know you've been in contact with other women Campbell was involved with. It is against the law to refuse to cooperate with a federal law enforcement official. It would be in your best interest to share the contents of whatever dossier you have assembled on Campbell and Rousseau. Do I make myself clear?"

I do not like strong-arm tactics so I ignored his question and asked one of my own. "Where has Dr. Rousseau been detained and by whom?"

Neither of them answered. I stared into the pale, cold blue eyes, then glanced over at Farraday. His inquisitive brown eyes were probably not as friendly as they looked. "Mr. Farraday, do you work for the CIA?"

"I do not."

"May I ask what your affiliation is?"

Baxter's eyes narrowed. Farraday leaned back in his chair, steepled his fingers, and regarded me for several moments. "I work for British Military Intelligence."

"MI-5 or MI-6?"

No answer.

"May I see some identification, please."

"I don't carry official identification. You're welcome to see my passport."

He reached into the inside left breast pocket of the blazer and handed me a blue passport with the heraldic crest on the outside of the standard text that said "United Kingdom of Great Britain and Northern Ireland." The photo inside matched the face of the man sitting in front of my desk. Michael J. Farraday, 18 Hampstead Lane, London NW3 England, was forty-one years old. I had no way of knowing if the document was authentic or phony. Or legitimately issued under a phony name. I handed it back to him.

"I understand your people lost two agents in Istanbul when Freddy went AWOL," I said conversationally. "And a U.S. Embassy employee died as well."

Farraday's left eyebrow climbed a fraction of an inch toward his hairline, but he ignored me. "We were hoping you'd be willing to share whatever information you've collected on Campbell." He glanced at my desk in the same manner as Baxter had. If he'd had the power of levitation, my desk drawers would have sprung open and spewed out their contents. I folded my hands together on the desktop to control their trembling, chewed the corner of my mouth, and said nothing. Downstairs, Dakota's toenails raced across the floor; the front door opened and closed. Zelda had left.

I looked at Baxter. "Do you know where Frederick Campbell is?"

Farraday looked at Baxter, whose jaw was clenched. No answer. Baxter's eyes got more narrow.

I glanced at the cell phone lying on my desk, but couldn't think of who to call, assuming these two androids would allow me to. In the aftermath of 9/11, I'd read stories of terrorist suspects who had been detained by the FBI for weeks without being allowed to call their family or an attorney. I'd never needed an attorney since I'd been in Friday Harbor and the ones I'd worked for handled mostly domestic relations cases. There was only one criminal attorney in all of San Juan County. My relationship with the duly elected sheriff was less than copacetic; I could well imagine his colorful response if I called and said that representatives of the FBI and MI-6 British Intelligence were detaining me and that my civil rights were being trampled on. I stared at the two men, wondering how the hell I could verify they were who they said they were. On the chance that they weren't legit, my request to check Baxter's bona fides by calling the nearest FBI office might start things unraveling. A small tongue of panic mixed with hysteria fluttered in my solar plexus. Feeling as if I had stumbled into an old outtake from *The X Files*, I decided to be diplomatic.

"I'd be happy to share the information I've collected, although most of it's redundant and a bunch of dead ends." I paused, looked at Baxter, then at Farraday. "What I need in return is help in locating Freddy before another woman dies. Do you know where he is?"

They looked quickly at each other, then at me. Both sat straighter in their respective chairs. "Be more specific," Baxter said in a sharp voice. "*What* women have died?"

"Diane Duvall, the assistant to the governor of California, was shot outside the Westin Hotel last Thursday after meeting with me. Campbell was blackmailing her."

"Why was he blackmailing her?" Baxter asked. Outside a car started up. I glanced out the window and watched Zelda's Morris Minor lurch down the driveway and into the street with Dakota in the backseat.

"A personal indiscretion."

"You said *women*." Farraday shifted in his chair, meticulously pulled up his right trouser leg and crossed his right leg over his left knee.

"Freddy's first wife, Gwendolyn Godfrey, died under what I would call suspicious circumstances, particularly since Campbell inherited her money."

The two exchanged another look. "We need to see your file," Baxter said, and leaned back in his chair. His jacket fell open and I saw the edge of a nylon shoulder holster.

I tried one more time. "Why have you come to Friday Harbor?"

Farraday cleared his throat. "We think Campbell may be here on San Juan Island."

I swallowed with difficulty. The only reason Freddy could have for being on the island was to kill my client! Or me! Because I now had the combined information of all the former wives I'd found, I, more than anyone else, was closer to the big picture. Somehow he knew. My mouth became so dry my tongue stuck to the upper palate and I barely managed to speak.

"Why do you think he's here?" Neither man answered me.

"I tried again. If you know where he is, why do you need me?" Something was awry here and the thought crossed my mind that perhaps these two had *nothing* to do with any official investigation. Perhaps they'd been sent by Freddy to get the file. After which I would be superfluous.

"We thought you might have discovered where he's hiding," Baxter answered.

I shook my head, both hands clasped so tightly that they were tingling. Both men stood up.

"We want your Rousseau file," Baxter said.

I looked up into eyes that had turned to pure ice. I didn't have a weapon in the office. I was alone in the building. If I flat out refused, the best case scenario was that I would be detained for obstructing justice or whatever story they might concoct. In the worst case, they were going to take the file and I'd end up like Diane Duvall. Either way, I wasn't going to win. Keeping my hands visible, I pulled out the left-hand desk drawer where I kept current case files.

The Rousseau file wasn't there.

I stared at the drawer for a moment, mind blank. *Merde à la treizième!* I riffled through the other files. Nothing. I stared at the open drawer and for a long minute I considered that the file had been stolen; then I remembered I'd given it to Zelda before I went to the dentist. Carefully I turned back to my two menacing visitors. "I believe my assistant was working with it," I said in as calm a voice as I could manage. "It should be downstairs."

I was sure Baxter had heard Zelda leave, but he motioned toward the door with his head and we trooped single file down the narrow, creaking stairs. A Schubert symphony wafted from the quadraphonic speakers and the lights were still on. I approached Zelda's desk, expecting to find the file on the cluttered desktop. The three of us stared at the desk: at the stack of *Bride* magazines, two romance novels with salacious dust jackets, a rainbow of Post-it notes stuck to the desk mat, a half-full sack of Canine Maintenance Science Diet, and the remains of a Danish pastry. But no Rousseau file. The tension in the room was palpable. I started jerking drawers open. I found a box of floppy disks, a number of CD's without their plastic jackets, recycled envelopes, blue plastic hair curlers, file labels, out-of-date postage stamps, and an unopened box of French condoms.

But no Rousseau file.

Where the hell was it? Had she lost it, or had she serendipitously realized what was transpiring upstairs and removed it for safekeeping?

Bent over the desk, considering my options, I heard the door open and saw Abigail come in. Baxter and Farraday pivoted.

"Hi, everyone, sorry I'm late. I need to borrow your copy machine. We're running out of flyers."

The two agents regarded Abigail in her bib overalls, long white plait bouncing around her shoulders. I heard Baxter sigh. Figuring I would create more havoc by asking Abigail to leave, I told her to go ahead and make her copies and turned to face the two agents. "I'm sorry, I honestly don't know where the file is. I know she was working on it last night. She must have taken it home with her and forgotten to bring it back."

Abigail hustled over to the copy machine and lifted the cover. Baxter gave me a piercing look that left little doubt as to what he thought of my office procedures. "What's her address?"

I scribbled what I hoped was a fictitious address on Black Gully Road on a pink Post-it and handed it to him. "She usually goes home for lunch," I lied.

"Her phone number?"

I hesitated, frowned, and added more fictitious information.

"Call us if you just *happen* to find the file." Baxter shoved a business card at me and lunged for the door, followed by Farraday, who had enough good breeding to nod to my mother, who was on her way in with Leonardo. I watched Baxter climb into the turquoise Subaru parked out front. Farraday followed and the Subaru tore away from the curb.

"Scotia, what's wrong?" Jewel Moon asked. "Your face is all white. And Zelda said she'd be here to watch Leonardo. Where is she? Who were those two men?"

Abigail leaned against the copy machine and watched the Subaru's departure with a thoughtful look on her face. I took a deep breath and tried to calm my voice. "Everything's okay, Mother, really. I didn't sleep very well last night because of the heat. Let me get my bag and we'll go get some lunch. Zelda's in the middle of planning a big event. I imagine she had a crisis and had to leave. Maybe Abigail would like to join us."

I called Zelda's cell phone number, left a message to call me ASAP, and locked up my office and the front door to the building, and the three of us walked over to Shirley's Café. After ordering the *soup du*

jour, we settled ourselves at the least dilapidated of
the tables under an ancient madrona tree. Jewel Moon
tied Leonardo's leash to a low branch. I made no attempt to join in the luncheon conversation, which was
comprised of my mother's description of her and Giovanni's participation in the anti–Vietnam War demonstrations in Berkeley years ago and Giovanni's brief
sojourn in jail near Sacramento. Abigail listened, blue
eyes sparkling, dunking pieces of peasant bread in the
thick cream of tomato soup, then added her own saga.
"Right after I started teaching, there was a brilliant
math teacher . . ."

I barely tasted the soup, unable to stop thinking
about the encounter with the two agents. It wouldn't
be more than half an hour before they discovered my
duplicity. Would they be back? I scowled at my cell
phone, willing Zelda to call. She didn't, but Kimberly
Korda did.

"Scotia, the kids and I are on our way to the airport.
What I called about is . . . you asked me if Forrest
had any . . . er . . . any medical problems."

"Does he?"

"Well, yes." There was a silence.

"What's the problem?"

"He has trouble . . . you know . . . getting it up.
And . . . uh . . . keeping it up."

"Does he take any medication?"

"Viagra." She giggled. "It really works, you know."

I didn't know, but I thanked her and promised to
call as soon as Freddy had been located, relieved that
Kimberly and her children were away from Orcas, at
least temporarily. I had no idea if Hannah von Suder
would follow my security suggestions. And if Dr.
Rousseau had been detained, that explained why I
hadn't heard from her. At least if she was in FBI
custody, she was safe for the moment.

I declined to accompany Jewel Moon and Abigail to
the Grange, where an itinerant oriental rug vendor was

peddling his wares. Jewel Moon said she was attending the Corona meeting that night and gave me a kiss on the cheek. My cell phone chirped. It was Zelda.

"Are they gone?" She was whispering.

"They're gone. Where are you?"

"I'm at home."

"You have the Rousseau file?"

"Yeah. I was on the phone when they came in. When the tall dude opened the door, I saw his shoulder holster. Are they bad guys or feds? Or is there a difference?"

'Supposedly one FBI and one British Intelligence."

"Supposedly?"

"Their ID could be phony."

"I see. If they're legit, they're *looking* for Freddy. If they're not, they could be *working* for him?"

"The sixty-four-million-dollar question."

"What shall I do? I'm picking up your mother at three thirty. The Coronas are going to see *Die Another Day* at four."

I pondered. When the two agents came back into town, they would be mad as the proverbial hatter, and they'd head straight for the Olde Gazette Building.

"Can you skip the Corona meeting and stay out of sight?" I asked.

"No way. How's this? I'll put on a disguise and borrow my neighbor's pickup truck. And they're not going to harass Jewel Moon or Abby."

I flashed on last night's dream. "That's probably true." I sighed. "Okay, leave the Rousseau file at Angela's when you pick up Jewel Moon. I'll get it from her. I'm going to Seattle tomorrow, back on Wednesday."

"Business or pleasure?"

"The latter."

Despite a few brief moments of panic that morning, I didn't actually believe I was in danger. If the agents were going to harm me, they'd had the opportunity. Nor did I believe Freddy was on San Juan Island. It was too small a place to hide out. He was either still in Seattle or had moved on to another big city. But since I didn't intend to give up the Rousseau file, I needed to find a place to hang out until I left for Seattle tomorrow.

I called Angela and told her about my visit from Baxter and Farraday and the wild goose chase I'd sent them on.

She replied, "About thirty minutes ago the dispatcher got a call from a guy whose car has a broken axle out on Black Gully Road. A 2002 turquoise Subaru. Wouldn't happen to belong to your friends, would it?"

"Sounds familiar. You know where they are now?"

"The dispatcher referred them to San Juan Towing. But Jed's out at Cape San Juan retrieving a disabled SUV from Wisconsin that missed a turn and tried to drive to Goose Island."

"So the Subaru may be stranded for a while. Pity."

"They'll make it back to town eventually. And they might just make a case for detaining you. Obstruction of justice, providing false information to a federal agent. You want to spend the night at my place and deal with it tomorrow when they've cooled down? I've got a bridge game tonight and Matt's playing poker with the boys, so you can have the place to yourself in the evening, but you'll have us keeping guard late at night."

I considered her offer. The alternatives would be to hole up at Nick's place or spend the night anchored out on *DragonSpray*. Either place, I'd be all alone if the agents came after me.

I accepted her invitation and hurried down to *DragonSpray* with a dock cart. There was no sign of either Henry or Calico on G dock. I left a note for Henry, grabbed what I needed for my visit to Nick's, and as a precaution, tucked the Beretta into my bag.

It was three forty-five when I got out to Angela's.

My mother's Jetta was in the driveway, a rolled up
red carpet protruding from one rear window. The door
was locked and there was no sign of Leonardo. I retrieved the extra key from under the faux dog turd in
the garden and let myself into the old kitchen. The
Rousseau file was on the counter along with a note
from Angela: *Leftovers in the fridge. Help yourself.
Leave a note if you want me to wake you in the
morning.*

I set up my laptop and leafed through the file. Hoping for some news of my client, I connected Angela's
telephone line to my laptop's modem and checked my
e-mail. I downloaded two new messages, neither of
them from Dr. Rousseau. The first was from Melissa;
*Mummy, haven't heard from you for a while. How is
Grandma's visit going? Can't wait for you to meet Justin. Love, M.*

I responded that Grandma and I were getting on
fine and that I would call her next week. I gave up
thinking about the case around five thirty, wandered
around the house feeling like a fish out of water, considered and rejected a walk down to the beach, and
ended up watching a rerun of *The Avengers*. In Angela's fridge I found a Tupperware container of lasagna
and an open bottle of California merlot. I microwaved
the pasta, carried my plate and wine into the living
room, and caught the last part of an *Ally McBeal* epi-
sode, then moved to the sofa bed in the sewing room
and fell asleep watching *Law and Order*. I did not
hear Angela, Matt, or Jewel Moon come in, and I had
a hard time opening my eyes when my cell phone
chirped. I scrambled to turn on the lamp and knocked
something off the table next to the sofa. I squinted at
the time. It was 1:48 and no caller ID was displayed.

"Scotia MacKinnon."

"Hi, boss, it's me."

"It's nearly two a.m. This better be good."

"It's good. I've just left your British agent. We closed up George's."

"Is that what you called to tell me? For Christ's sake, Zelda, it's the middle of the night! Couldn't this have waited until tomorrow?" I was snappish and didn't care. I couldn't remember when I'd had an uninterrupted night's sleep.

"What I called to *tell* you," she snapped back, "is that I think they really *are* legit."

"I see. I'm sorry. Tell me."

"I don't think Baxter is his real name, but Farraday wouldn't tell me what it was. Anyway, you know the woman who was killed in Istanbul? Moira somebody, the embassy employee?"

I was wide awake. "Moira St. Martin?"

"Yeah. I'll bet you dollars to doughnuts she's related to Baxter. Like a daughter or a sister."

"They didn't tell you that, did they?" No operative would ever be forthcoming to some female he met in a bar. It just would not happen. Their training was too intense, the fear too great, the repercussions too serious.

"No, they didn't tell me anything. They said they were insurance adjusters. But I spent all afternoon thinking about that *Crustacean* article and I got to thinking about the woman who was killed and that she was somebody's daughter or sister. If that somebody happened to be CIA or FBI, well, what do you think? I mean, isn't Baxter a bit long in the tooth for active duty?"

"It's an interesting theory. Did they recognize you from the office?"

She guffawed. "In my Cher wig, with black eyelashes, burgundy lipstick, and four-inch heels? Not a chance. I told him I was a cocktail waitress at Roche Harbor."

"What about Abby and Jewel Moon?"

"'Jewel Moon couldn't take the smoke at George's. They had a burger and left before Baxter and Farraday arrived. The two boys spent a good deal of the evening moaning about the roads on the island and our lousy taxi service. You'll be happy to hear the little Subaru may be out of commission for several days until the rental company can get the parts shipped up to the island. There aren't any more rental cars available until next week. And apparently the Seven Swans is not up to Baxter's standards either. Not only is it ten miles out of town, but there are swans on the bed sheets, swans on the towels, and stuffed swans in the dining room. He left about eleven in a foul mood."

I was too tired to respond to the pun. "What about Farraday?"

"He seemed a lot more human after his buddy left. He's a real cutie, and smart, too. We talked about opera. If he weren't the enemy, I could get interested. Never done it with a limey. Anyway, I'll let you get back to your beauty rest. I'm going over to Lopez in the morning to check out the chateau. I'll be back at noon to work on Freddy's e-mail. I have an idea."

I turned out the light, contemplating Zelda's theory about Baxter and the dead woman in Istanbul. If she was right, Raheela wasn't the only one who wanted him dead. Just before I drifted off, I wondered if the agents were right and that Freddy really was on San Juan Island.

18

Getting on and off the island in the month of July is either a challenge or a disaster. It all depends on your frame of mind. On a summer Friday afternoon it's not unusual to wait six or seven hours for space on a westbound sailing. Fortunately I was traveling eastbound on a Tuesday. There was room on the 10:05 and I arrived in Anacortes at 11:55. After driving San Juan Island's two-lane roads with a maximum speed limit of forty-five, it always takes me half an hour or so to generate the adrenalin required to survive on I-5 in four-lane freeway traffic moving at eighty.

It seemed strange to be going to Seattle in the middle of the week—and in the middle of a case as bizarre as the Rousseau investigation—but an overnight in Nick's new condo might provide some needed inspiration. A month ago, after negotiating a seven-figure out-of-court settlement for a client in a case involving a cruise line accused of dumping sewage in the waters of San Juan de Fuca, he had invested his fee in a Queen Anne condo with walls of windows overlooking water and mountains. I'd spent only one weekend there since he moved in, but the view and the ambience were almost enough to make me give up Friday Harbor, should I be asked to.

The traffic thickened north of Everett, slowed to a crawl for half an hour past the Everett Mall Parkway exit, then thinned out. I exited at Mercer Street and drove around Lake Union and over to Doc Freeman's on Eighth Avenue. I found a replacement bilge pump, spent half an hour browsing the store, and added two new dock lines and a set of strip charts for the Gulf Islands. The Volvo turned over on the fifth try and I had an hour before I was due at the condo. Just time enough to check out the lingerie department at Bon Marché.

The pink teddy was a sinful integration of soft lace and pink satin, accompanied by an equally sinful price tag. I spread the garment out on Nick's king-size bed, stripped down to the buff, and headed for the shower in the huge, tiled master bath. I'd left the Volvo with Keith, the security guard, as Nick had instructed. Keith said that he would put it in one of the guest parking spaces a bit later and that I should call down when I needed it. The four-story building with its old red brick facade presented a weathered, historical look. The parking garage for owners was located under the building, in the back. Lush landscaping covered the grounds, and a waist-high brick and stone wall surrounded the property.

I had called Nick when I got up to the fourth floor unit. He needed another hour to finish up and then he'd be home. "There's a bottle of Pinot Grigio in the refrigerator. Help yourself. We're eating in. Can't wait to see you."

Late afternoon sun streamed through the bedroom window, which looked out onto Elliot Bay and the wooded islands of Vashon and Bainbridge. I wrapped myself in a thick terry bath sheet and stretched out on the bed with a flute of the Pinot Grigio. I couldn't remember how long it had been since I'd had time to myself or a real vacation. Lately, life seemed to be one mad dash from crisis to crisis. The muscles in my neck and shoulders began to relax. Now that I was off the island, I realized the extent I'd gotten personally involved in the Rousseau case—a case that grew more bizarre by the day, with a client who might have been detained for possible terrorist connections. Perhaps she and Freddy deserved each other.

I finished the wine, donned the pink teddy under the burgundy shirt and trousers. The long, dark blue scarf with a red rose that I hadn't been able to resist at the Bon added what the French call a je ne sais quoi. I brushed my hair, added a quick touch of mascara to my lashes and wide gold hoops to my ears. I padded across the warm hardwood floor out to the kitchen. I didn't hear the key in the door. When I turned away from the refrigerator with the bottle of wine, I turned directly into Nick's arms and a long, anything-but-innocent kiss.

"God, but you smell good enough to eat," he said. "Sorry to be so late. I was trying to get everything I needed for the Mexico trip. Tomorrow morning's clear. I thought if I took you to lunch, you'd drive me to the airport before you head back north."

I nuzzled his neck. "It would be a pleasure."

"Let me get out of these work clothes and into something comfortable." He glanced down at my feet. "Great toenails," he said with a grin. "Love that shade of pink. Or is it mauve?"

"Misty mauve."

His work clothes consisted of a well-tailored charcoal gray suit that fit his six-foot four-inch frame as if it had been tailored by a Saville Row virtuoso. He pulled off the patterned blue and maroon tie, paused at the console in the dining room wall, and twisted a knob. Something by Schumann drifted from the surround-sound speakers. "Be right back. Don't go away." He backtracked, kissed me on both cheeks, and disappeared into the bedroom.

The oriental rug and mahogany dining set had belonged to Nick's parents, but the two facing ivory brocade couches were new, as were the two end tables and the Chinese porcelain lamps. There were no hangings on the windows yet, and several large framed graphics leaned against one wall. A thick scrapbook lay on the coffee table between the couches. It was Nick's ongoing project of compiling his family history and tracing the family's origins in Hungary and Russia.

Nick's family had escaped from Budapest when the Russians overran the city with tanks in 1956. They had made their way to Canada and ultimately to San Francisco. Nick's father, a mid-level bureaucrat in Budapest, ended up working on the docks in San Francisco. His mother was the daughter of a Hungarian symphonic musician and a Russian artist. For the past several years Nick had been tracking down Canadian immigration records and corresponding with several Hungarian genealogical groups. Then last year he'd located a cousin, the son of his mother's brother, who lived in Paris. Together they had traced the family ties to the early nineteenth century in Russia.

I sat on the sofa and flipped through the pages. He'd added another branch to the genealogical tree: a great-great-grandfather named Anatoly Rostokov. I closed the book and was about to get up when I spotted a swath of silky green fabric between the sofa cushions. I pulled it out. It was the scarf Chantal had been wearing when I'd had lunch at her condo last week.

What the hell was it doing in Nick's sofa?

"What you got there, love?"

"Nick, this scarf belongs to Chantal Rousseau."

He shrugged. "She was up here on Friday. She probably dropped it. Can I refill that glass for you?"

"Up here? What was she doing here?"

He stared at me and burst out laughing. "Do I see the green-eyed monster circling?"

"Green-eyed monster is right. What was Chantal Rousseau doing here?"

"Hey, calm down. Andy came by to pick up a brief

I reviewed for him. Crystal and Chantal were working on stuff for a charity ball. Andy and Crystal were leaving for an Alaska cruise on Sunday. I offered them a bon voyage drink. No big deal." The phone rang. "I'll get that. Come on out to the kitchen."

As I watched Nick's retreating back, I counted to ten and tried to act like an adult.

You do not own Nick, Scotia.

He has a perfect right to offer cocktails to friends.

Even your sexy client.

The problem was I couldn't erase the image of Chantal in her white one-shoulder dinner dress cooing at Nick, "I would love to see zee Double-O-Seven tapes when you are back on zee island." And I suspected that Crystal Cooper had had a hand in arranging the little cocktail foursome on Friday.

I followed Nick into the kitchen. "That was Keith. He had a bit of trouble starting the Volvo. I told him you've been having problems with it. He offered to take a closer look in the morning. Scotty, I think you should get a new car. In fact, I have an idea. Tony, my partner, has been lusting after a new Alfa. I think he'd sell you the old Alfa Berlina real cheap. He's kept it in cherry condition. Why don't we go look at it tomorrow on our way to lunch?"

"The Volvo is just fine." My voice was still icy. "Tony can afford an Alfa. I can't."

Nick put his arms around me. "Scotty, don't be angry at me. I swear to God, that green scarf doesn't mean anything. And I wasn't happy to have to spend an hour entertaining when I wanted to do my homework so I'd have more time with you. Now grab a bar stool and tell me what progress you've made tracking down Chantal's ex while I assemble the ingredients for the perfect Anastazi Martini." He opened a cupboard door and took down the blue bottle of Sapphire gin and the shaker.

"She's been detained for questioning about her Islamic charity," I said.

He spun around, frowning. "Again?"

"What do you mean 'again'?"

He rubbled his forehead. "She wanted it kept quiet, but Andy told me she was questioned a couple of weeks ago. He said they cleared her. Who told you she'd been detained?"

"She hasn't returned my calls for several days and yesterday I had a visit from two men professing to be FBI and British Intelligence. They claim they're after her ex. They said she'd been detained. Not a nice pair."

"Shit, I can't even call Andy."

"I'm sure if she needs help, we'll hear from her." *And you probably before me.*

"You're right," he said slowly. "You think there could be anything to the allegations?"

"She's a hard one to figure. Might be, might not."

Nick upended the blue bottle with its speed pourer over the stainless steel shaker half-filled with cracked ice and poured for what I knew was exactly twenty-one seconds. He added what looked like two drops of dry vermouth, covered the shaker, held it at a slight angle, and shook it gently with an up and down motion. The resultant concoction was pale and shimmering. He sipped appreciatively and his frown disappeared. He took a bag of fresh vegetables from the fridge and began to chop them. Unbidden, my thoughts wandered back to the case. I glanced at the TV and wondered if there was any news on the Duvall shooting. And in spite of myself, I began to worry about my client. Supposing the two "agents" had been lying. Supposing she had been killed and they didn't want me looking for her. I seldom have headaches, but I could feel one beginning behind my eyes. I chewed on a thumbnail.

Nick looked up. "You're obsessing about this case, aren't you?"

I nodded, tempted to tell him about the *Crustacean* article.

"I think some light entertainment is in order for tonight. How about a good spy movie?"

I almost choked on my drink and laughed in spite of myself. "Which, of course, means Double-O-Seven."

"Of course. By the way, did you know that the double-O designation came from a code that was broken during the First World War? And that there were several other agents in the Bond series with the alleged double-O license to kill?"

I shook my head, took a clean cocktail glass from the shelf to the right of the sink, added ice and soda water. "No, dear, I did not know either of those facts."

"Double-O-Two was assumed to have been assassinated by Francisco Scaramanga in Beirut in 1969. However, he comes back in *The Man with the Golden Gun* and dies in the arms of a belly dancer."

"And the others?"

"Double-O-Three was discovered very dead in Siberia with a microchip around his neck. I'm embarrassed to admit I've forgotten what happened to Double-O-Four and -Five. Six, who was once Bond's best friend and then became his worst enemy, was supposedly executed by a Russian colonel but turned up again in *Goldeneye*."

"And Eight and Nine?"

"Eight is very interesting. In *Goldfinger,* M threatens to replace Bond with Double-O-Eight, 'Because, James, Double-O-Eight follows orders, not instincts.' He grinned, pleased at his excellent imitation of the fictitious, crusty head of MI-6. "But Eight never actually turns up in any of the films And Double-O-Nine is my favorite. He was supposedly assassinated at the beginning of *Octopussy,* but despite his mortal wounds, manages to crawl to the British Embassy to deliver the Fabergé egg to the British government."

"Awesome. I'll be happy to watch any of the Connery Bonds."

"No Brosnans?"

I shook my head and sidled closer. "Sean Connery is the second most beautiful man in the world."

19

It wasn't until later that I realized it was the explosion that had awakened me. I'd come breathlessly awake, mouth dry, grateful to have escaped the two hooded figures in my dream that had pursued me through narrow, twisting alleyways for what seemed an eternity. I shook my head to clear it and sat up in the dim room. We'd left one window open last night but closed the blinds. Nick was sleeping deeply. The clock on the bedside table said 7:48. I shivered. The temperature must have dropped overnight. I crept out of bed, retrieved my blue nightgown from the floor and pulled it over my head, then used the bathroom. Nick opened one eye when I slid back under the silver gray coverlet. He mumbled something I interpreted as a complaint about being awakened in the middle of the night and pulled me into his arms.

Five minutes later, the blue nightgown was back on the floor, this time on Nick's side. An hour later, we were awakened by pounding on the front door.

"Who the hell is that?" Nick grabbed a white terry robe from the foot of the bed and went out, closing the bedroom door. I heard the front door open, then voices, one male, one female. There was a sharp exclamation from Nick, another exchange, and then the front door closed. Nick returned to the bedroom, his face pale.

I sat up in bed. "Is it Melissa," I gasped, "or one of yours?"

"Neither," he said slowly, sitting on the bed and holding me close. "It's your car. That was the police and the condo association president. The police'll be back in an hour to interview you. We better get dressed."

"*My car?* What do you mean, my car? What's wrong with the Volvo?" *It wasn't Melissa.* Relief flooded over me.

"It blew up in the garage. Keith's in critical condition."

"Keith?" I frowned. The concierge or security man or whoever he was had said he would park my car. I remembered he phoned before dinner. *"Keith's had a bit of trouble starting the Volvo. . . . He's going to take a closer look in the morning."* And now he was in the hospital.

"There was no reason for the Volvo to blow up. My God, Nick. We'll have to call the hospital."

He nodded. "Scotty, if this has anything to do with the Rousseau investigation, then you've got a real tiger by the tail."

I nodded, thinking he didn't know the half of it, wondering where the tiger would pounce next.

The police officers, a tall Asian male with a sergeant's badge and a thin, medium-height, African-American woman who introduced herself as Lieutenant Andersen, returned in an hour as promised. Their initial sympathy for the demise of the Volvo dissolved somewhat when they saw my Washington private investigator's license. I gave a statement to the effect that as far as I knew, the Volvo had only been suffering from an occasional reluctance to start and I had no idea who might have sneaked into the garage and blown it up. At my insistence, they confirmed that fragments of a small bomb had been found near the remains of the car. The Volvo had been totaled, and two other cars in the immediate area had been damaged. The garage was closed off with yellow tape, the Seattle P.D. bomb squad had arrived, and the area was being treated as a crime scene. No, I would not be allowed into the garage to view the remains of my car.

"Would you describe the cases you are currently investigating."

"I have three current cases, Lieutenant. One involves the missing heir to an estate in the San Juans who was last sighted in Singapore. Another is a client in Friday Harbor who is unhappy with the property settlement from her ex-husband. The third involves a contested child custody case." The truth, so help me, God. Just not all of it.

"That's it? Nothing else?" Her tone indicated her disbelief that I could possibly pay the rent with only three cases. She glanced at Nick, who was leaning against the wall in the foyer, arms folded.

"That's it," I said.

"Did any of the parties in these cases know you were in Seattle?"

As far as I knew, only Zelda, Angela, and my mother knew where I was. "Not to my knowledge."

"What about the ex-husband of your client? What's his name and address?"

"His name is Forbes Cameron and he's also known as Frederick Campbell. I've spent the last week trying to locate him. Unsuccessfully, I might add."

"What was the purpose of your visit to Seattle?"

I glanced at Nick. "She's visiting me," he answered.

The lieutenant checked my investigator's license again, gave me an inscrutable look, and asked where they could find me if they needed to question me. I gave her my card and she instructed me to call if I located the missing ex-husband. After checking Nick's identification and verifying that neither of us had any outstanding warrants, they departed.

Nick pulled me into his arms and we stood quietly in the embrace for a long time. "Scotty, I'm starving. Let's go out, grab some lunch somewhere. I'll call my assistant and get her to book me on a later flight to L.A. Then we're going to look at the Alfa Berlina." I was in too much of a state of shock to reiterate that I couldn't afford an Alfa.

At The Blue Plate Diner a mile down the hill from Nick's place we ordered scrambled eggs with home fries, sourdough toast, and big mugs of French roast. Nick called Tony Nakano on the cell. "Tony's already bought the new Alfa. They didn't want to give him what he thought he should get on the Berlina, so he decided to sell it privately. He's calling Michigo right now to tell her we're coming by."

I nodded. It was true that I would have to get a new car. But despite the fact that Albert, my third husband, had collected classic cars, I had always chosen to drive something practical: an old VW van when I was a student, a Honda Civic when we were in San Diego, and the Volvo after we moved to San Francisco. Vehicles that were safe, low-profile, and not expensive. The last thing I wanted was to mortgage my lifestyle for a fancy car.

The Nakanos lived in a striking brown-shingled craftsman-style house in the North Capitol Hill area. The two story dwelling had an old-world look with staggered gables and beautifully finished wooden steps leading up to a porch and an elaborate, carved wooden door with stained glass. Michigo answered Nick's knock and led us to the two-car garage under the house. I took one look at the trim little dark green sedan and smiled. It was old and a little funky but classy in a European way. The interior was a soft tan leather, but it was a long way from being a high-profile sports car.

Michigo instructed us about the garage door opener,

handed Nick the car keys and what looked like a spec sheet, and drove off in her little Toyota to pick up her daughter. Nick peered over my shoulder while I scanned the list of details on the Berlina. "Please note," he said. "Remote lock, remote unlock, remote ignition. Tony had them retrofitted when he added the CD player." The Berlina also sported a tachometer, air-conditioning, and heated leather bucket seats, and it was in pristine condition. There was no price listed.

"Shall we take it for a drive?" Nick dangled the key. I stared at it and stared at the classy little car, afraid that if I got in and drove it, I wouldn't be able to give it up. He opened the driver's door for me and I settled into the sculptured bucket seat that made me feel like I was wearing the car instead of driving it. Nick folded his tall frame into the passenger's seat. I turned the key in the ignition, the engine turned over, and I backed gingerly out of the garage.

It didn't take more than ten blocks and one long hill to know I had found my car. "Will it do?" Nick asked.

"It's wonderful. A low-key sedan that drives like a sports car."

"Then don't put it in the garage. You can drive it home. I'll call Tony and settle up later."

"What do you mean, settle up later? How much is it?"

"It's a late birthday gift, Scotty. Or an early Christmas gift. Whatever. It's for you."

I stared at him. Over the years, I'd received gifts from Nick, usually of a personal nature, but never anything as significant as this. I looked at the car again, knowing that it would not have strings attached, and knowing that Nick could afford it. I felt tears starting to well up, whether from the aftermath of the morning's events or because the little green car meant a deepening of our relationship, I wasn't sure. I leaned over, gave him a long kiss, and scrambled out of the Berlina before I started to blubber.

*   *   *

I dropped Nick at the airporter office on Lake
Union instead of driving him all the way out to SEA-
TAC. "I'm worried about you, Scotty," he said with
a frown when he hugged me good-bye. "If you think
there's any connection between the Rousseau case and
what happened to your car or the Duvall shooting,
then turn over the information to the police and let
them carry on. And until this case is closed, for God's
sake, use the remote ignition."

I sat for a few minutes in the parking lot after the
airporter bus had pulled away, mentally reliving the past
two days, the destruction of the Volvo and the injuries
to Keith, trying to recover some of my equilibrium
before I took on the afternoon freeway traffic. Was
the bomb meant for me or was it some random act of
domestic terrorism? Was I supposed to be the one in
the ICU at Harborview instead of Keith? I checked
around the parking lot, which had cleared out after
the shuttle left. The two remaining cars appeared to
be empty. No one lurked around the door to the terminal. It is not my style to go around looking over
my shoulder. For the umpteenth time I reviewed
Freddy's trail of destruction. The longer I thought
about it, the angrier I got. It was time to confront the
ogre and I had a couple of ideas about how to make
that happen. The quickest one was to look for the
ogre where he'd last been sighted, the Rose and Thistle Club. The second idea would require more thought.

Forty-three Carlyle Place stood at the end of a
quiet, tree-lined cul-de-sac. Thick strands of ivy covered the front of the dark-red Georgian-style structure. I locked the Berlina with the remote, put on a
Mary Sunshine smile, and sauntered up the walkway. I
rang the bell located to one side of the stained, carved
wooden door with its round peephole.

"Yes, madam?" Anthony Hopkins's double blocked
the doorway. Behind him I glimpsed a spacious foyer

with large floor tiles the color of a Mexican sunrise and beyond, an ancient elevator with heavy brass grating.

"Good morning. I was wondering if Frederick Campbell is in? I'm a friend of his sister Marianne."

"Mr. Campbell is not in residence. Would you care to leave a card?" I took a card from my pocket and handed it to Anthony. "When do you expect Freddy?"

He examined my business card. "I have no idea, madam."

I thanked Anthony for his time and felt his eyes on my back as I turned away. Halfway to the Berlina I heard the heavy door close with a decisive click. Anthony made a very good firewall.

Half an hour later, I inched my way up the on-ramp to I-5 north, and headed for home, frustrated that my first ploy had not worked. The afternoon traffic thinned north of Everett, the Berlina drove like a dream, and I began laying out ploy number two, which would require help from Jared. A ploy that I hoped would not backfire.

20

"There's something wrong with the phone lines," Zelda said when I got to the office on Thursday morning. "There's a faint hum and half the time when a call came in yesterday, no one was on the line. It just happened again." Zelda scowled at her receiver. I checked my cubby and found a message from Hannah von Suder from yesterday afternoon.

"Call Centurytel and report it," I said. "Some of these lines are really old. Probably need replacing."

"*That'll* cost an arm and a leg."

I left her grumbling over the insatiable greed of the phone company and climbed wearily upstairs. It had been nearly eleven before I'd gotten to bed last night. I'd slept badly again and wanted nothing so much as to get some closure on the Rousseau case. Each day I felt more deeply mired in the ugly minutiae of Freddy's behavior. I called Hannah back and got her answering machine. The phone on my desk had a call log and I checked for any callers who hadn't left a message. There were two: one from Jared and one with an international number. I dialed the international number first.

"Farraday."

Merde! Now I was in for it! Hanging up wasn't an option, since he probably had caller ID. "Scotia MacKinnon, Mr. Farraday. I noticed you called yesterday."

"Thank you for ringing back. I was wondering if we could meet? I think it could be mutually beneficial. Perhaps this afternoon?"

The last thing I wanted to do was meet with someone who wanted to steal the Rousseau file, but the "mutually beneficial" hooked me. It was Baxter who had done the strong-arming on Tuesday. And a public place should be safe.

"The Book Café at four o'clock? It's on Spring Street across from the church."

"I'll look forward to it."

I hung up, wondering what had motivated Farraday to change his strategy, and immediately the phone rang.

"Scotia MacKinnon."

"Ms. MacKinnon, this is Larry Lonngren. I'm a detective with the San Juan County Sheriff's office. I'm investigating the death of a woman from Santa Maria Island. Her name is Hannah von Suder. Your name and phone number were found on her desk. Could you tell me what your relationship is with her?"

Another dead wife! That effing bastard! I stared out the window, trying to steady my pounding heart.

"Ms. MacKinnon?"

"Yes, detective. I talked with Ms. von Suder by telephone last week. I think it was Tuesday. It was in connection with an investigation I'm doing for a Friday Harbor client."

"Could you be a little more specific?"

'My client's husband—I believe his name is Frederick Campbell, although he has a number of aliases—was formerly married to Ms. von Suder. Or may still be married to her. There are a number of irregularities in the case. I spoke to Ms. von Suder's parents, also."

"How can we find this Campbell?"

"That's what I was hired to find out. I haven't located him yet."

"What is your client's name?"

"Dr. Chantal Rousseau. She's an internist at the Friday Harbor Medical Clinic."

"May I have her number, please?" Impatience was creeping into his voice.

I started to say that I thought she'd been detained by the FBI, but I knew the next question would be how did I know that, and then I would have to explain Baxter and Farraday. Instead, I decided to let the chips fall where they might and gave him Dr. Rousseau's two phone numbers. Then I flipped through my bag and found the card for Lieutenant Andersen's phone number at the Seattle P.D. and left her a message asking about Keith and what she had found out about the source of the bomb. Finally, I returned Jared's call and agreed to join him for lunch at Pablo's.

When I went downstairs for coffee, Zelda was still ranting about the phone. "I called Centurytel," she said. "They'll check out the problem this afternoon. If it's internal wiring, we'll have to pay for it."

I headed for the stairs without comment.

"Do you think someone's tapped our phones?" she asked.

I stopped and considered. When you bug somebody's phone, it's to find out something that you don't know, or to gather incriminating evidence, or to find out if somebody knows something about you that you don't want them to know. And if it's done by a professional, you'd never know it had been done unless you hired a professional "sweeper" to check the lines. So if there was a hum on the lines, then either we'd been tapped by an amateur or it was a matter of old wiring. 'I hope not, but it's not impossible. Let's see what Centurytel has to say."

I fervently hoped it was a wire problem. If Freddy had tapped our phones or hired someone to do it, then he would have had prior knowledge of my meeting with Diane Duvall and known what Hannah von

Suder had told me. In fact, he would know everything I'd discussed with everyone. Not a pleasant thought.

And if Freddy hadn't tapped the phones, I could think of two other possibilities, neither of them local boys.

I went upstairs and called Bernie Morgan in Seattle. He thought I was calling about Diane Duvall.

"Bad news on the Duvall shooting," he said. "We can't link the guy we pulled in—the nut in the Civil War uniform—to the shooting. Weapon doesn't match the bullet, no police record, no gunpowder traces, and the gun is so old it probably wouldn't even fire. There is nothing to prove he ever knew Duvall. The California governor is screaming bloody murder and we've got two detectives working around the clock on it. So far they've come up with zilch."

"My car was blown up on Wednesday, Bernie, and a man was injured. Can you tell me if Lieutenant Andersen found out anything about it?"

"Hold on. Not so fast. Where did this bombing happen?" I supplied Nick's address and tapped my fingernails on the desk impatiently, glanced out the window. "Scotia, I'll call you or have Andersen call you back."

When the phone rang fifteen minutes later, it was not Lieutenant Andersen, it was Jewel Moon. She had spent the morning at the Historical Museum and was going to leave tomorrow. Could we have dinner and talk about my having a psychic reading?

My client had been detained by the FBI.

My car had been bombed.

And my mother wanted me to have psychic reading.

I took a deep breath, my head spinning with conflicting emotions. I truly regretted not having spent more time with her. Once again, my personal life was being overwhelmed by my investigations. But the way things were going, I was grateful that she would be

safely back in Mendocino by Saturday and I'd have
one less person to worry about.

"I'd love to take you to dinner tonight, Mother. Do
you want me to pick you up?"

"Raheela and I are going to help Abby get ready
for her new photo exhibit at the Wildlife Gallery. I'll
come down to the boat when I finish. Will you be
there by five o'clock?"

"I'll be there." I hung up. An hour should be ample
time for Farraday and me to play our little head games.

"What do you know about the Santa Maria murder?" I asked, settling into the padded wrought iron
chair across from Jared and reaching for a tortilla chip.
He poured a can of ginger ale into my glass before
answering.

"Hannah von Suder, Caucasian female, owner of
the Santa Maria Winery, shot in the head with a 25-
caliber bullet. She was found on a rocky overlook with
lots of dry moss. Hard to find footprints. There are a
number of deer trails leading up there. She fell face
down, but the shooter could have been in any number
of locations, either on the ground or in a tree. Apparently she went for a three- or four-mile run every
morning. None of the employees recalls hearing a
shot."

"That's the same caliber as the bullet that killed
Diane Duvall."

Jared frowned and rubbed his eyes. "Duvall? Sorry,
I've had a crazy last few days. What's her connection
with the von Suder killing?"

"Hannah von Suder was married to Freddy Campbell before he married my client."

"Good God! And Duvall was. . . ?"

"Being blackmailed by Campbell. Until she stopped
paying."

He blew air through his front teeth and shook his
head. "You sure do pick 'em."

"That's only the beginning. On Wednesday morning my car was blown up. Demolished."

"My God, Scotia! Here in Friday Harbor?"

"No, it was parked at Nick's condo in Seattle. The condo security man was badly injured.

"Do the police know about the Duvall woman's connection to your case?"

I waited until Pablo took our order for enchiladas suizas and replenished the bowl of salsa. "Yes. And I've told them there might be a connection to my client's former P.I., the one who was shot outside his office a couple of weeks ago." I took a deep breath and shook my head. "What is the sheriff doing about the von Suder shooting?"

"There was a resident special deputy on the scene when I got there, and then Nigel sent a new detective by the name of Lonngren and the deputy medical examiner. Lonngren is from Portland. Seems pretty sharp."

"I talked to Lonngren this morning. I gave him the basic facts from my investigation, but I didn't tell him about the Istanbul stuff. It's too convoluted."

He shook his head. "That was over two years ago."

"Yes, and it was also just the beginning." We stared at each other for a long minute. "How are we going to stop him, Jared?"

"You've established his M.O.: Find an affluent woman, get introduced by the right people, romance her, marry her, rob her, and disappear. But now there's a new factor in the equation. Which is why the ex-wives are dying."

I stared at him, hating what he was telling me. "It's me. The new factor is me."

As I left Pablo's I couldn't stop thinking about what Jared had said and walked down to the Port office to pick up a duplicate parking permit for the Berlina. My lousy mood did not improve when I found a pink and white parking citation decorating the windshield of the little green sedan. At the port administration office, the blond-haired clerk with smudges of magenta lipstick on her front teeth told me I would have to buy a new permit unless I had proof that I had sold the Volvo. I considered telling her the truth, but Friday Harbor is a small town, and I knew that by tomorrow morning at least fifteen people would know that the town's female private investigator had had her car bombed. I muttered something to the effect that I had lost the bill of sale and began filling out the application.

I put the new permit on the Berlina and walked slowly back to the office, thinking of Hannah as she was before she met Freddy: a successful manager of a winery in the bucolic Sonoma Valley of Northern California. Then came the fortune seeker, the "love bandit," who ultimately left her lying dead on a rocky hillside. Hannah von Suder had not been an attractive woman. Had it ever occurred to her that Fletcher might be too good to be true?

I knew very well that my job was to uncover facts and present them to my client. Way back in San Diego, I had trained myself not to become emotionally involved in my cases and to recognize when my job was finished. Nevertheless, I felt a wave of icy anger wash through my veins. It was time Frederick Campbell got his just desserts.

It was after three when I returned to the office. Zelda was communing with her computer, shoulders hunched in front of the monitor, something by Wagner blaring from the speakers. I returned a call from Bernie Morgan.

"Scotia, I don't think the bombing had anything to do with you. Andersen did a check on the condo owners in the building, including your friend, Mr. Anastazi. The penthouse is owned by one Oscar Higueros Ramsey who's got an arrest record as long as your arm. Drugs, high priced call girls in Los Angeles, kiddie porn. Owns a late model Volvo sports car that someone might have confused with your Volvo.''

I didn't know how anyone could have confused the Volvo wagon with a late model anything, but I let him go on.

"By the time we got to check out the penthouse, Oscar and his girlfriend were gone and we haven't been able to locate them. It was a lightweight bomb, probably placed in the gas tank. Apparently designed to minimize casualties. If somebody had wanted to plant a serious bomb, your friend's building wouldn't be standing. I'd say it was a warning to Oscar. He probably stepped on someone's turf. So relax. Your car just happened to be in the wrong place at the wrong time."

"What about Keith, the security man who was in the car when the bomb went off?"

"I'll ask Andersen to call you. Anything else?"

"It's possible my phone line's been bugged."

"Welcome to the world of crime. You ever think of moving somewhere safe?"

I didn't think it was funny.

21

Farraday was already at the Book Café when I arrived, seated at one of the small bistro tables in between the tall stacks of used books, reading *Our Man in Havana,* an empty espresso cup on the table. I nodded to him and ordered a café au lait. He stood up when I came over to the table, then sat and closed the book. I spooned up some of the whipped cream on top of the coffee, wanting him to initiate the conversation.

"The first thing I want to do, Ms. MacKinnon, is apologize for our behavior on Monday. It was inexcusable. All I can say is that Baxter sometimes gets carried away."

I wondered if he was going to play the good cop–bad cop routine. "Apparently he prefers strong-arm tactics," I said. "And I really didn't have the Rousseau file."

He smiled. "No, but I'll bet you've recovered it."

I took a sip of the steaming drink and didn't answer.

"I asked you to meet me because I think we both have the same goal: to find Frederick Campbell."

"Neither of us has been particularly successful, have we?"

"You really don't know where he is?"

"I really don't know where he is. I don't even know

where my client is. And the women he's been involved with are being murdered, one by one."

"You mean Duvall?"

"I mean Duvall. I mean Hannah von Suder, who was shot this morning. And, of course, there's the old unsolved murder of his first wife."

He rubbed his forehead without speaking.

"Is Dr. Rousseau still being detained?" I asked. "*Has* she been funding the terrorists?"

"Sorry, I can't answer that."

"Do you still think Freddy is here on the island?"

"He was in Seattle last week, but last night he was seen boarding the seven-thirty ferry in Anacortes."

I frowned. Did that mean Freddy was on the same ferry I took? That he'd seen me at the Rose and Thistle Club and followed me here? *Merde!* "That ferry stopped at three islands before it got here," I said.

"I know. And he didn't get off here."

"So he got off on Shaw, Orcas, or Lopez. Are you working with the sheriff?"

He shook his head.

"Why not?"

"Sorry, I'm not at—"

"—liberty to say," I finished for him. "Are you a bounty hunter?"

He raised his eyebrows and smiled crookedly. "A bounty hunter? You mean like America's Most Wanted?" He smiled. "No, I'm not a bounty hunter. Nor is Baxter. This has nothing to do with a bounty."

"What are you going to do with Freddy if you catch up with him?" I asked.

"I *will* catch up with him."

"You didn't answer my question."

Another crooked smile. "Ms. MacKinnon, you are obviously a smart woman and you have a background in law enforcement. I think you know the answers to the questions you're asking me and you know why I can't answer them." His smile disappeared and he chewed on a corner of his lip. "Without being offensive, I'd like to suggest that you may be out of your depth. Campbell is a nasty customer."

I regarded him over my coffee cup. I agreed with him and I believed that he actually did work for British Military Intelligence, as he had said.

"What do you want from me?" I asked.

"I'm assuming you want Campbell captured as much as I do. Though since you work for a fee, your motivation may be more mercenary than mine."

"I don't take cases on contingency, Mr. Farraday," I said in a cold voice. "I will get paid whether I find him or not. If I want Freddy captured, it's because I've talked with four of the women he swindled out of significant amounts of money. Three of those women were financially ruined, two are dead. And if you count his first wife, the number goes up to three. I want him stopped."

"I would like to help with that task. Do you have anything in the . . . shall we call it the 'recovered file' . . . that might help me?"

"All that I'm sure of is that he swindled those women, though even that would be difficult to prove, since in two of the cases he had power of attorney. The woman he blackmailed probably wouldn't have testified against him, but since she's dead, that's moot anyway. I suspect there's a connection between Diane Duvall's death last week, Hannah von Suder's death this morning, and the bomb that blew up my car . . . even if the police think differently. But there's no real evidence except for the caliber of the bullet used in both shootings. A halfway good defense lawyer could convince a jury that that could have been a coincidence. And even if he's ever convicted of swindling, he'll be back on the street in three years."

"So may I assume that if you learn where he's hiding in the islands, you'll call me?"

I probed the tawny brown eyes that met mine without wavering. I took in the well-defined dark brows, the determined chin, the nose that was somewhere between Roman and Semitic. I considered my obvious lack of success in locating my quarry. And finally, I thought about what Jared had said about me being the new factor in Freddy's M.O. Since neither Farraday nor Baxter had enlisted the help of the local authorities, either their hunt was a personal vendetta or else, as the *Crustacean* article had wagered, Freddy was on MI-6 most-wanted list.

"Why is the FBI involved in hunting for Freddy?"

"They're not."

I thought about Zelda's supposition—that Baxter was related to the embassy employee killed in Istanbul—and tried again. "Does Baxter have a personal stake in this? Like maybe he's related to the woman in Istanbul? Moira St. Martin?"

He played with his spoon, finally raised his eyes with a slight shrug. "All I can tell you is that Freddy's connection to the FBI was ironic and purely coincidental."

"How so?"

"When she was detained, your client suspected that Freddy had turned her in and she told the people who were holding her about him and about how you were looking for him. Baxter found out and that led us to you."

I stared at him. Freddy had reported Chantal to the FBI to get her into trouble! And in so doing, he had overplayed his hand and inadvertently led Baxter and Farraday to me. Ironic indeed.

I considered what I knew about "wet operations." "Mr. Farraday, is your operation one that might require a raincoat, shall we say?"

There was a long silence before he said wryly, "A raincoat or perhaps an umbrella."

The *Crustacean* article had been right on the money!

"I'll call you if I find out anything," I said.

He handed me a white business card that simply said Michael J. Farraday. There was a phone number written on it in blue ink. I gave him my card and we stood up. "A good tale," I said, nodding toward the book he'd been reading.

"My fifth reading. Le Carré tried some of the same devices in *Tailor of Panama,* but Greene does it better." He followed me to the door and it occurred to me that if Freddy had been in Seattle until yesterday, he couldn't have tapped my phone. Farraday opened the door for me.

"Did Baxter bug my office or tap the phone line?" I asked abruptly.

"I told him you'd find it." He rolled his eyes and put on his dark glasses. "He's not very good at that sort of thing."

"Tell him to take the tap off by tomorrow A.M. or I'll send him the bill for the sweeping."

I walked outside, scanned the street in both directions, saw nothing out of the ordinary. Down the street the Bank of the Islands clock read 71 degrees at 4:55 P.M. wind NE 10. Two men were entering the consignment shop across the street. A gray van that said "Secret Garden" on the side pulled to the curb in front of the Book Café. Lily MacGregor, our island florist, got out, opened the back of the van, and headed for the church next door with two baskets of white dahlias. I nodded to Farraday and hurried down Spring Street, wondering what I'd just agreed to. And with whom.

"When is Giovanni returning to Mendocino?" I faced my mother across a small table with a red-checked cloth at the Bistro Café. I made a monumental effort to stop thinking about the Rousseau case and reached for another piece of warm rye bread.

"He's getting into San Francisco on Saturday. I'm

going to drive straight down I-5 and meet him, then we can drive up the coast together. How was your trip to Seattle? Did you have a nice evening with Nick?"

The door to the café opened and a tall, well-dressed man came in. I searched his face and watched while he joined his female companion in the corner of the restaurant. He didn't look at all like Freddy.

"Scotia, you seem preoccupied tonight. Did you have a nice evening with Nick when you were in Seattle? Did you go somewhere special?"

"Sorry, Mother. Yes, we had a nice evening. He's about to leave for Mexico so we had dinner at his condo."

"Why's he going to Mexico?"

I stared at her blankly, realizing I had been so preoccupied with my own problems I had forgotten to ask. "I believe he has a client in Los Angeles who's doing some kind of underwater recovery off the coast of Mexico." It was probably partly true.

"You've been together a long time, haven't you. Do you think you'll ever get married or live together?"

It was a "mother question." "It seems to be working fine. As in 'if it's not broken, don't fix it.' "

"I know what you mean. I think marriage can ruin perfectly good relationships. All that forced togetherness. But I do miss Giovanni."

The waitress brought our Caesar salads and twisted the pepper grinder over each plate.

"I had a reading with Rainbow yesterday," my mother said, fork poised over her salad. "She said I could move forward now. I told her about our little talk on the boat and our wonderful sail. She'll do a reading for you if you like." She reached into her linen jacket and put a card beside me. PSYCHIC READINGS, TAROT, SPIRITUAL COUNSELING, it said.

"Thank you, Mother." My straw bag was on the floor beside my chair. I unzipped it, slid the card into a side pocket and felt the smooth metal of my little

Beretta I'd been carrying since I returned from Seattle on Wednesday.

"I hope you've had a nice time here, Mother. I'm sorry I've been so busy."

"Oh, Scotia, I've had a wonderful time! I loved hanging out with Abby and Raheela. *I* was feeling guilty that I didn't spend more time with *you*. But maybe I made a difference in Abby's work for the whales. What do you think?"

"I think when the *Gazette* comes out tomorrow with the picture of you three chained to the tree, Joe Tracy is going to be a lot more amenable to changing his whale watching procedures. I'll be sure that you get a copy. And I think we should both stop feeling guilty."

The waitress removed our salad plates and served the Sesame Ginger Chicken with mashed potatoes while my mother launched into a lengthy narration about a friend of hers who was building a winery in the hills east of Mendocino. I thought about Hannah von Suder and wondered what she had wanted to tell me. I replayed my conversation with Farraday. I believed that Farraday was legit, that he either worked for MI-5 or MI-6, and was on a special assignment to find Freddy. He had obliquely admitted that his assignment was a "wet operation," what the CIA termed an "executive action." If I gave Farraday information that would allow him to find Freddy, then the trail of swindled and murdered women would end. It would also mean that I was giving tacit approval to circumventing the U.S. justice system.

22

My mother left on the 6:00 A.M. ferry to the mainland on Friday morning. I bought her a cup of coffee, hugged her, and promised more sailing lessons whenever she returned. I did not promise to have a reading with Rainbow.

I stood on the sidewalk on Front Street, watching the white vessel move slowly away from the docks in the early mist. Across San Juan Channel lay Shaw Island, one of the islands the ferry had stopped at on Thursday night when I returned. That particular sailing did not stop at Santa Maria. If Freddy had been on board, he would have had to disembark on Shaw or Orcas or Lopez and catch the interisland ferry the next morning. That would have put him on Santa Maria in time to lie in wait for poor Hannah von Suder when she went off for her morning run.

Was he still on Santa Maria?

I was out of leads and there was nothing calling me to the office. Unless I could think of some way to lure Freddy from his hiding place, I would have to wait for him to act. I trudged up the street to the health club, swam thirty-five laps, spent fifteen minutes soaking in the whirlpool tub, then dressed and headed up to the Olde Gazette Building, all the time toying with an idea that might smoke Freddy out.

The lights were on at New Millennium, the coffee

brewed. Something symphonic filled the office, but
Zelda was absent. A note in my cubby advised that
she'd gone off to find a blue garter for Bronwyn
O'Banion and what did I think of her late night work?
I read the peach-colored Post-it slip attached to two
printed e-mail messages.

E-mail from emorts8591@aol . . . Two sent
messages. Everything else deleted, no new
mail, but I'll keep monitoring it. I've earned
my money on this one. Z. 1:37 a.m. P.S.
Password is a Scottish castle and the name of
his investment company spelled backwards
plus year of birth backwards

Hallelujah! She'd done it. She'd breached Freddy's
password and gotten into his e-mail! Maybe now we
could track him!

Both messages had been sent on Wednesday, two
days ago. The first was to christgood@bsg.law.uk.com,
Freddy's barrister chum.

Chris: About to take the leap again. Had a
fabulous run of luck on-line last week and
a number of loose ends to tie up. Pity you can't
make the festivities this time. But no mind,
K. and I will have a glass of the bubbly for
you as we sail off to Bora Bora. Regards to
your mum. F.

The second was to jehane1675@aol.com

Kathleen darling: I am counting the hours. I
have the tickets in hand. See you Friday. All
my love always, W.

Taking the two messages together, the meaning was
perfectly clear: Freddy, in a new "W" persona, was

about to be joined once more in holy matrimony to someone named Kathleen, then they would depart on an exotic honeymoon. Probably booked on a cruise ship with a casino and funded by the starry-eyed bride . . . until Freddy's "funds" arrived. Whether Diane was a "loose end"—or Hannah—was purely academic at this point. The more important question was, where was he meeting Kathleen on Friday?

I glanced at the clutter on Zelda's desk, the stack of magazines and Lopez wedding "To Do" lists. If Freddy and Kathleen were getting married in the area, there might be an announcement in a local newspaper. I'd have to go to the library and check all the area papers. But first I wanted to run something by Jared.

"Let me get this straight," he said when I got him on the phone. "You want me to put a story on-line about the von Suder shooting indicating that evidence points to Freddy? He's going to come after you, Scotia."

Jared had recently starting doing a weekend on-line edition of the *Gazette.* It was a long shot, but I was desperate to find Freddy.

I thought about Farraday. "We'll be ready for him."

"You're sure?"

"I'm sure. I'll get reinforcements, Jared. As it is now, I don't know where he is or when he's going to strike."

"Okay, I'll post it this afternoon along with some community announcements. Be careful. It's hard to put the cover back on Pandora's box once it's opened."

There were footsteps on the stairs as I hung up. It was Angela, paying me a visit in her official capacity.

"Nigel is on the warpath," she said. "He just came back from Santa Maria with the assistant prosecutor. The von Suder shooting destroys his campaign promise to keep crime down. He wants an explanation for the shooting, like right now. Today. This afternoon. Since the woman had a bullet through her head, he hasn't been able to think of any way to label it an accidental death, though if he can't arrest someone, he'll probably blame it on an out-of-season deer hunter."

"How can I help?"

"I've been asked to assist Detective Lonngren. He said he talked to you, but he doesn't think you were being straight with him. And Nigel is ready to get a subpoena if you refuse to share information. He wants your file."

Sheriff Nigel Bishop wanted *my* file? That had to be a first.

"Nigel does not need to get a subpoena," I said, reaching into my file drawer and pulling out the ever-thickening file. "Let's make copies and you can take it with you."

Angela stood beside me in the alcove that housed the copy machine. As I pulled out the various reports, clippings, and notes from interviews, I gave her an oral summary of what I'd learned in the past twelve days. I hesitated when I came to my typed notes on the interview with Diane Duvall, regretting that I would have to break my promise of confidentiality. When I got to the *Crustacean* article, she read it and pursed her lips. "Jesus Christ, I think we've got a nutcase on our hands. This is definitely not going to make Nigel happy."

"There's probably a lot of stuff in here that's not going to make him happy. Assuming he believes it. Of course, if he doesn't, it will be a case of Ms. Mac-Kinnon causing trouble again."

I copied the last document, describing my initial meeting with Dr. Rousseau.

"What's your client's take on all this?" Angela asked. "She must be scared out of her wits."

"If I can believe the two agents who visited me last week, Dr. Rousseau has been detained on suspicion of funneling money to Islamic terrorists. She hasn't returned my calls for over a week."

"FBI?"

"That's my guess." I inserted the stack of copied documents into a manila envelope. Angela tucked it under her arm and headed for the door. "Much appreciated, Ms. MacKinnon. I'm sure we'll be in touch." She flashed me a grin and was gone.

I locked up and hurried down Guard Street to the library for my wedding announcement research. The copies Angela took with her did not contain any notes on my last meeting with Farraday.

Two hours later, I reluctantly concluded that my library search was for nothing. I'd read the wedding columns of newspapers from the entire Puget Sound area: Seattle, Tacoma, Everett, Bellingham, Bellevue, and Olympia. I'd even checked the Portland and Vancouver papers. I found no photos of men I could identify as Freddy, nor any engagement announcements I could match to any of his various personas or possible personas. Either Freddy and Kathleen were keeping the wedding a secret, or his new victim was from out of the area. I tidied up the stack of newspapers on the library table and made my way back up Guard Street, wondering if Jared had posted the von Suder story on-line yet.

Zelda was about to lock up New Millennium when I came up the walk. Head down, arms full of packages, she nodded in my direction. "On my way to Lopez," she said breathlessly. "Rehearsal dinner tonight. If Jean Pierre calls while you're in the office, would you tell him I'll call him when I get back tomorrow night?"

I nodded and watched her scurry to the little Morris. The phone rang as I stepped into the office. I sat down at Zelda's desk to answer it. It was Nick.

"Scotty, I just got a call from Chantal Rousseau.

She's *was* detained by the FBI, but they've let her go and she thinks they've still got her under surveillance. She's positive her ex sent an anonymous tip to the FBI. She wanted me to represent her. What's going on with your investigation for her?"

"Another dead ex-wife."

"Are you *serious?*"

"Unfortunately, yes. The sheriff has requested my file on the investigation. I hope to God he gets a warrant for the arrest, so if Freddy does show up, they can nab him. Are you going to represent her?"

"Not my field. I referred her to a guy I know. By the way, the trip to Mexico has been postponed. I'll be back on Sunday. I'll call you, maybe come up to the island. Be careful with Forbes or whoever the hell he is."

I reached across the desk to hang up the phone and knocked a book to the floor. It fell open and the dust jacket slid off. I picked it up. It was B. K. O'Banion's most recent novel, *The Legacy of the Rose.* I was replacing the dust jacket when the door behind me opened. A lean, dark-haired man in his thirties in an open-collar white polo shirt and faded blue jeans and sandals came in. "Good evening, madame. I am Jean Pierre. I am looking for Zelda." He smiled, his teeth white against his tanned face. He was so beautiful that for the span of a few seconds I wished I was thirty again. Poor Sheldon didn't stand a chance.

"I'm Scotia MacKinnon, Jean Pierre. I share the office with Zelda."

"I call her at home and to her cell phone. She does not answer. Is she here?"

"She had to go to Lopez. She said she'll call you tomorrow night."

Crestfallen, he thanked me and left.

I put *The Legacy of the Rose* back on the desk, staring at the publicity blurb on the back, which ended with an invitation to the reader to contact the author at jehane@bkobanion.com. I felt goose bumps on my forearms and the hairs on the back of my neck stood up. Freddy's e-mail had been to jehane1675@aol.com. I grabbed one of the wedding invitations and read it.

Mrs. Fiona Livingston
requests the honor of your presence
at the marriage of her daughter
Bronwyn Kathleen
to F. Wesley Caswell
on Saturday the nineteenth of July
two thousand and three
at one o'clock in the afternoon
The garden at the Château
Number One Fleur-de-lis Road
Lopez Island, Washington

Bronwyn *Kathleen!* Good God, it had been right in front of my face for two weeks and I hadn't seen it.

23

I had to let Farraday know that Freddy was on Lopez and would be getting married tomorrow. Then I had to get over to Lopez. To let Kathleen know about Freddy, to stop the wedding, to see if I could find any more incriminating evidence—phony ID, possibly a weapon or ammunition—and to prevent Freddy from disappearing. Most important of all, to make sure no one got hurt.

I needed to do so many things at once that my head was spinning. I ran upstairs and made a list: *Call Farraday. Call Angela: warrant? Call Zelda. Call Dr. Rousseau. Check for* Gazette *on-line story. Get over to Lopez on the next ferry.*

I called Dr. Rousseau, left a message telling her I thought I had found Freddy and that he was marrying Bronwyn O'Banion on Lopez Island on Saturday. She was to call me and be sure to take extra security precautions.

I called Farraday. "This cell phone customer is out of range," intoned a computerized voice. *Merde!* If Baxter had tapped my phone lines, the two of them were going to know exactly what I was up to, anyway. At this juncture, who the hell cared!

The dispatcher at the Sheriff's department informed me that Deputy Petersen was out of the office. I called

her at home. "What's the status of the warrant? Did
you get it?" I asked.

"We summarized all the info in your file and the
undersheriff took it to the judge this afternoon. He
hasn't heard back about the warrant. Nigel's gone over
to Santa Maria with the Washington State Police
crime scene team. We've also contacted Seattle P.D.
Any new developments in your investigation?"

I told her about Freddy's e-mail and the e-mail address and what I had concluded.

"You're basing this all on an *e-mail message*? There
are probably a hundred Kathleens in Seattle alone.
Or more!"

"It fits, Angela. F. Wesley Caswell is "F.W.C." The
same initials Freddy has kept throughout. Jehane is
Bronwyn O'Banion. I'm 90 percent sure Frederick
Campbell is marrying her tomorrow."

"Are you sure this isn't just wishful thinking? This
is a celebrity wedding we're talking about. If you're
wrong, Scotia, Nigel will have your head. And so will
a lot of other people."

"Yeah, I know. Talk to you later."

"Scotia? Don't hang up! Matt just came in." I heard
Matt's baritone in the background, then she was back.
"He says there's a feature on Channel 7 news about
the von Suder shooting. Both your name and Campbell's are mentioned. Did you know about it?"

"Uh, I knew Jared was going to post a feature on it
on-line. I sort of thought it might smoke Freddy out."

"*Smoke him out?* Now I *know* you're out of your
mind."

"Yeah. Catch you later."

I hung up, chastened but still convinced I was right
about the names. But I'd better find out what I'd un-
leashed. I clicked up my Internet browser and went
to the *Gazette On-line* Web site. The article was
very succinct.

Napa Valley Wine Heiress Shot
on Santa Maria Island

The body of Hannah von Suder, 52, was found
this morning on Santa Maria Island a mile from
the old Franciscan convent that Ms. von Suder
was renovating. The two servants on the property, Rafael and Cecilia Gomez, confirmed that
Ms. von Suder was in the habit of going for an
early morning run on the three-hundred-acre
property she purchased only a few months ago.
She usually returned to the convent by eight
thirty for breakfast. When she failed to appear
by ten o'clock, Mr. Gomez went looking for her,
then returned to the convent and called the sheriff's office. Deputy Angela Petersen responded
to the call. Detective Ronald Longrenn has confirmed that no footprints or other evidence was
found. Deputy Petersen confirmed that the sheriff's department had received a report of a
prowler on the property in the past week. Sheriff
Nigel Bishop believes Ms. von Suder may have
been hit by a stray bullet from an out-of-season
deer hunter. The sheriff says he has no reason
to believe the killing was intentional.

Ms. von Suder is the only daughter of Helga
and Henry von Suder of St. Helena, California.
She purchased the convent property with the intent of turning it into a winery and a B&B. Ms.
von Suder was previously married to Fletcher
Curtis of San Francisco. According to local investigator Scotia MacKinnon, Fletcher Curtis may
also be known as Frederick Campbell or Forbes
Cameron or Forrest Clark, and may still be married to at least two other women, one on Orcas
Island and one in Seattle. Additionally, there is
reason to believe that Fletcher Curtis may have
some connection to Diane Duvall, the special as-

sistant to the governor of California who was killed last week outside the Westin Hotel in Seattle. In both the Duvall and von Suder shootings, the bullet was fired from a 25-caliber weapon.

Following the autopsy, Ms. von Suder's body will be returned to California.

Nothing like getting what you asked for. When I'd made the suggestion to Jared, I'd wanted to smoke Freddy out, but I hadn't expected things to develop quite this way. The worst-case scenario would be if Freddy or any of the wedding guests happened to catch the evening news. If they did, a whole lot of stuff was going to hit the fan that I hadn't counted on and Freddy was going to disappear.

Until the sheriff got a warrant, I had to coordinate with Farraday.

It was five thirty. I didn't know what time the O'Banion-Caswell rehearsal dinner was, but it had to be soon. Zelda answered on the second ring. "Yes!?"

She sounded so jumpy I almost didn't recognize her voice.

"It's Scotia. I know you're probably frantic right now, but listen carefully. It's important. If you're around other people, don't react. Do you understand?"

"Yes."

"I know this sounds farfetched, but the man Bronwyn is marrying is Frederick Campbell. Freddy."

There was no response. "Did you hear what I said?"

"Yes."

"What time is the wedding rehearsal?"

"At seven."

"Is it in the house?"

"No, in the garden."

"The rehearsal dinner?"

"At the Islander Lodge in Lopez Village at eight thirty

tonight. Everybody will be leaving here at around eight."

"Private cars or taxi?"

"Both."

"I'm coming over on the ferry. How will I find the house?"

She gave me directions from the ferry. "When you get to Fleur-de-lis Road, follow the road until it dead-ends at the horse pasture. If you turn right through the white gate there, you'll come to a gray and white French chateau. If you don't want to come to the house, you can park your car under the trees in the lane beside the pasture."

"Is the fiancé staying at the house tonight or in the village?"

"Here."

"Are you going to the dinner?"

"No." Her voice fell to a whisper. "There's a problem with Chloe and Bronwyn's on the warpath. Something about the prenuptial agreement. I've got to go."

"One more thing," I said quickly. "Do whatever you have to, but try to make sure no one looks at the evening news. I'll explain later. Oh, see if you can get me a place to lay my head in the village tonight." I hung up the phone, locked up the Rousseau file, and looked for my ferry schedule. It was missing. I checked the ferry Web site. The next and last ferry of the evening to Lopez left at eight fifteen.

I hung up the phone, locked up everything, and left the building. Summertime Friday night was in full swing. Vehicles crawled up Spring Street in futile search of a parking spot. Heavy metal poured from the open doors of George's Tavern. I hurried down Second Street, paused at the doorway of the tavern, and scanned the crowd. There was no sign of either Farraday or Baxter.

Compared to the foot traffic on the main dock, G dock was relatively quiet. There were no lights on

Pumpkin Seed and no furry feline greeted me. My mind in high gear, I was making up a plan as I went along, and if I missed the ferry, things were going to get a lot more complicated. I unlocked *DragonSpray,* changed into black cotton pants and an old black long-sleeved T-shirt. My canvas rucksack was in the aft cabin. I found my shoulder holster and tucked an extra clip of ammo into the rucksack, then added the other necessities for the night. Flashlight, bottle of water, surgical gloves, a pair of pliers, a set of lock picks, a little hand-held copier, and my two-way radios.

I moved back to my cabin, opened the hanging locker, and pulled out a black cardigan sweater I'd been meaning to give to the thrift shop. It would cover the shoulder holster and the night might get cool. I grabbed a change of underwear, a pale green linen dress with a long jacket, and bone-colored sandals in case I needed camouflage on Saturday. On the shelf in the locker, I found a straw hat that had a blond ponytail attached, grabbed a pair of dark glasses from the nav table, checked for car keys. I locked all the hatches, put out food and water for Calico, and checked to be sure her aft porthole was open.

Remote ignition in hand, I raced up the dock and up the steps by the yacht club to the parking lot. Haunted by the memory of the bombed-out Volvo, I scanned the lot for any movement, stood twenty yards or so from the Berlina, and clicked the remote Unlock button. The lights flashed and the door locks popped up. I pressed the ignition button and the engine came to life. Tentatively, I approached the car, opened the driver's side door, and slid in. Nothing happened. I exhaled a long breath I hadn't known I was holding.

I was the tenth car in line for the ferry. At 8:17 the huge *Evergreen State* reversed slowly past the pilings and out into the crowded harbor. At 8:46 we rounded Upright Head and pulled into the Lopez dock. Lopez roads are winding and rural, often unmarked, flanked by long grasses and thick stands of Douglas fir and madrona. For the last mile on Dill Road I was sure I was lost; then I found the sign for Fleur-de-lis Road and kept driving until I ran into the horse pasture. The fence was the expensive white three-rail type you see in pictures of Kentucky thoroughbred farms. Three horses were grazing in the middle of the pasture.

The clock on the dashboard said 9:07. About now the best man was giving his toast to the bride, which meant I had an hour to do what I wanted to do. Or less. I cruised slowly along beside the horse pasture and stopped under a large madrona tree. My cell phone rang. It was Zelda.

"Where are you?"

"In the lane by the pasture. Who's at the house?"

"The housekeeper, Chloe, and me. The housekeeper is asleep and Chloe's barricaded in her room."

"What's the best way into the house? I don't want either of them to see me."

"There's a side door before you get to the main entrance. I'll have it open."

"Turn off as many lights as you can."

I locked the car and shouldered my rucksack. A few yards from the car I spotted a clump of white balloons with curly white ribbon. The long winding drive to the chateau was overhung with trees and ended in a gracious circle in front of a sprawling, elegant masterpiece of gray stone and white stucco with steeply pitched roofs and massive chimneys. Twilight was deepening and the ground-level lights along the driveway were on. To the right of the driveway was what had to be a carriage house—perhaps chauffeur's quarters—connected to the main house with an overhead walkway. Two or three of the downstairs rooms were lighted, but the upper floor was dark. Four vehicles were parked along the driveway, including a vintage white Chrysler convertible with the top down, a white Nissan Altima, and Zelda's Morris.

I kept to the close-cropped lawn under the trees
and saw the side door open on the dark side of the
house. I slipped inside, motioned to Zelda for silence.

"Caswell is really Freddy?" she whispered.

"I'm almost positive. I want to get into his room.
Where is it?"

"Second floor in the front overlooking the driveway."

She pointed across the room to a stairway. "At the
top of the stairs turn right. It's the third room on
the right."

"When do you expect them back?"

She shrugged. "They didn't leave until eight fifteen.
Chloe turned up at the rehearsal with blue hair, dirty
bra straps, and magenta lipstick. When Caswell com-
mented on her appearance, she said she hoped he
died."

"Not a good beginning."

"What vehicle does Freddy have?"

"White Jag. Bronwyn rode with her mother in the
Mercedes."

"What about the TV? Anyone watch the news?"

"I don't think so. As soon as they left, I disconnected the main cable. Chloe came storming out of
her room when she couldn't get MTV. I told her I'd
check it out. I think she's watching a video."

"Is she going to complain when they get back?"

"Probably. I'll think of something."

"Where's Chloe's room?"

"Back of the house overlooking the pasture. Housekeeper's on the first floor behind the kitchen."

I showed Zelda how to use the two-way radio by
pressing a button that would signal me with a tone.
"Press this when the first headlight comes up the
drive. Don't wait to find out who it is. Is there a back
stairway to the second floor?"

She nodded. "There's a long corridor, then the
stairs at the back that go down to the kitchen. Keep

on going and you'll come to the overhead walkway.
It comes out in the guest apartment over the garage.
I unlocked the door."

"Will Freddy's room be locked?"

She nodded and handed me a key. "Lock it up and
I'll get the key from you later."

"Where am I sleeping tonight?"

"Lopez Village Guest House. They don't lock their
doors. Martha, one of the owners, will leave you a
note." She handed me a piece of paper. "I drew a map.
It's pretty easy to find. If you get lost, there's a
phone number."

I stuffed the paper in my pants pocket and gave her
a quick hug. "If all goes well, you won't see me until
tomorrow. What time's the wedding?"

"One o'clock."

"See you there."

The key to Freddy's room turned silently. I slipped
inside and closed the door. The large, carpeted room
was still lit with the late evening light. A king-size
bed with a blue-and-white flowered coverlet faced an
elaborate armoire of some pale wood. French doors
opened onto a balcony overlooking the drive. I checked
the drop from the balcony. Not a viable escape route.
On the other side of the bed I found a walk-in closet,
mirrored dressing room, and a marble bath that
smelled of soap and a man's cologne. A leather shaving kit lay on the marble sink. I unzipped it: Poco
Rabanne shaving cream and cologne, Tom's of Maine
toothpaste, and a small brown plastic vial. The pre-
scription was for Viagra, issued by a Seattle doctor
and filled at a Seattle pharmacy. I closed the kit, recalling Kimberly Korda's report about Freddy's "medical problem." Freddy was prepared for his marital
duties.

Several men's shirts hung in the closet, along with
a black leather bomber jacket and a maroon plastic

bag that said Seattle Formal Wear. Both shirts were
monogrammed. The pockets of the bomber jacket
were empty. I returned to the bedroom, checked the
drawers on the wide bureau of the armoire. All were
empty except for two Star Wars videos. A black suitcase lay on the luggage rack secured with a four-digit
combination padlock. It opened with the same four
digits of his birth date backward that had unlocked
his e-mail. Was MI-6's most wanted getting careless?
I raised the lid of the suitcase.

I liked Freddy's taste in undergarments: blue glen
plaid boxers, size 36, all monogrammed; classic blue
pajamas with notches on the collar, monogrammed;
one unopened package of bird's-eye cotton socks from
Brooks Brothers, two striped twill ties. I felt underneath the clothing and pulled out a rectangular box.
Inside on the dark felt were two sets of cuff links,
each sporting the "F.W.C." in an elegant script. I replaced the jewelry box and felt around the edges of
the suitcase, ran my fingers across the smooth silk that
lined the bottom and felt something underneath the
silk. I could find no opening in the lining. Again I felt
along the edges, found the minuscule metal tab of an
invisible zipper in the far left-hand corner under the
pocket. I pulled out a man's passport. Inside were various documents and a laminated card. I glanced out
the French doors, saw lights through the trees. I
grabbed my little copier from the rucksack and ducked
quickly into the closet, hoping I could depend on
Zelda. I examined the various cards and papers and
gave a sigh of relief. I hadn't been wrong.

The laminated card was an Oregon driver's license
issued a month ago to Franklin Wesley Caswell, 3497
Wisteria Drive, Portland, Oregon. Date of birth May
14, 1960. Height 6'1", weight 176 lbs. Hazel eyes,
brown hair. The man in the photo had a mustache,
longish dark hair and a well-trimmed beard. Only the
aristocratic nose and high forehead gave him away. I

unfolded the documents and found six birth certificates, all issued in Florida, in different names for a
male child to various sets of parents. The last document in the case was a U.S. passport issued to the
same Franklin Wesley Caswell. I spread the certificates on the floor of the closet, tried to keep my hands
from trembling, and photographed the certificates and
the Oregon driver's license.

I hurried back into the bedroom, saw headlights
somewhere out near the end of the driveway. There
was no signal from Zelda and it was too late to worry
about whether I had replaced the documents in the
case in the same order I'd found them. I slid the passport case into the secret zippered compartment, feeling my hands sweating inside the gloves, hearing a
car's engine below the balcony. I was about to close
the compartment when my right hand touched what
felt like a book. I pulled it out and shone the flashlight
on it. Inside my pocket my radio began its insistent
two-tone signal. I pulled it out and muted it, riffled
through the pages. It was a journal, written in French
in small, precise handwriting. The first entry was dated
10 mars 2001. The last one was dated four days ago.
Several days and sometimes weeks elapsed between
the entries, a few of which were in what I thought
was Russian. I read the first paragraph. *"Arrivé a Los
Angeles heir. Ce soir j'ai recontré une femme qui travaille dans le bureau du gouverneur de la Californie.
L'aventure a commencé. . . ."*

I zipped up the tiny secret compartment, relocked
the suitcase, and threw the copier, flashlight, and the
journal in the rucksack. I stood for a second at the
door, heard nothing, opened it a crack.

Laughter and voices from below, then a burst of
music. The corridor was empty. I locked the door,
turned right, and speed-walked down the long carpeted corridor past three more closed doors. Halfway
down the hall I heard voices behind me coming up

the stairs, a man's and a woman's. I kept on going, found the stairway that descended to the kitchen. I paused, heard ice cubes tumble into a glass. A door slammed loudly, followed by a high-pitched female tirade which left no doubt about how the speaker felt about "sucky lavender shoes." I followed the jog in the corridor, came to a heavy carved wooden door, opened it, and found myself in a windowless corridor which I assumed was the overhead walkway. I opened the door to the chauffeur's quarters and locked it behind me.

I had gotten what I wanted. And probably a lot more.

24

It was nearly midnight before the lights in the O'Banion house went out and I dared emerge from the guest apartment. I left the lights in the Berlina off until I was a mile away, then checked for pursuing lights in my rearview mirror all of the five or six miles to Lopez Village. After several wrong turns, I found the Lopez Village Guest House at the end of an unlighted, winding rural lane that was probably picturesque by day and by night just flat-out exasperating. I got out of the Berlina, opened the big metal gate, drove through, and closed the gate. Martha had left a note for me. My room was the Petunia Room on the second floor, the bathroom was down the hall, breakfast was from seven to nine thirty.

There was a light on in the Petunia Room. I put the rucksack on the desk in front of the windows, closed the pale yellow blinds, and removed the black cardigan. I put the Beretta in the table next to the bed and removed my shoulder holster, wishing I had a glass of wine or a cup of tea. The miniature Seth Thomas clock on the mantel above the fireplace showed 12:48. I was grubby from stumbling and falling in the pitch-black road near the horse pasture and I wanted a shower. I needed to call Angela and Farraday. I wanted to call Zelda but didn't dare risk it. And then I wanted to crawl into the big bed and read

Freddy's journal from cover to cover, assuming I could stay awake that long.

A shower removed the grime but did nothing to banish the fear that I was wearing like a second skin. Not so much fear for myself, although there was that, too, as apprehension for what Freddy might do if he discovered that he'd been made. Or if someone told him about the news article or the on-line announcement. I hadn't found a weapon in his room, which meant he had it with him. If he checked his suitcase or the hidden compartment when he got back—as any well-trained intelligence person would do—he would know someone had been there. In the past, Zelda has not proved to be a good liar. With the proper persuasion, Freddy would know where to find me in ten minutes.

I'd forgotten to pack pj's. Fortunately the doors to the Rose Room and the Dahlia Room remained closed when I paraded back from the shower wrapped in a voluminous bath sheet. I dialed Angela's number, then noticed that there were only two service bars on the cell phone display. Not nearly enough to get connected. I pulled on my dirty pants and T-shirt and padded downstairs to use the phone under the sign that said "LOCAL CALLS ONLY."

Matt answered after six rings and called Angela to the phone. I tried to summarize my evening's activities. "Did the sheriff get the warrant?"

"We'll know in the morning," she answered. "I'll call you."

"There's no cell phone service here. I'll have to call you."

I hung up and called Jared, gave him the same summary I'd given Angela. But I needed a favor from him. "Please call Farraday and tell him where I am and that he needs to get his ass over here tomorrow if he wants Freddy." I gave him the number. "It's an international number. I'll reimburse you."

"Who's Farraday?"

Hadn't I told him? "He claims to be British Intelligence and he's looking for Freddy. Will you please call him? I don't have cell phone service here."

"Scotia, I know you and Nigel don't get along, but he should be handling this."

I spoke very slowly. "Jared, I would be happy to have Nigel handle it, but if he doesn't get a warrant, he's not going to do anything. Freddy is going to get married and take off, someone else is going to die, and we'll all be back at square one." I was so exhausted I thought I was going to cry. "Jared, as a favor to me, call Farraday. Please."

'He's the reinforcements you were talking about, isn't he?"

"Yes."

"I'll call him. Give me the number again. But I think you're making a mistake. And call me if I can do anything."

Back upstairs, I locked the door, removed my pants and shirt, checked the safety on the Beretta and put it under my pillow, crawled naked under the lily coverlet, and began reading.

Arrivé a Los Angeles heir. Ce soir j'ai recontré une femme qui travaille dans le bureau du gouverneur de la Californie. L'aventure a commencé.

Arrived in Los Angeles yesterday. This evening I met a woman who works in the office of the California governor. The adventure has begun.

I continued reading, turning the pages through the deadly roller-coaster escapades of a frighteningly accomplished Casanova con man.

Freddy's meeting with Diane Duvall, whom he referred to as "moneybags."

His elation during the tryst on Coronado Island when she agreed to divorce her husband. Rage when she broke off the clandestine relationship. Gloating triumph when the monthly payments began.

Elation once more when he met Kimberly Korda, who appeared to be perfect for his devices: newly rich, madly in love with him, and—because she was less than glamorous—so terribly grateful for his attentions. After the Duvall interlude, he refined his modus operandi. There were no more married women and the prenuptial agreement with a mutual power of attorney—which he hadn't expected Kimberly to sign—obviated the need for blackmail.

Throughout the journal, the comments about and descriptions of each woman were cryptic. After the mention of Los Angeles in the first entry, there were no further indications of geography, no full names or initials. Without the information on the women I already had, including the recent hacked e-mail from Freddy to Christopher Goodfellow and to "Kathleen," it would have been impossible to identify the women. Chantal and her mother were *"la jolie coquette and la folle berbère"*; Kimberly he called *"la maigre,"* Hannah was *"la maman gâteau."*

With Hannah, Freddy thought he had hit the jackpot: almost a million dollars by the time she divided up her interest in von Suder Cellars. A million dollars that was gobbled up by the voracious maw of his gambling addiction.

There were random mentions of wins or losses at gambling—usually roulette, with occasional forays into blackjack and baccarat. And throughout, soliloquies on ingenious ways to "beat the house" and the joys of on-line gaming. Taken as a whole, the journal was a how-to manual for the con man in search of madame bountiful. An oeuvre that I hoped would help to put Freddy behind bars for bigamy and murder one.

Assuming Farraday didn't get him first.

Fatigued to the marrow of my bones, I checked the Beretta under my pillow, drifted into a thin, half sleep, and spent what was left of the night in pursuit of dervishlike women in black wedding veils.

*   *   *

I awoke on Saturday morning to the chiming of the little Seth Thomas. I counted the eight tones and sat up in bed. It had been after three when I'd finished the journal and I didn't remember anything after that. I checked my cell phone: still not enough bars to send or receive a call. I dressed, used the bathroom, brushed the tangles from my hair, applied makeup. I was downstairs by eight thirty. The breakfast was lavish, orchestrated by Martha's husband, Terence. I declined the bacon and mushroom omelette and took my juice and coffee, croissant, and strawberry jam into the library to an antique table and stared out at the crisp sunny day that was perfect for a wedding. Several minutes later, Terence put his head around the door to the library. "You planning on catching the ferry anywhere this morning, Ms. MacKinnon?"

"No, Terence, I'm not."

'Good thing. The reverse gear went out last night and they rammed the dock. Won't be any ferries docking there today."

Won't be any ferries docking there today. Hand poised over the dish of jam, I tried to assimilate what Terence had said. If there were no ferries, how would the wedding take place? And how would Farraday get to Lopez? Could he charter a plane? A fast boat? Supposing the judge did not sign the warrant and nobody came over? Then what? Could I make a citizen's arrest?

I carried my dishes to the kitchen and called Angela from the LOCAL CALLS ONLY phone. She was at work and did not have good news. "The judge wouldn't sign the warrant," she reported. "Said there was no real evidence in the Rousseau file or anything the crime scene team found that indicates that Frederick Campbell might have killed von Suder. No fingerprints, no footprints, no DNA, no corroborating witnesses. The Duvall shooting is out of his jurisdiction."

"What about the photograph? Kimberly identified it as the man she married and the man in the wedding photo with Hannah. Couldn't they at least *question* the guy?"

"No good enough."

"What about the *Crustacean* article? And the Istanbul incident?"

"He said you've been reading too many spy novels." She paused, then added, "Scotia, maybe you should just give it up. You don't even know where your client is. Take the weekend off; get a little perspective on it."

"Thanks, Angela." I hung up and called Jared but couldn't find him to ask if he'd gotten through to Farraday. The ferries weren't docking at Lopez. The sheriff wasn't going to get involved. In four hours or so, Frederick W. Campbell a.k.a. F. Wesley Caswell, was going to marry Bronwyn Kathleen O'Banion. And if she signed the prenup and the mutual power of attorney, nobody could help her.

I needed a plan. And then I was going to a wedding.

25

The garden behind the six-foot-high wall of river stones was larger than I'd expected, and inside, it was moist and warm and fragrant with flowers. Purple and white rhododendrons, daylilies, and red roses over-flowed the meandering flagstone paths. Blue dragon-flies darted and dived above the congregation. Large stone urns brimming with gigantic pink blooms decorated the ends of pathways. Behind the wedding party a tall, ornate stone fountain gurgled.

I'd arrived at the château around twelve fifteen. An eager young man in a white cap embroidered with the names of the wedding couple pointed me to a parking spot at the bottom of the drive below a white Cadillac. I walked up the drive, noting the white Jag parked under the overhead walkway. I'd found Zelda in the sewing room making last-second alterations on a bridesmaid's dress. She said she hadn't seen Freddy since he'd come back from the rehearsal dinner last night.

I mingled with the other guests, chatting with the bride's gregarious grandfather and a cousin of her mother and drifted out to the garden with the first bars of "Pa-chelbel's Canon." Rows of white folding chairs sur-rounded the fountain in semicircles. I found a seat in the last row beside a well-dressed dark-haired man in a pale gray suit. I spotted Zelda's flame-colored top-knot six rows ahead of me.

Pachelbel was replaced by something by Bach. The pastor in a white cassock and purple soutane, accompanied by four men in white dinner jackets filed into the garden. I searched the men's faces for the man I had been hunting, quickly eliminating the tall, bald man with a goatee who looked like a rabbi as well a the short, rotund one with a fringe of light brown hair and the red-haired gentleman with horn-rimmed glasses.

That left only the tall, dark-haired man in tinted glasses with a well-trimmed beard. As he passed down the aisle, I realized with a shock it was the man I had seen with Bronwyn on Thursday night when I was having dinner with Jewel Moon. I also realized that the slightly shaggy, darker hair and the beard were an excellent disguise. The closely-shaven, well-turned-out Los Angeles financial advisor had been replaced by the bearded Northwest male.

A female soloist sang an impressive rendition of "Ave Maria." The harpist paused, then the female entourage was summoned by the unmistakable first bars of Lohengrin. First came two flower girls strewing rose petals upon the crowd. Then three bridesmaids in lavender and the matron of honor in petal pink. Chloe had apparently undergone a change of heart and was wearing the "sucky" high-heeled lavender satin sandals with rhinestone buckles. Her gait down the flagstone path was wobbly, but no outbursts occurred. And finally, there was Bronwyn O'Banion in Vera Wang. As modest and virginal in the filmy white veil as forty-something can appear, she radiated bliss in the strapless white organza creation with its dramatic tiered train.

"Dearly beloved, we are gathered here together . . ."
All heads swiveled toward the front and the soft

murmurs ceased. The pastor turned a page and peered at his notes.

I checked my watch. It was one twenty. It turned out that Terence had been wrong about the ferry. The dock had been repaired by nine o'clock and the caterer and the guests had arrived in a timely fashion. When I'd finally gotten within range of a cell tower, I'd found a message from Farraday. "We are en route. Don't do anything." That was over three hours ago. Would they get here before Freddy realized the trap was closing? I stared at the broad back of the man in the white dinner jacket that I'd been hunting for two weeks. I'd gotten a quick look at him when he'd come in.

"*. . . therefore, if any man can show a just cause why they may not be lawfully joined together . . .*"

I glanced across the garden at the large wooden gate, looking for Farraday, and did a double take. Just inside, white silk shirt and pants belted seductively over her curvaceous body, stood Chantal Rousseau. She held a white beaded bag against her chest with both hands and her gaze was riveted on the couple in front of the flowing fountain. I tried to breathe, swallowed, considered getting up, then changed my mind.

"*. . . by God's law or the laws of the realm . . .*"

Was Chantal going to accost Freddy? Break up the wedding in a dramatic confrontation? Tell Bronwyn she was marrying a bigamist? I'd seriously considered trying to get Bronwyn alone before the wedding to tell her what was coming down, but if she didn't believe me and tipped Freddy off, he would flee. If Chantal confronted Freddy before Farraday arrived, or if I tried to detain him, the outcome would be the same. Or worse.

"*. . . let him now speak, or else hereafter forever hold his peace.*"

The pastor looked up with a beatific smile and

scanned the rows of faces. I watched Chantal, waiting for the dramatic outburst. She frowned and fumbled with her bag. I watched her fingers slide the zipper open. She reached into the bag and I knew exactly what she was going to do. Chantal Rousseau and Michael Farraday belonged to the same school of criminal justice.

"Franklin Wesley Caswell, wilt thou have this woman to be thy wedded wife, to live together in the holy estate . . ."

Freddy turned toward his bride, a tender smile lighting his handsome profile.

I stood up, ignored the puzzled glances of the well-dressed man beside me, and moved swiftly around the perimeter of the garden toward the gate.

". . . of matrimony, for richer, for poorer, so long as ye both shall live?"

A large, black iron urn from some previous century blocked my view of the gate. I circled a bed of purple foxglove, nearly tripping on the protruding edge of the flagstone walkway. I had a clear view of my client at this point. She had the gun out and no one in the garden but me was aware that "so long as ye both shall live" was apt to be very brief indeed. She stared at the weapon, then moved her gaze to the wedding party lined up by the fountain.

"Bronwyn Kathleen O'Banion, wilt thou have this man to be thy wedded husband . . ."

I heard the click as she cocked the hammer. From the front row of chairs where Mrs. Livingston, the mother of the bride, was sitting, I heard a stifled sob. I pulled the Beretta from the back waistband of my slacks, removed the safety, held it low by my side.

"I Bronwyn, take thee, Franklin, to have and to hold, from this day forward"—

Chantal raised the gun to eye level and took a stance right out of a rerun of *Charlie's Angels.* I was still fifty feet away and I knew I wasn't going to reach her in time.

—*"for better for worse, for richer for poorer . . ."*

"Dr. Rousseau, stop! It's not—" My shout was loud, but the shot was louder. If Chantal had been aiming for Freddy's heart, she missed and the two shots that followed in quick succession hit the stone fountain. A red stain appeared on the upper left sleeve of Freddy's white dinner jacket. He stumbled and half fell on his side against the stone fountain, right arm clutching his left shoulder. For several seconds, there was total silence. All eyes were riveted on the drama at the front of the garden. No heads turned; no one moved from their seat. Bronwyn stared at her betrothed, then shrieked, and tore the Vera Wang veil away from her face.

I lunged and slammed Chantal's arm hard as she was preparing to fire again. The gun flew out of her hands and bounced off the garden wall. She swung on me and hissed her fury with words I was glad I didn't understand. I shoved her to one side and she tumbled awkwardly against the black urn, still spitting obscenities, and slid down the garden wall, one leg bent beneath her body. I turned and dived for the gun a second after it was kicked away by a man's well-shined black shoe. In the nanosecond during which I was processing the information that the black shoe was attached to a leg in black trousers above which there was a white dinner jacket, my right wrist was twisted painfully behind me and I was relieved of the Beretta. My hat and fake pony tail tumbled to the ground and I felt the hard metal of the gun through my linen shirt.

"Unlatch the gate. Do it now." The voice was low, British, and not one you would argue with. The cologne was spicy and masculine. I didn't need to see the stained left sleeve to know who the voice belonged to.

As the gun prodded me toward the gate, I heard

chairs falling over. I got one glance at the horrified faces of the guests, spotted Zelda elbowing her way through the throng, cell phone to her ear. Chloe was at her heels. The photographer from *Village Life* was snapping away with all the zest of a paparazzo. With my free left hand, I lifted the iron latch on the heavy gate. Freddy kicked it and it swung outward. He twisted my arm a few degrees higher and shoved me out of the garden. He had transferred the gun to his left hand. I expected he would kill me at that moment and make a run for it. "Latch the gate," he commanded. I did as I was told, awkwardly, with my left hand.

"Where are you taking me?"

"On a little journey and you're not going to return." He prodded me roughly along the path that ran between the house and the stone wall of the garden. The pain from my twisted arm made me light-headed. I stumbled twice, the last time falling hard to one knee on the gravel.

"Get up! You've caused me enough trouble."

He grabbed my arm and pulled me to my feet.

"Why did you kill Diane Duvall?"

"The old cow talked. I told her what would happen."

"How did you know she talked?"

"Let's just say Duvall's secretary has a thing for older men. She'd have been okay and von Suder too if you hadn't started meddling. You signed their death sentences. Get moving."

We were out in the driveway, running past the parked cars and the startled faces of the two young parking attendants.

"Why *did* you blow up my car?"

Freddy jerked me to a stop beside the white Jaguar XJ8. He looked at me in surprise. "Don't be an idiot. I'm not a terrorist."

Parked behind the Jag was a tan Ford Windstar. The sliding door on the driver's side was open.

Freddy shoved me toward the Jag. "Get in on the driver's side," he ordered. "It's not locked."

I refused to move, certain that if I got in the car and he forced me to drive away, I was dead. Over to my right, a figure moved on the veranda. Freddy jabbed me hard in the ribs with the barrel of the gun. A cacophony of voices rose in the garden. Someone was battering the gate.

Freddy twisted my arm higher. Furious, I kicked sideways, lunged hard against his chest, and brought my head up under his chin. He wrenched my arm higher and snarled, "Get into the bloody—" He moved to open the car door, the gun momentarily drifted away from my head, and I heard the two quick puffs of sound made by a silenced weapon.

My twisted arm slid free. Freddy's legs buckled; he fell against the car and slid to the ground. His gun— my Beretta .380—tumbled under the Jag and I saw the two small holes in his forehead. In seconds, Baxter and Farraday grabbed Freddy's limp body, half dragged, half carried him to the Ford Windstar, lifted him bodily into the backseat, and raced away in a spin of tires on loose gravel.

I watched the Windstar fishtail out of the driveway. I swallowed and rubbed my aching arm and checked my bloody kneecap. The latch burst off the garden gate, and the gate hit the wall behind it. Led by the photographer, the first of the shocked guests made their way warily and silently along the path beside the house and stood staring at me. Zelda had called the Lopez deputy, she said, and Dr. Rousseau was still lying in the garden. She hadn't even tried to run away. Grandpa, his dark blue tie askew, cast a disgusted look at the disappearing Windstar and shook his head.

"If those two'd've asked me, I'd've told them I already called the EMS unit for Wes. You think they know how to find the clinic in the village?" He closed the open door of the Jaguar, frowned, stooped stiffly, and picked up my Beretta between his thumb and forefinger.

A tan Chevy Blazer with a bubble on the top turned into the driveway. "Grandpa," I said, "I don't think they're headed to the clinic."

26

The ringing phone awoke me on Sunday morning. I moved carefully in my bed on *DragonSpray,* arm and shoulder muscles screaming, right knee stiff, and picked up the phone with my left hand. It was Angela. The tan Ford Windstar that Baxter and Farraday had used to kidnap Freddy belonged to Fisherman's Bay Transportation, she told me. It was found abandoned at MacKay Harbor, but no one had seen any of the three men. A woman who lived near the harbor recalled seeing a floatplane taking off on Saturday afternoon but was vague about the time.

"Dr. Rousseau's attorney flew up from Seattle this morning and got his client released on bail," Angela continued. "The sheriff was in a huff about the whole thing and suggested that since it was apparent that Dr. Rousseau's former husband—Freddy—was a felon, perhaps the doctor shot him in self-defense. I'm sorry I gave you a hard time yesterday, Scotia," she said. "I probably got a bit officious." I told her not to worry and thanked her for the call.

Slowly and with great effort, I climbed up the companionway and walked up to the shower, thinking that I would have to remember to refund the balance of Dr. Rousseau's retainer that I hadn't used for expenses and services rendered. She might need it for attorney fees. The heat wave had sucked fog in from the Pacific. It poured up San Juan Channel in a great grayish white blanket and swirled around the masts in the harbor. The phone was ringing when I got back to the boat. It was Nick. He'd just seen the Channel 7 News feature story.

"Scotty, your name is all over the news. Are you all right? My God, why didn't you call me last night?"

"By the time I got back to Friday Harbor and had my arm x-rayed, I was beyond conversation. I just came back to the boat and crashed."

"The news says you were injured."

I glanced ruefully at the sling on my left arm and my bandaged right knee. "A sprained arm, a bloody knee, and some bruised ribs. Nothing that won't heal in a week or so."

"The two mystery men who kidnapped Freddy in the Ford van, were they the agents that visited you?"

"Affirmative."

Nick whistled. "And they just *disappeared?*"

"Apparently. Bizarre, huh? And Freddy claimed he never bombed the Volvo."

"He's right. I had a call from Lieutenant Andersen. They've got the guy in custody who made the bomb. It was intended for a Volvo sports car that belonged to a guy named Ramsey who lived in the penthouse. Big-time drug dealer. Lovely neighborhood I've moved into."

"How is Keith?"

"He's out of the ICU and is going to recover. The condo association is going to help his family until he can work again. Scotty, shall I come up? We could hang out at my house for a while."

"I can't think of anything I'd like better."

Ten minutes later the phone rang again. This time it was Melissa.

"Mother, are you *okay?* I was watching the news on the satellite channel. There was a story about a shooting on Lopez. They said you were there and were taken *hostage*! And that a woman *shot* the bride-groom."

I gave her a sanitized version of the interrupted O'Banion–Caswell nuptials, assured her I'd be healed in a few days, and inquired about life on the ranch.

"Yesterday was so awesome. Up in the high desert here above the ranch, there's a band of wild mustangs that's managed by the Bureau of Land Management. The ranch bought four of the excess horses—two yearlings and a two-year-old and a four-year-old palomino. The wrangler is going to gentle them. Isn't that cool?"

"Very cool."

"And, Mom, I'm sorry I got mad at you about Justin. You're right about his being too old. His daughter is almost as old a I am. It's pretty weird. We're just going to be friends."

"Sounds good. You still want to stop off here on your way back to school?"

"I do. Talk to you later. Love you."

I made a big breakfast of scrambled eggs and sourdough toast and carried it up to the cockpit. Tucked under the canvas dodger in the swirling mist, I sipped my coffee and listened to the clanging bell on Reid Rock. Spreading Raheela's *confiture d'orange* on my toast, I puzzled over the obsessions that had kept Freddy going from one con to the next, one courtship and wedding and theft to another. Or, in Freddy's own words, from one *aventure* to another. If Dr. Rousseau hadn't hired me, how long would he have gotten away with the cons?

Chantal Rousseau's behavior, unacceptable by civilized standards, might be perfectly understandable in a Berber village: Whether her original motive in hiring me was to find Freddy so that she could carry out her own brand of frontier justice, I didn't know. But as for shooting the bastard, what woman who's been seduced and abandoned—never mind financially ruined— hasn't fantasized about revenge?

At four o'clock I ventured out to replenish the larder, met Jared for coffee, and decided to go by the office to check my e-mail. There was only one.

Raincoat no longer needed. I'm off on holiday. Do you have a bikini?

Below the message, a tiny falcon fluttered across the screen.

Acknowledgments

The author wishes to thank the following individuals for their input to *The Dead Wives Society:* Philip Bauso, Jennifer Conway, Jack Cory, Roberta Crist, Penelope De Paoli, Donna Donahoo, Sabrina Duncan, Janet Gallaher, Martin Garren, Jr., Nancy Hird, Cynthia Hubbard-Tripp, Michelle Kirsch, Mona Meeker, Ramsey Milne, Robert Stamm, Louise Wells, Rudi and Bill Weissinger, Gerard Woldvedt, and Jon Zerby.

With special thanks to Helen Bowie, who burned the midnight oil with me; to my editor Ellen Edwards; and to Annelise Robey of the Jane Rotrosen Agency, who suggested the title.

And with all due respect to the San Juan County Sheriff's Department, the author begs forgiveness for taking outrageous liberties with local law enforcement procedures and personalities.

COMING IN SEPTEMBER 2003 FROM SIGNET MYSTERY

BETTER TO REST
A Liam Campbell Mystery
by Dana Stabenow   0-451-20960-5

Just when his personal life starts to heat up, Liam
Campbell must put it on hold...after the grisly discovery
of a severed hand leads him to a crashed WWII Army
plane frozen precariously in a glacier.

HIGH STAKES
8 Sure-Bet Stories of Gambling and Crime
Edited by Robert J. Randisi   0-451-21018-2

Eight exciting stories of high-rolling intrigue from
today's best authors make up this unique collection that
looks at the chances we take, the laws we break, and
the fortunes we hope to make. Featuring tales by
New York Times bestselling authors Lawrence Block,
Leslie Glass, and Donald E. Westlake.

DANA STABENOW

BETTER TO REST: *A Liam Campbell Mystery*
0-451-20702-5
Alaska state trooper Sergeant Liam Campbell is the representative of law and order in the fishing village of Newenham—yet struggles to keep his own life on an even keel. Now, just when his future is starting to heat up, he delves into a case of a downed WWII army plane found mysteriously frozen in a glacier.

NOTHING GOLD CAN STAY
0-451-20230-9
Shocked by a series of brutal, unexplainable murders, Alaska State Trooper Liam Campbell embarks on a desperate journey into the heart of the Alaskan Bush country—in search of the terrible, earth-shattering truth...

SO SURE OF DEATH
0-451-19944-8
Liam Campbell has lost more than most men lose in a lifetime: his wife and young son are dead; his budding career is in a deep freeze ever since five people died on his Anchorage watch. Demoted from sergeant to trooper, exiled to Newenham, a town teeming with fiercely independent Natives, he lives on a leaky gillnetter moored in Bristol Bay, brooding on how to put down roots on dry land again and rekindle his relationship with bush pilot Wyanet Chouinard, who won his heart long ago, and then broke it.